GULLEYTOWN

GULLEYTOWN

Rix County

JOHN BARKSDALE

authorHOUSE®

AuthorHouse™ LLC
1663 Liberty Drive
Bloomington, IN 47403
www.authorhouse.com
Phone: 1-800-839-8640

Published by AuthorHouse   02/17/2014

ISBN: 978-1-4918-6381-7 (sc)
ISBN: 978-1-4918-6395-4 (e)

Library of Congress Control Number: 2014902732

CHAPTER 1

From its creation the life that was given to me has been filled with complications and disaster. Hurt that involves much more than pain has been a cornerstone of my existence for as far back as memory will allow. So much hurt that I've lost count of the many days and occurrences that my survival was somehow managed, and I escaped the grasp of death, whether it was through the hands of others or my very own. A look back over the course of my many encounters with futility has forced one certain realization, all which has not open up a grave to me, has in one way or another most decidedly persuaded me to bend to my knees in reference for surviving.

Within this giant world that we have all been given to reside, I am a particle of one even tinier. And it seems that all the inhabitants that have chosen to dwell here also are in some manner familiar with certain components of my life, though only a precious few of them are in knowledge of the complete story of my troubled life.

If ever an account was given of my life any description would be incomplete without the inclusion of my fascination and love for fireflies. Lightning bugs might be what you would probably refer to them as if you are anywhere near as aged as I am. A bonding affection is what I carry for them and it developed as naturally as any thing could during the years of my youth. I chuckle at the memories because that was a very long time ago. Back in those times there wasn't a catalogue of options available to the young populace to occupy ones time like there are now. Never even knew that this tiny creature existed until I stumbled upon what seemed like thousands of them one evening. Reachable and unhurried, they danced in their glow out over an open field before me and I've been hooked from that moment forward. They are seasonal beings, and with only them I am an impatient observer. But wait I must until the waning moments of the sun, right at the point when darkness comes to capture up its glow, and at that point they appear from the dusk almost like magic. At my advanced age, I'm far from my youth, but nothing about aging has dull my affection for them. I still wait for those exact moments to enjoy the beauty of my precious lighting bugs.

Age and time have taught me that life doesn't always deal out what one expects or wants. I certainly never expected nor did I want to experience any of the crippling limitations longevity sometimes offers but I most certainly have. Although I have not been hobbled or rendered disabled by any of the illness or diseases that oftentimes maneuver into the life to cripple the elderly, I have been stricken by limitations. For a period reaching backwards towards ten years, I really have not been able to observe as I would like the true glowing beauty of my lamped-tailed lighting bugs. Over the before mentioned timeframe a horrific tragedy occurred within this small world in which I exist. A tragedy set in motion by senselessness and one that ended in dreadful horror, where one precious life after another was murdered from existence. I said murders and I meant awful murders and they were all troubling. They were the kind of murders that baffled our small surroundings and shook at the lives of decent soles. There is this mystical place that overflows with wonder that has become a part of our environment and made a home in our tiny world. The tragedy in which I speak occurred not very far from this mysterious place and it is my observation that it was because of the proximity that these ungodly deeds were committed to this indescribable place that an amazing event was set in motion. An event that culminated in miracles occurring that are yet to be explained, and the partial destruction of my vision. I was in no way personally engage in anything that transpired to set off this unbelievable event. My only involvement was to be awake and away from my bed in a position to look down upon it. For my transgression I was cursed into limitations, having to settle with observing my harmless lighting bugs and all other forms of life through a vision that is truly not my own.

I am here to tell you a story, in fact I believe I was chosen to tell you this tale, and oh what an unimaginable one it is. We have yet to even set pace properly and at this point, exposing my troublesome eyesight and who I am is getting a little ahead or where I need to begin, so for now, at this early stage of my introduction to you, I'll spare you the full disclosure of how my once glorious vision got to be so limited, and besides, there are far more interesting occurrences that I wish to include you in on first.

OFTEN TIMES BEFORE but not one minute later than five every morning I awaken to greet a new day by climbing away from the tugging sheets of my bed to capture a reflection in the mirror. From my scalp grows a shade of hair that matches the color of dying snow. At my age its texture and thickness still manages to surprise me every time I attempt to pull a comb through it. Another reason it surprises me is that it's faded several shades lighter than any of the strands I witness growing from the mane of the deep roots of my father before his introduction to final destiny came twenty one years ago in a single car accident that finished him off without head or hair. My father and his truly beautiful head of hair died in an unforgiving bend of the road in one of our communities that through the years has claimed more than its fair share. So many lives have been snatched from existence where my father succumbed that the small portion of roadway has been given a description, by the locals.

It's called Dead Man's curve.

Rix County, Georgia is the place of my birth and it's also the place where you can find Dead Man's curve.

Rix is one of those small southern settings where the name of the town serves also as the name of the county. Checkered about its landscape and most prominently along some of the main streets within the city limits are grand antebellum mansions. All of the homes varying in degrees of impressiveness and each and every one restored to some measure to adequately capture the quality of its past whether being lived in currently or not. Other than for the appeal that these imposing old homes might carry for ardent tourist or individuals passing through, I can think of nothing else on the surface about this small county other than its friendly people that would appear alluring or somehow different in some manner from any other one in the south. Certainly nothing attracting enough that might encourage a visitor to return to such a place.

Rix is a southern town, and I do stress the word southern, and one with its fair share of old and forgotten ways. Residents are cordial and extremely pleasant with waves and smiles in abundance. And the children are what formulate the community. All the value behind all the smiles is centered on them and it expands out to incorporate everyone else. There is no doubting this fact and the community shares in the responsibility for raising them.

Rix Georgia is a livable lovable town but it is not without its faults. The smiling faces captured under the southern sun reside in separate places when there is no longer any sunlight. Rix is a municipality mostly divided, one where whites have settled in on one side of town and black on the other, and the rails of rusted train tracks separate them and their communities of Stansburg and Gulleytown.

The location of Dead Man's curve is near Gulleytown and it seems to always be a daily centerpiece of discussion for someone in the township regardless of their community.

There is another particular area positioned not a great distance from Dead Man's curve and it is an area held in supremely high regards by some, almost holy. Outside of the borders of the Rix, nothing is known to any individual or establishment about this place. Within the county the populace has such little knowledge to the whereabouts of the area that they rely on folklore and or speculation. Scores do not even believe in its existence. To be down right truthful towards the matter, there are only a handful of the community's older residents that have any evidential knowledge that this particular area actually exists and we don't dare speak out publicly about it, not even amongst ourselves. But exist it does, and when I tell you this place is uniquely special, I truly mean godly.

Within the boundaries of this small Northeast Georgia County sits a portion of land unlike any other tract of earth that you can dream up. Only special individuals warrant an invitation upon it and those are only allowed trespass upon these hollowed grounds under truly extraordinary reasons. This place I make reference too is called Sacred Hills, and it is the county of Rix, Georgia's very own gift from God.

Sacred Hills is one of the centerpieces of this tale and for no other reason but that is why I must end my silence and discuss this hallowed place.

At this premature stage of our story, it is much too early to center all of my attention on the topic of Sacred Hills but we'll most certainly revisit this true marvel a little later, and I promise that at that time, I will give to you my full knowledge of this place of miracles.

THOSE WORN DOWN railroad tracks in Rix that have not been used in more than two decades other than to separate the white Stansburg community from the blacks in Gulleytown have no reference to me and where I live. The small home in which I reside is not on either side of them. There isn't any form of mountain or peak that elevates from any section of county, although you would be hard pressed to believe that fact if you ever ventured out to my home. The small area of the county in which I live is called Taylorsville. It sits about five miles outside of the city limits and the road that delivers you here seems to never stop rising until it runs right up to the porch of my property.

Time and the elements of nature have certainly had a fair taste of this old home and that goes especially for the floorboard of my porch but its declining condition bothers me very little. If it did, I would not spend as much time as I do there and that is practically all of the daylight of every day, rain or sunshine. This old porch, my favorite rocking chair and the weight that I bare down into them have been creating cracking melodies for more years than I care to remember. It is from this seated location that I have looked down over the county that I have lived in for all my life like it was a far off share of the front lawn of my property.

From up here in Taylorsville, I have lived a long and more often than needed troubled life. I have grieved tremendously but I have been abundantly blessed also. The blessing nearest my heart was when I became a grandparent. It may seem a little off-centered but I treasure that label even more than I did the title of mother and I have my own selfish reasons for that.

Because of this advanced age that I have attained, the generation aging beneath me refers to my stage of maturity as fragile, but my appearance before their younger eyes makes little difference to me at all now, although, at one particular time in my life, it meant everything.

This world and all things functioning within it I view through a distorted vision that resembles a strong rain cloud. I no longer can see the many different shades of black or whites or any of the other bursting iridescent colors. Most certainly, I do have limitations in my vision but these restrictions have not settled my life into sadness. Instead they have allowed me to capture life in its simplest form. I most certainly wish that I could see my beautiful lighting bugs as they truly appear but that is little reason to seek change in the vision that has clouded my sight. Instead, I have risen up like this inclining property in which I reside to just be thankful for all the things I do have and to appreciate the blessing of just having life, because it could have very well been snatched away also instead of just my vision.

At birth, my parents delivered to me the name of Anna Withers and I was referred to as exactly that for my first fifty or so years of life, but I was freed of that name on one intensely bright day and given in its stead the most beautiful title that has ever filtered through my ears, and it was given to me by my irreplaceable grandchild.

He pointed up to me, smiled and then mumbled.

"Ms. Sadie."

To this very day I am troubled to explain exactly where he arrived at this new description for me but in accordance with my wishes, it has been by that name and only that name that I have been referred to since.

A body of water called Between River serves as a divider for this county and the state of Georgia to a neighboring state to the Northeast. It is exactly twenty seven point two miles from the tattered one post mailbox that begins my property. I have never traveled far enough away from my home to have ever seen this river nor that state on the other side of it and I do not expect I ever will.

Around these parts I have been called a homer and it speaks to the fact that I have not an idea in the world what is available to me less than thirty miles from this house. And that revelation more than anything else gives the best impression of how much I leave this home and my rocking chair that I will tell this tale to you from.

Murder, untimely deaths and the bitterest form of hatred imaginable in no way form a simple life but it certainly is a life that I can attest too.

I live alone in my home and I live exactly that way almost all the time now. I was married once but it's been a little over twenty five years since I withstood the loss of the husband I loved so dearly. I was blessed to become the mother of only one child and she was taken away from me also by a murdering husband. A man who deprived me of his dreadful presence also on the very same day when he shotgun-sprayed their brain fragments over one of the walls in a bedroom of their home. This occurred five years behind the birth of my only grandchild.

The story of my life would be one befitting for a good book, for it is a tale of its own filled with many twists and tragedies but the story I wish to tell you this evening is not my own. It belongs to Rix, and by that I mean all of Rix, County, Taylorsville, Gulleytown and Stansburg. It is a desperate and ugly tale highlighted with some unsavory characters and it's centered on top of this unimaginable secret that this county has sheltered for far too many years.

This is also a spiritual tale, one that is brimming with spirits and many of them yet to rest. For reasons that I am not fully aware of, these wandering spirits have chosen me as the vessel to deliver their tale, and my agreement to follow their wishes will keep me awake and away from any of my own rest this evening.

This tale is one that expands back over many years, so adjust as best you can to the timetable I have developed.

On the floorboards down next to me and my rocker I keep a wooden footstool. Never remember ever putting my feet up on it but it has been here as long as I have and it is the only other item on my porch and most folks that visit utilize it to perch down on when we are talking for long sitting. It's not the most comfortable arrangement, but I'm sure it will hold any warm body steady if nothing else.

Relax yourself down somewhere if you have got a little time to spend with an elderly lady that has a tale to tell. Up here in Taylorsville I don't get to entertain much but I would love to have your company for as long as you can stay. And who knows, over the course of your visit, maybe something magical will occur. It has in the past. And if it does, maybe it will provide some settlement and rest to those wandering spirits, and maybe it will bring on an appearance of my wonderful lighting bugs.

FRIDAY, JUNE 14, 1999

DANDLER

WEST OFF OF GEORGIA'S HIGHWAY 44, a small opening appears. The road leads to the very last property on the western shoulder of Rix before travelers enter into Fandale, the next county over. The road is unceremonious and under the cast of nightfall could very easily be missed if not specifically sought. The small opening allows access to a home completely unavailable to view from highway 44 until a number of apples trees that line both sides are passed and a modest hill is crested. Down on the other side of the hill sitting on very flat land, a small ranch home becomes available that is backed by a large catfish pond. Both are tucked neatly away from society seemingly in a small world all their own. The homeowners are Rix County coroner 59-year-old Dennis Jacobs and his wife of many years Fanny, both life time residents of Rix. The couple resides alone on the spacious, dutiful property they love and own and neither would dare to live any place else. Of late however, the property that Dennis cared so much for had been offering him more difficulties than he could mentally handle and none more ghastly and complex than the event taking place within his unlit home on this specific night.

In blood-soaked underclothing, Dennis raced through his home in horror. He stumbled from one corner of it to another. His small green eyes appeared to be spinning as he gazed out of the windows of the home over the shadowy landscape of the large property that he and his beloved Fanny called home.

Dennis Jacobs was a heavy human. He weighed up close to four hundred pounds. He was a spongy mountain of a man. On more than one occasion during his dashes of terrified madness, the mammoth male had slipped from his bare feet in a very bruising manner down to the floor in pools of blood. Blood smeared over most of the wooden floors of the entire home and every single movement made by Dennis served only to make them bloodier as more heavy droplets fell away from one of his hands.

There was someone else inside of the home with Dennis and Fanny and that someone was uninvited and most certainly unwanted.

But the individual was there nonetheless, and haunting the longtime county coroner in every direction his eyes visited.

The romp of madden horror had begun in the Jacobs' bedroom. Detaching himself from a window, Dennis raced for the kitchen to a window there to examine what was going on outside before slugging back to the window in his bedroom. Behind Dennis on the bed lay a body so cruelly punctured that bone-chippings lay exposed on its torso. Turning away from the window again, Dennis crashed into his bed like he never knew it was in the room, the collision toppled him into a crawl that took him over the mutilated body. There were small night dressers near the head of both sides of the bed. Without getting to his feet, the coroner fumbled through a drawer in one of them to obtain a handgun that was secured there.

The huge man groaned while making a giant roll that took him squashing back over the gory body and completely off of the bed into a hard crack against the bloody floor. Dennis had not attempted to protect himself and the fall broke a bone that came jaggedly out of his arm above the wrist. Below the wrist in that same hand, Dennis Jacobs continued to hold firmly to a mass of mangled flesh and bone. In spite of this injury and without even a grimace against the pain, Dennis rose back to his feet again as quickly as he could and burst towards the door. His right arm no longer fully under his control as it partially dangled, Dennis rammed it into the frame of the doorway as he exited.

From the master bedroom a short hallway opened up to a quaint kitchen. Not pausing at all Dennis rumbled forward. After circling the kitchen table, he screamed out as he crashed through a large window that looked out over the rear of the property. This act ripped him open cruelly. Gashing holes were in his face and torso, and the fall nearly broke the county coroner's neck but he merely yielded to it. It didn't stop him. In a smashing thump Dennis spotted the grass red beneath the large bay window of his kitchen. He struggled but somehow made it to his feet again, and in a torturous voice, he screamed.

"Leave me alone! Please . . . God almighty . . . I'm sorry!"

EXISTING WITHIN RIX COUNTY and positioned precisely in between Gulleytown and Stansburg there lays this wondrous setting. There is no history of its origination and no documented record that it is even a part of the land map of the county. Nothing at all to prove its existence other than word of mouth and word of mouth describes it as a gift from the heavens, one that is remarkably mystifying. Pure and unfiltered mythology surrounds this site and there is not a place like it anywhere else in this land. By certain individuals with some knowledge of this area it has been referred to as a misplaced curse but others view it as a sheltering blessing. It depends on who you are in Rix and where you were born whether you carry one view or the other. Miracles and nothing else resides over this special place and there is no disputing that, and I for one have been blessed in some ways and not so blessed in others to have had the opportunity to have seen one of these miracles from afar with my own eyes. The opportunity presented itself to me nearly ten years ago while I sat rocking away in this very chair.

Here begins the tale.

MID-OCTOBER 1989

It was early Fall of the year. A Friday night high school football game had recently ended, eight teenagers coupled off into pairs all had agreed earlier during school that day to meet up at a log cabin home. The cabin was owned by Henly Blackmon who was mayor of Rix at the time and father to Lawrence Blackmon, one of the teenagers agreeing to meet up and the Rix County Fighting Trojans popular young quarterback.

Purposely the teenagers had all agreed to not include any of their parents of their plans after the ballgame. Mayor Henly Blackmon expected his son to be hanging out around the town square like most teenagers usually did after Friday night games or enjoying some teen event that kept them away from homes after ballgames. That would not be the case on this Friday night. Seventeen year old Lawrence had invited his girlfriend Susan McCoy, his three closet friends and their girlfriends over to a second home that his parents owned that sit above a large lake located in the Stansburg community where some of the kids lived.

Arriving at the cabin right with Lawrence and Susan around ten-thirty was Calbert Davis and his girlfriend Kim Hopkins. On their heels were Gary Simms and Solomon Builder riding in a vehicle together. They were followed minutes later by both boys' girlfriends,

Latosha Williams and Carla Freeman. Before eleven that evening everyone invited had arrived at the expansive property and was inside the log cabin that sits on over one hundred acres of mostly flat wooded land except for the area immediately surrounding the cabin. The lake fronted it, there, the soil soften and descended sharply. That's why the town called it Sunken Lake.

Following the Fighting Trojans victory most of the teenagers who were all juniors and seniors had consumed an absorbent amount of alcohol and it had pushed them towards different stages of anomalous behavior, some of it typical for kids their age, but a portion of it was nothing close to normal and that portion would end the night in tragedy and reshape all of their futures.

BY TWELVE FORTY-FIVE, Latosha, Kim and Susan, the girlfriends of Gary Simms, Calbert Davis and Lawrence Blackmon were out of the cabin all waiting inside of the blue, four-door Ford that Latosha Williams had driven out to Sunken Lake. She was attempting to arrive home before one when a curfew went into affect for not only her, but all the girls who were members of the varsity cheerleader squad.

Latosha's best friend Clara Freeman was holding everyone up. She was out of her mind intoxicated and had begged off degrees of persuasion to leave with the rest of the girls but was committed instead to remain locked behind a bedroom door with her boyfriend Solomon Builder. Clara had decided to catch a ride back to Gulleytown with her boyfriend whenever he and Gary Simms decided to cross back over the rail tracks from the mostly white section of the Rix that they were in now.

The homes of Susan McCoy and Kim Hopkins were in Stansburg so Latosha would not have to drive far to reach them. She had enough time to get everyone home before curfew without having to rush if Clara would just come to her senses and leave with her as they had planned.

After dropping off Susan and Kim, Latosha was all alone in the small car when she crossed over the railroad tracks into Gulleytown and was safely inside of the home she shared with her mother and two younger sisters with another five minutes to spare before her curfew.

THERE WAS NEVER enough time in any day to meet the satisfaction of Clara Freeman when it came to being in the presence of Solomon Builder. Clara Freeman loved her handsome boyfriend with every bit of her heart and would trust him with her life because she knew his love for her was identical. There would be indeed punishment to endure for missing curfew but under the irresponsible conditions she had placed herself in, she could not decipher what the term meant. And it didn't much matter to Clara. Nothing did. She was with Solomon, the only boy she had ever thought of. The night was a very special one for her. It was the one that in which Clara lost her virginity. And this committed her to Solomon even more, and when that was coupled with all the alcohol she had consumed, it forced her to push away the plans she had made with Latosha in meeting their curfew. Clara Freeman lay inside of a log cabin bedroom existing in a world of satisfaction different than any she had ever known, and she existed there for the most part without awareness. Beer and alcohol had seen to that.

Solomon Builder was referred to as Slay by all the people that knew and loved him. It was a nickname he had been called for years and it excited him to extended lengths to hear Clara call his name. It seemed that no one could whisper his name like her. Slay Builder was under the same teenage crush of love that consumed his girlfriend and there appeared to be no one in Rix that didn't know of it. The night had been very special for him also. He had received a couple of excellent scores for tests done earlier in school and in overtime of the game, Slay had scored his teams winning touchdown. Being with Clara the way that he had and the enjoyment they both received from it was just perfect for a boy caught up in his first love. Neither he nor Clara knew much about sex, but they both had enjoyed sharing it. The entire night would have been perfect if he would have been able to stop Clara from drinking too much. Arriving at the cabin, Slay had taken a sip from one beer. It was only the suds from the top of the can but it was enough to build his guilt. Slay's parents, Edward and Thomasina Builder had not raised their only child to partake in any spirits. Slay also knew that his parents would not take kindly to him having sex before marriage but he worried less about that than the alcohol consumption.

As a country preacher Slay's father earned a living traveling to churches where ever they would have him, he went from town to town as a guest pastor but had no specific church of his own. Whatever monies Edward Builder earned from speaking the word was assisted by the weekly check his wife pulled in as the day manager of the local dollar store.

When not at church or work, the Builders stayed secluded in their home. There they sheltered their son and the young man thrived in the environment, and it didn't include deprivation because everything the respectable boy ever desired Edward and Thomasina Builder made available to him. He was all they wanted in a son and they were all he needed as parents.

The Builders raised their son in the community of Gulleytown. By the time Slay had reached the age of seven, older residents in the community had tagged him with a nick-name of Slayer simply because he always seemed to be going from one home to another swatting at flies. By the time he had reached his teens Slayer had been shorten to Slay, and the name has stuck since that day.

THERE WERE THREE bedrooms within the lake cabin home above Sunken Lake, Clara and Slay had lay together in one of them for almost two hours before he finally rose and after covering her nakedness with a sheet, walked from the room to a bathroom that was on the other side of the bedroom's door. In a total state of unconsciousness from all of her earlier drinking Clara Freeman lay all alone.

All four teenage boys that had arrived at the cabin remained there and three of them were on the outside of the cabin next to the next to the bedroom window where Slay had moments ago left Clara. One of the teenagers had witness some of the sexual expression that had taken place on the other side of the window and it was enough to feed his own desires.

Lawrence Blackmon was already aflame with lust before his arrival outside near the window. What he witnessed there between his two friends only served to elevate his desires, and he had a predetermined idea of just how to extinguish his flame.

"Ok that's it . . . Slay just did it . . . he gave the signal. And I'm first this time, no matter what."

"First my ass man . . . that's that man's girl in there and he ain't' gave you no signal," Gary Simms said in frustration.

13

He was outside of the window also, but unlike Lawrence, he and Calbert Davis had not looked in on their friends. Everyone referred to Gary Simms as Big Simms because he was exactly that. He had a large bald head that looked as if it had been stuffed down onto bullish shoulders and he stood right at six-four. His legs were enormous. Big Simms was one of those individuals that appeared to be the same size from his ankles all the way up to his head and he was by far the best and most physical athlete on their football team.

Although he was pretty drunk himself, Big Simms was sober enough to know that what his good friend Lawrence had been doing outside of the cabin looking in on their other friends was not right and he wanted nothing to do with it or what Lawrence's intentions now were. With his knees up in the front of his chest, Big Simms had his back against the cabin while sitting on the ground below where Lawrence was standing. Calbert Davis stood on the other side of Lawrence with his back brushing lightly against the structure.

After hearing Lawrence's intentions Gary Simms pulled up to his feet to draw at his friend's arm.

"What the fuck's wrong with you Lawrence? Slay ain't tryna let nobody be with his lady, and you know that better than I do!"

"What you doing Big Simms . . . turn me a loose," Lawrence exclaimed as he struggled but couldn't break the hold that Gary Simms had captured him with.

"I'm the one standing up here watching, and I ain't blind. Slay just went out the room and that's the signal we always use."

Lawrence's words were more pleading then convincing. "Come on Big Simms, you know he knows that we're all out here waiting on the signal. That's how we do it all the time. If it was me in there instead of him, he'd be right out here with you guys doing the same thing we doing . . . ain't that right Calbert?"

Lawrence had blue eyes that carried a frozen stillness to them all the time. His eyes were so still that it almost appeared that ice was a part of his pupils.

Those frozen blue eyes raced from viewing Big Simms over to the bluer eyes of Calbert Davis. The teenager was not at all in the right frame of mind to receive them, or the question that had arrived with them.

In exact size alone, Calbert was hulking, almost thirty pounds heavier than Big Simms. But for a young man in ownership of so much girth, his voice was velvety soft. Older women always complimented him on how charmingly smooth it was. But whenever Calbert felt pressured or closed-in on by individuals or his surroundings, a pronounced form of stuttering uprooted everything that was usually easy and normal for him.

The question by Lawrence and the drunken stupor that they all were in pushed Calbert chest-deep into unwanted pressure and jump-started his stammering.

"I d-don't kno-know 'bout that La-Lawrence . . . Slays never did-did nothing li-like that out here with us and-and plus he's got Cl-cl-clara in there."

With a look of incredulous delivered to both his teammates Lawrence proclaimed, "What you mean you don't know? What the hell is wrong you two? Now turn me a loose Big Simms . . . and stop acting stupid!"

With a grunting effort Lawrence flung his arm free and began making his way around the cabin for the front door.

Disappointed, Big Simms first glared in Calbert's direction before rushing to overtake the pace of his other unsteady friend before Lawrence could reach the front corner of the home. After catching up Big Simms spun Lawrence towards him with a bit of violence.

"Hold up!"

"For what . . ." Lawrence half shouted while staggering backwards but quickly stood straight again.

"Look man we violating already. Just by being back there by that window is a violation of every code we ever stood for and now to top it all off you're about to mess things all the way up with some bullshit that you know ain't right. We fucked up man but come on . . . think straight. You and Calbert both know that every girl we've ever snuck out here was never nobody's girlfriends. Think about it Lawrence. This is your folk's house," Big Simms said with emphasis. "You're the one who set the off limit rules on watching each others girls out here. I guess now the rule don't go for you, and now you tryna totally disrespect the man by believing he wants you to freak his lady while she's drunk." He pointed a finger, "Now nobody but you been with this bullshit since you pulled us around here and I for one ain't 'bout to sit here and let it go no further."

"Big-big-big S-s-s-simms is r-r-r-right Lawrence." Calbert had followed their every step to where they had come to a stop.

15

"Shut the hell up Biggun!" An aggressive finger accompanied Lawrence's angry voice as he addressed Calbert by the name he had begin calling him every since hearing a coach refer to Calbert as that while playing football as children. The words were strong enough to back the huge teenager up a half of a step after he had come right up off of Big Simms' back.

"There was one thing you said that was right Big Simms . . . this is my folk's property. I don't know what the hell done gotten into you, but I get to run what's goes on out here . . . not you. And I'm saying fuck all them codes you talking about. The rules have changed." He sniffed before continuing, "I see you forgot to mention that every girl we done had out here to freak before has been white. Don't remember you raising no issues about that. Now that we finally got somebody in there that's your own color, you all of a sudden got problems with what we doing and how we do it."

Big Simms had released the arm of Lawrence once they were facing one another. He struggle in his attempt but did recapture it.

Lawrence's face had flushed and he forced out his feelings through lips that had tightened.

"For all I care, you can get your ass back into that junk truck and head back over to the other side of the tracks. Me and Calbert about to get us our first shot at a black girl tonight . . . now get your fucking hands off of me and don't put 'em on me again!"

Using his entire body, Lawrence swung his wrist free. Every word he had spoken had served to enrage his large friend who stood staring at him in total disbelief for a half a moment. And then with perfect quickness, Big Simms lowered his shoulders and exploded into Lawrence shoulder first like he had tackled several ball carriers earlier that night. The vicious blow took Lawrence off his feet into a violent collision with the cabin. It sent Lawrence down so fast that it seemed as if the ground raised up to collect him.

On impact with the cabin Big Simms entire body folded inward like an accordion. In his assault on Lawrence, his large head had clubbed against the logs that framed the home. Bent abnormally, Big Simms appeared to linger for a moment up against the cabin before crumbling in a face first dive right down on top of Lawrence.

With concern rising up to frame his face, most of the white in Calbert's eyes showed as he rushed over to assist.

CALBERT DAVIS had met Gary Simms at the age of six on a playground right off of the town square in Rix and since that day they had been best of friends, this was an entire year prior to him ever knowing Slay or Lawrence. Calbert did not share the caramel skin tone nor did he own a pair of small brown eyes like those of Gary Simms's, but his meaty-shaved head and massive size twinned that of his now raspy breathing unconscious friend.

CALBERT ROLLED the large boy over to his back and then slid both of his arms down next to his side after Lawrence's feet had pulled one of them away while the shaken teenager attempted to stand again after coming from beneath the weight of Big Simms's attack.

"You crazy fuck . . . what's wrong with you?!"

Drawing back, Lawrence kicked out in his own attack for the fallen teenager but it was thwarted by Calbert who caught Lawrence's leg and shoved him backwards into the home again.

"Leave him alone Lawrence, c-c-can't you see he's hurt." Calbert leveled Lawrence with a jumbled look of concern mixed with distaste. He continued to watch as his friend turned immediately away. Calbert was kneeling as he looked away from Lawrence to whisper to Gary Simms.

"Big Si-simms, you alright . . . can you hear m-m-m-me?"

Lawrence stepped closer before kneeling down also and was instantly greeted with the labored breathing of Gary Simms.

"Biggun, look at you worrying like a little wimp, Big Simms is gonna be fine. He just knocked himself out being stupid that's all."

Lawrence pushed against one of Calbert's shoulders to stand again.

"Stop worrying like a girl Biggun. Big Simms is alright. You see he's breathing and all, just let him lay there and sleep off one of them six packs and he'll be fine. I promise. Now come on and get up because he ain't going nowhere any time soon so there ain't no need for us to be tryna wake him up or move him right now. Let's go inside and have some fun like we started."

"You-you-you crazy or something Lawrence . . . Big Simms is hurt man!"

"Hurt! Biggun, Big Simms ain't no more hurt then you were last Tuesday when he knocked you silly in practice. You were out just like this 'til coach woke you up with some of that smelling salt. You were alright when you woke up and Big Simms will be too, he'll just have a knot on that big head for being stupid." Lawrence nudged Calbert with one of his knees, "now come on Biggun . . . get up and let's go."

Nothing that Lawrence said made much sense to Calbert so the boy's attention remained where it had been all along on Gary Simms. He lingered over his fallen friend for several moments while Lawrence continued to try to persuade him away and then suddenly there was total silence between them. Without another word being spoken, Calbert allowed himself to be back-collared and pulled clumsily from outside into the cabin and to the bedroom where Clara still lay having not moved from the position she had held since Slay had left her.

The bedroom that Clara lay in was not very big at all and once Calbert had followed Lawrence into it, it became even smaller. The room was furnished but only sparsely. A large shelf of rows centered one wall with nothing on either side of it but there was a door at the end of the wall that open to a small closet. It was partially open. Two chairs with wooden arm sit out a couple of feet in front of the bed. They held the discarded clothing of Clara Freeman and Slay Builder. Behind the chairs up next to the bed down on the floor was a giant trunk that was pad locked and as wooden as everything else in the room. The trunk ran the length of the four post bed that Clara lay slightly off center on.

The door to the bedroom that the teenagers had just walked through opened up to the window where Lawrence had watched Clara and Slay through. A few feet down the wall from the door was a fireplace that was stacked from the pine floor boards all the way up to the ceiling with large stones. Calbert came to a solid but uncomfortable rest against the stones, leaning with his back to the fireplace. He skillfully trained his eyes for a rotation that included the window and the back of the door, but away from Clara.

A bathroom was located next door. The sound of water running could be heard coming from it, indicating that Slay Builder was possibly taking a shower.

Lawrence was wearing a dark gray wind suit with a large Nike emblem stretched across the back of it that glowed fluorescently whenever the surroundings were dark. He freed himself from both jacket and pants and then snickered as he staggered over to the bed. The moment Lawrence had wanted had finally arrived but he would be acting alone. This fact was obvious to him even in his condition

18

of intoxication. Gary Simms, his biggest objector had knocked himself unconscious, and although Calbert no longer tried to stop him, it was clear there wasn't even an intention on his behalf to even look in the direction of their friend Clara Freeman. For a very brief period, Calbert did center his focus over her but for only long enough to release a heavy sigh. He then pulled it away to look through the window towards the vehicles sitting in a designated parking area a small distance away from the cabin. Calbert's focus through the window was for only several moments before he closed down on his eyelids completely to deny himself from any view.

As Lawrence pulled away the sheet covering Clara, she rambled something that was undecipherable but it was alluring to Lawrence. That tiny sound of gibberish coupled with her innocence pushed Lawrence into more snickers as he took in every inch of her small but shapely body.

Lying motionless on her back, Clara was completely exposed when Lawrence kissed at her face and then her neck. He went down from there to the top of her breast. All actions that drew no response, even the full weight of his body on top of her did nothing to awaken Clara.

Lawrence snickered again and it was much louder this time because he was well aware that it would take a small miracle for the girl he had known as a friend since they were both twelve to open her eyes anytime soon. Lawrence's pursuit towards the desires boiling within him had grown more aggressively when the small room all of a sudden brightens a bit as the door that led into it was opened.

THE SOUND of water could still be heard in the room on the other side of the wall where the bathroom was, Slay Builder had taken a long shower and had left the water running on purpose so that when he carried Clara in there would not have to be any adjustments made to ensure her comfort.

Wrapping the young man's waist was a towel that descended all the way down to his ankles, other than that the teenager was naked.

Solomon 'Slay' Builder was no where close to being as huge as his two teammates and good friends Calbert Davis and Gary Simms but he was a bit larger than Lawrence and much stronger. His body fat was lesser than any team member and he worked out like a man possessed.

Slay's entire upper body was water-spotted from the shower and the small droplets seemed to cling to his every muscle as he re-entered the bedroom from the hall. His expression showed betrayal. It showed hurt and it was plain to see. It was a wounded incurable hurt that his large friend Calbert Davis would never get an opportunity to observe because his eyes were never open to witness it.

On the bed in front of Slay, Lawrence Blackmon had closed his eyes momentarily also and they had been that way for mere seconds prior to the door being opened as he continued to force his body against Clara who still offered no response.

Slay Builder stopped his forward motion right on the inside of the doorway and just stood there as if he was framing the moment. The heart-broken teenager inhaled the atmosphere and allowed his deep hurt to escape through nostrils that had begun to flare. For only a few brief moments, Slay allowed his attention to move away from what was occurring before him to focus on where Calbert stood, but it then went instantly back to the bed again before he introduced any of his feelings verbally.

"You mortherfuckers!" It came out of him in a winded fashion after he had inhaled deeply.

After a couple of running steps, Slay launched for the bed, his angry scream seemed to arrive atop of Lawrence at the exact moment as he did to violently separate his friend from Clara.

The bed was not in the center of the room and it was not up against any wall either. There was about a two foot separation from bed and wall. Expanding out from beneath the bed in each direction was a hand woven rug, circular in its pattern. It was there for comfort to separate the coolness of the wooden floor cabin from the inhabitant's bare feet.

The collision created by Slay as he slammed in to Lawrence eventually landed them in a thud down to the floor with both teenagers partially on the rug but mostly on the flooring, and they both were completely naked now as the towel came undone on contact that wrapped the waist of Slay Builder.

The disturbing shout and the battle going on down on the floor forced Calbert's eyes to open again.

The diminutive body of Clara Freeman absorbed the full jolting force of the two teenagers as Slay crashed into Lawrence, but the impact had no effect in pulling her out of her incoherent state, nor would anything that would come on the heels of it.

"Why Lawrence," Slay strained out while pounding away with his fist to do damage to Lawrence.

"I thought you were but I see you never were my friend!"

"Slay! Wait . . . nothing happen man! Nothing happen . . . get off . . . get off me!"

It was as if Lawrence had not said a word. Slay continued punching him in every area aimed in his face and head. Lawrence discontinued his pleas to be heard and began to fight back but with little affect. Desperate and having very little left in his ability to defend himself, Lawrence immediately begin to scratch and claw at Slay's face which only served to enrage even more the teenager on top of him.

With his teeth set in a clench, Slay Builder instantly stopped pounding down. He looked into the eyes of Lawrence as his friend continued clawing, kicking and spitting and without uttering another word cupped his hands into a lock around Lawrence's neck. This action squashed out a scream coming up from beneath him. Slay then begin to squeeze so tightly that Lawrence's skin could be seen pinching up in some area between his thick fingers.

Muffled and strained into a whisper were the next words that came up out of Lawrence.

"Help . . . please! I can't . . . I can't breath."

The words had no affect on Slay Builder. Whatever the sounds were that came up from Lawrence only seem to anger him more. Measuring the strength struggling beneath him, Slay felt it as it begin to fade and with his hands remaining locked raised and adjusted his body weight to place both of his knees up and onto the chest of Lawrence Blackmon. He then positioned to push down even heavier in an attempt to squeeze every bit of life from the friend he had called his best for nearly nine years.

Slay Builder's head slowly begin to tilt to an angle on one side and from there a tear dropped from his eyes down into the shoulder length golden strands of Lawrence's hair.

The fingers scraping at Slay's face had lost all strength and there were no longer any desperate pleas for help, only whimpers.

From the moment that Calbert Davis had become aware of Slay Builder's presence in the room, he had remained where he stood and had instructed himself to remain completely clear of everything because he felt that Lawrence deserved a good thrashing for the behavior he had displayed, but he could not allow this to continue on any longer.

The bed Clara was on had tall posts on each corner, as though being forced, Calbert approached it and used the first post he came upon to assist him in almost a swing toward his friends' positioning on the floor. He delivered an uncomfortable stare to Clara Freeman and allowed it to linger while standing behind Slay Builder. Calbert's focus and every movement from that point forward appeared mechanical as his attention drifted from the bed and came back to the struggle occurring on the floor.

Lawrence's legs were no longer kicking out. One lay straight and still while the other pushed up and down slowly as if he was attempting to push away. Calbert stepped closer until he was standing between them. He then leaned slightly forward to look over the tighten shoulders of one of his best friends and down into the icy blue pleading eyes of one his other best friends, Lawrence Blackmon.

The sight was a disturbing one for Calbert, so disturbing that he instantly closed his eyes again in order to not continue to frame the picture of the true ugliness of one of his friends squeezing the life from the other. Without uttering a word, Calbert kept his eyes closed as he drew an arm back above his shoulders and swung down at Slay with much more force than he really intended too, and much more force than he really had too.

The fire iron poke was right next to the fireplace where Calbert had been standing, he never even remembered picking it up, but it was in his hand and he had used it to club at Slay Builder who never saw it coming.

There was a moment of stillness as every moment appeared to be suspended and the room fell suddenly quiet It only took seconds but it seemed like much longer, Slay fell heavily, down and to the left of where Lawrence was. Both of his arms folded inward and were trapped beneath the weight of his body. His head lay twisted off of the rug towards Lawrence but his body crumbled in the other direction. Slay Builder lay awkwardly motionless.

On the floor beside Slay, Lawrence was grasping for more air. He moaned and coughed until his breathing pattern came back close to normalcy.

After his dreadful action had silenced the entire cabin, Calbert crumbled hard to his knees, his head bowed into cupped hands. His body heaved and he made no attempt at all to hold back tears that had begin coming in uncontrollable torrents.

A half minute had stolen by but it crawled past more like it was half an hour instead and nothing had changed. Everyone remained where they were until Lawrence mustered enough strength to finally struggle up from beneath Slay's lower body to rest his back against the bed. There was still some laboring in his breathing as his focus settled on what had become of Slay Builder. His friend was in such a mess that Lawrence could hardly look at him. Lawrence tried but his emotions crest up to take an explosive leap from his chest. Lawrence quickly looked away from Slay and it helped him manage to keep everything in check. He then felt about his throat gingerly as if this action would some how return him comfort and then looked over to Calbert, whose own emotions were dealing him a hand that he was not playing very well.

Lawrence stood up to circle around the mess heaped on the floor and wrestled back into his clothing and then finally spoke.

"This ain't good Biggun . . . this ain't good at all."

Right there before them, Slay Builder was piled up and not moving but neither boy had dared to get any closer to see how badly their friend was hurt. They were both scared and both praying that the worst had not happen but it appeared obvious.

Lawrence's breathing pattern had come back to as close to normal as the present situation was going to allow. He stepped cautiously forward to push at Calbert.

"Get up Biggun . . . we gotta see how bad he's hurt."

The touch from Lawrence cringed Calbert slightly. The heavy crying he had fallen into didn't end but Calbert did manage to stand and with Lawrence bending next to him got a better angle of the damage his hands had caused to their friend.

Before both boys could back away, Lawrence was shuddering hard at what he had just gotten a close up look at.

In the closely cropped hair above one of Slay Builder's ears was a large hole and it remained filled with the fire tool that Calbert had clubbed at him with.

Blood sprayed across Lawrence's face. It was the blood of Slay Builder that Lawrence didn't even notice was there. And there was so much of it running from the fallen boy's head that some of the blood had already traveled over to soak into the rug he still lay on top of, and even more was pooling up on the floor planks.

In a direction that was head on Calbert could not even look at Slay anymore, there was just too much of his friend that was no longer there. From the corner of his eyes and from beneath his brow at different angles is how he looked at him until he finally just couldn't look at Slay at all anymore. Calbert twisted and went around the bed. He had moved over closer to where Clara remained and with the care a mother would give, gathered her small body into his arms while pleading for her to awake. Calbert did this until he was startled again by a hand pushing at his back.

"Biggun, come on. I think we need to get away from this room so . . . so we can think. Everything closing in on me in here, we've got to get out of here for a minute so we can try to think this thing out."

Hearing Lawrence's voice, Calbert completely covered Clara with the sheet she had once lay beneath while still trying to will her back to consciousness.

"Come on Biggun . . . what you doing? She out of it man. She ain't waking up no time soon so just leave her alone."

"Lawrence . . . we . . . we done messed up. We need an ambulance. Everybody's hurt. Get an ambulance for Slay. Go call them for everybody . . . now Lawrence."

"Ambulance," Lawrence muttered.

"Yeah, c-c-call them right now."

Lawrence begun stammering, "Wait, wait a minute Biggun, slow down a little bit. We need to do some figuring first before we go calling folks out here."

"Fi-fi-figuring, what we figuring?"

"I don't know Biggun but it's a lot going on you know. We at least need to be together on what we are going to say before they get here. Don't you think we at least need to know that before we start calling folks?"

Calbert attempted to speak but Lawrence headed him off.

"Look, let's first get from in here from around all of this . . . ." Calbert never looked in his direction as Lawrence glanced down to Slay Builder in his settled position before immediately continuing. "Biggun, I need you to hear me please. I'm telling you that I can't really breathe any more standing in here. We need some fresh air, it'll be good for both of us and then maybe we can figure out who to call and what to do about Slay and Big Simms."

Calbert still held Clara in his arms, but without another word of protest he placed her back gently on the bed and insured she remained covered before allowing Lawrence to draw him from the room. Although the actions of Calbert were willing and not forced, they were in total contrast to how he was truly feeling inside.

Attached to the front of the cabin was a porch that ran its length. Banisters of logs framed it in a rectangular fashion except where three narrow steps lead up onto it. The huge frame of Calbert plugged those steps as he sat legs wide facing Sunken Lake with tears in his eyes. Lawrence Blackmon paced in back of him and while doing so made statements and produced ideas that Calbert didn't much understand or agree with. In fact, Calbert never replied to anything that Lawrence spoke about until the name of Big Simms was mentioned.

"Biggun I'm telling you the first thing I think we should do is go around there and get him. Bring Big Simms back around front with us."

"For what . . . what we need to do that for? When we were inside you said we needed to come out here to figure out who to call and what to say; now you want to move Big Simms when earlier you wanted to just leave him back there. Slay's laying in there dead and if he's not he'll be done bleed to death soon while we out here just wasting time while you suppose to be thinking. The more we sit out here thinking the more me-me-messing up we doing. The man is in there dead Lawrence!"

"You think I don't already know that," Lawrence shouted. "And don't be saying that anymore. What we're going to do is worry about who's alive out here first and what to do and say about what happened to them. And that's why I'm saying to get Big Simms so we can make sure that he's still straight and get him around from the side of the cabin."

"Now-now-now you wanna make sure he's straight. We should have been thinking about that at first. We shouldna been around there in the first place to have to leave him back there . . . and now look what' happen . . . Slays dead."

"Damn Biggun, I told you to stop saying that! And while you at it stop all of that damn crying! I'm thinking because I'm trying to help. You the one that killed him, you dumb fuck. Now shut up and go get Big Simms like I told you."

In the manner that he had fallen, Gary Simms was still positioned. Calbert first tried feverishly to awaken him but his friend gave no response. He then braced the large teen up against the home before going deep beneath the arms of Gary Simms. Alone and in a very troubled state, Calbert strained to drag the dead weight of his friend to the front of the residence. Once there, he placed Gary Simms a couple of feet to the right of the center of the steps he had only minutes ago sat on.

Lawrence had remained on the porch while Calbert went to haul back Gary Simms. He allowed one of his legs to ride a portion of the banister as he sat while he waited for Calbert to look up his way.

"He's still alive, right?"

"He still won't wa-wa wake up, but he's still breathing hard . . . now what?"

"Ok good." Lawrence pushed both of his palms out in a gesture of relaxation. "Now we just keep calming ourselves down. Clara and Big Simms we know both should be fine as soon as they wake up, and Biggun," he paused, "we both know that Slay is gone so let's get our story straight about what we was doing out here and why what happen to him did."

"It was an accident Lawrence, we-we-we'll tell the sh-sheriff just that and he'll see it when he comes."

With a solemn face Lawrence followed what Calbert had offered and then gave in return, "Yeah Biggun, it was an accident. We sho' didn't plan it. But what about my dad, what's he going to think when he finds out? That's what got me. I don't think we should call the sheriff right off, we better call him first."

Standing over Gary Simms, Calbert's disapproval to what was just said was plain and obvious. Calbert moved away from his fallen friend and made a small leap up onto the porch to make sure that Lawrence was more than aware of it.

"What you talking about? You-you-you know how your d-d-dad acted the last time he caught us all out here."

"Man that stuff don't matter no more . . . this is different. Big Simms is hurt, and Slay is . . . ." Lawrence didn't want to say the word. He shook away his last image of Solomon Builder and then took a couple of moments to regain full control before getting back on track.

"Look at us Biggun, we drunk, not just me and you, Clara and Big Simms too. I don't believe that's good for this situation. We don't need to call the sheriff right off; you never know how it could end up. My dad's got influence. The Sheriff will listen to whatever he says. He always does."

"Alright, ca-ca-call somebody else then if you don't wanna call the sheriff. What about Slay's dad or even Big Simms folks, but not your dad man. He won't understand this . . . he won't even try too."

The argument went on intensely for several minutes and it appeared that a pattern was being laid. Calbert relinquished his fight and caved in to Lawrence again.

Confused and more nervous than he had ever been in his life was how Calbert Davis felt as he eased back down to a seat while Lawrence Blackmon scurried back into the cabin to phone his father.

It took less than ten minutes for a car to arrive and it was the longest ten minutes both boys ever had to wait through.

Although it was located directly in front of one of Rix County Mayor Henly Blackmon's home, Sunken Lake was not apart of his personal property nor any other individual for that matter. It was not a portion of any state or county park. It was just a beautiful lake that the county of Rix did however manage for its inhabitants and all that came to visit. And they came from all over to boat, fish and picnic around it. There was a dark history that went hand-in-hand with the lake and surroundings part and it was almost as big as the body of water and mostly sordid.

The road leading out to Sunken Lake and the cabin where the boys were was a two lane no passing one that bent into one curve after another.

Calbert and Lawrence looked on as a long car sped from the road and pulled onto the unpaved drive. It was a small stretch of road that ended at a small graveled parking area. It was to the left of the cabin and across several yards of grass from the window where Clara Freeman and her boyfriend Solomon Builder still remained.

The white Lincoln town car lunged to a stop next to where Gary Simms' rusted red pick up truck and a car driven out by Lawrence were parked. It was only matters of seconds before the slamming of a car door would burst open the eerie silence of what had become of the night.

At fifty-two-years of age, Henly Blackmon could still run but he half-trotted over the parking area and across the lawn instead towards his log cabin. Halfway between the parking area and where the cabin was he was met by his son Lawrence.

MAYOR HENLY BLACKMON was a bear of a man. He was as tall as Calbert and carried at least fifty more pounds of adult weight than the still maturing teenager. Henly was a divisive man to say the least and he pulled no punches on his thoughts and the way he lived his life. He was serving out a second term as mayor of Rix and most outsiders wondered how he could be elected to a first term. For whatever the case, Henly Blackmon had been elected as mayor to Rix on back to back terms and would without a doubt be elected a third time if he decided to run again. And for those people that made unbecoming remarks about him and all that he stood for, none of those individuals ever said things of that nature before Henly's ruby red face and pink puffy eyes.

A LARGE ARM had been drawn back before he came within reach of his son. Henly slapped the boy so hard that it tilted them both off balance.

"What the hell is wrong with your face boy? It wasn't like that after the ball game."

Stunned but not surprised by his father's action, Lawrence gathered back his balance almost immediately and reflectively pushed his hands up to touch around the swollen areas of his face along with the drying blood from his battle with Slay Builder that he had completely forgotten was there. Withdrawing his hands, Lawrence decided against responding directly to his father's question, he decided instead to release the ugliest detail of the night's disaster right away.

"He's dead daddy . . . Slays dead!"

"Hell, you practically told me and anybody else that might have been listening that over the phone when you called. What I wanna know from you is what the hell that boy's doing back out here again on my property anyway? He ain't suppose to be out here boy."

It was a cold, very cold disregarding take for the lost of a life.

Calbert had closed his eyes in frustration and his head was bowed and shaking in disapproval. He had lived only long enough to be in his late teens, but from a lifetime of experience, he knew full well the type of individual Henly Blackmon was, and had predicted the events would play out as they had begun with him involved. He regretted it even more for allowing Lawrence to call his father.

"For fun Daddy . . . we were just out here celebrating a little after the game. I'm sorry for bringing folks out here, but we were just celebrating, and now . . . and now . . . Slay is dead." The boy was almost frantic. "We got into this fight . . . and Calbert ended up hitting him. It killed him Daddy . . . Slay's really dead!"

Disgust carved at the face of Henly Blackmon as he watched his son. He took Lawrence in from the deepest point of his son's eyes all the way down his body to the running shoes. Henly then looked him back up in the same fashion and made a mental note that his son had re-positioned out of arms reach from him.

Calbert had regained a seat on the steps and was only a few feet away from where he had laid Gary Simms out in a prone position on the ground.

Henly curled the fingers on one of his hands and positioned them near his mouth. He then glared past Lawrence and over to Calbert but came quickly back to his son with his thoughts and a pointed finger.

"You say that this all started from a simple fight?"

"Yeah."

In a tight lunge Henly Blackmon was on top on his son again to deliver another jarring slap that Lawrence stood up against better this time in a manner of anticipating the action.

"Sorry Daddy, I meant yes sir, me and Slay were fighting."

"Waist breath, it seems that's all I do when it comes to you because you never listen to a damn thing. I been warning you every since you been old enough to understand to stay away from their kind but you just won't let it sink in. Maybe this is what it had to take to smarten you up."

Henly inched ever closer to Lawrence to issue his next inquiry, which pushed his son to gain a little more length in distance by leaning a few inches back.

"Are you sure the boys dead?"

"Yes sir, bloods every where. It's just every where."

CALBERT PLACED a hand down to push away from his seat and the other one on a portion of the banister where it ended for the opening of the steps, he then rose to his feet.

Lawrence suddenly began shedding tears for the first time, but the movement behind him by Calbert pulled away his father's attention, although only momentarily.

"That's him on the ground there?"

"No sir, that's Big Simms"

"What the hell did you say, that's who!? Who the . . . ."

"Wait Daddy, please let me explain," Lawrence rushed out.

"I'm listening," Henly produced in a scowled whispered that was laced with discontentment.

Lawrence knew his father well and was very much aware of the slippery track he was own as it relates to how unpredictable the man standing before him was and that was irregardless to their relationship to each other. He attempted to choose his words carefully before sniffing out.

"It was all about celebrating the win against Lincoln County. I got Big Simms, Slay and Calbert to come out to the cabin. We got to drinking and funning around and we all was kind of wrestling and Big Simms kind of fell off balance and hit his head against the house and didn't get up. We checked him, and we don't think nothings seriously wrong. Ah," Lawrence paused and began scrambling his thoughts for the proper cover for the next lie he had to expose to his father.

"This girl name Clara . . . she's Slay's girlfriend. She's in there with him, and she's passed out too."

There was an attack forthcoming again that Lawrence expected. He took a blinding blow to the temple that sent him directly to the ground followed by a painful kick that landed right below his sternum and it left him writhing in pain. The assault ended as quickly as it began and Henly queried.

"I'm listening. Tell me all about y'all wrestling her down and the house knocking her out too. Isn't that what happened Lawrence?"

Lawrence Blackmon's core burned from the assault that had just taken place but he knew he had very little time to recover. He had to make it back to his feet to meet his father's glare or the battering would just continue. He struggle but stood and then answered.

"No . . . no sir . . . I wasn't gonna say that. Clara's just drunk. She's had too much to drink and passed out."

"Let me make sure I got your score card correct Lawrence; you got one nigger passed out, one knocked out and one dead." He pointed towards Calbert as he finished the despicable statement, "I guess if you do something about this piece of dog shit here you'll have a perfect game going."

Calbert Davis moved to a position to stand wide over Gary Simms like a guarding angel on the second of witnessing Henly Blackmon striding by Lawrence towards his direction. Calbert stiffened as the mayor of Rix came to within a foot of his position but released a bit of the rigidness as Henly turned back to further acknowledge his son.

"You put a permanent end to all that damn crying and from right here you take on the ritual of being a man. When you grow balls big enough to make a kill, you damn sure better be man enough to stand up to whatever it takes to get your behind out from under the consequences of it."

"But it wasn't something we meant to do daddy. It was an accident, and we just panicked behind it."

"No real man ever panics for any reason and it don't matter what the circumstances are boy. Been telling you that since you been about eight or nine but you won't get your head out of your ass to listen. And secondly, there's no such thing as an accident when it comes to situations like this. A decision was made, the result was death and that's cut and dry."

FOR MOST of the adult life of Henly Tallmadge Blackmon he had worn a banana hat and his selection was irregardless to the weather. Standing on his own property in the early morning hours of a new day less than twenty four inches from being up against the chest of Calbert Davis, the hat the mayor had chosen to place down over his graying strands had a two inch white ban circling it. Young Calbert like most of Rix constituents had never seen him with it off and at this point of the morning Henly was already sweating beneath it. The hat was removed momentarily as Henly dug into the pockets of khaki pants for a handkerchief to wipe away perspiration from his forehead.

Calbert was yet to be formerly acknowledged by the mayor even though he had been referenced in an insulting manner. He remained standing as tall as he could manage over his friend Gary Simms. The large teenager's eyes had barely lifted up above sweeping over the grass since the moment Lawrence had telephoned Henly Blackmon, ensuring his father's involvement in their tragic dilemma. Calbert's focus was still low when it needed to be up to meet the focus of Henly Blackmon after the mayor had turned from Lawrence to him.

Not impressed in any method by the individual that stood before him, Henly scowled and then looked straight through Calbert to the open cabin door. He allowed his focus to settle there and then addressed Lawrence again with more vileness without turning around to look upon him.

"You've always been on your own little nigger bandwagon." Henly bit into his lower lip several times before continuing. "Come on with the rest of your little story Lawrence, what other smut did you bring out here tonight besides the ones you've mention already, and you better stay on the level with me boy?" Henly turned and took several steps in the direction of his son but stopped well before he got to Lawrence.

"Big Simms' girlfriend was here, but she left before the fight started with Susan and Kim."

"Oh goodness I'm thinking now. Boy please don't tell me that you been out here trading out white girls for that smut nigger in there . . . is that what this is all boils down to Lawrence?"

If the look of death could wear a face of identity, it would be the one that Henly presented to his young son at that very moment. Lawrence ate it and after a hard swallow he replied and didn't dare look away.

"No sir. Nothing like that went on out here, I promise."

"For now I'm taking your word on that," Henly snarled. "How long has it been since those other girls left?"

"Probably twenty to twenty-five minutes before I called you, maybe more, I ain't exactly for sure on that."

Henly turned so that each of his sides were directly towards both Calbert and Lawrence before motioning them with his hand, "both of you two come over here."

Lawrence had discontinued crying but there was still moisture about his eyes, he wiped them dryer than he ever thought was possible and afterwards took the short steps necessary to place him within striking distance to his father again.

Although Calbert Davis didn't know it and at that exact moment would not have believe it, his friend Lawrence never really wanted to call Henly to assist them, but he had too. Lawrence knew that if he had not reached out to his father, the possibilities were enormous that neither he nor Calbert would be waking up to a sunrise. And that belief held even if they were locked in a jail cell. Some craftiness by Lawrence had for the moment diffuse that concern.

Calbert now became his central apprehension. The evidence was clear; Henly never thought very much of any of Lawrence's friend and specifically Calbert Davis and his displeasure had been voiced to both teens.

CALBERT DAVIS was polite. He was uncomplicated and he had a quiet demeanor. In spite of his calm aura, Calbert was still one of the more popular kids in school. He was the lone individual that all kids went to for assistance with their homework and he always put in the extra necessary effort to maintain scores that were near the top percent of his class.

A REQUEST HAD been made of Calbert but he had remained anchored above Gary Simms as if he had not been aware of it.

With every bit of clarity that was available to him, Lawrence saw the fiery frustration as it crept into the hairless face of Henly Blackmon. The elder man's upper lip trembled as it curved upwards.

Lawrence breathed a little easier as Calbert finally released his position and took several slow steps and he continued walking in this manner until he was on the opposite side of Henly from Lawrence. Calbert did so within a time frame that the frustration of the mayor had not boiled over into a negative confrontation, but what Calbert said to him most certainly did.

"Ma-ma-mayor Blackmon, this was an accident and it's really all my fault that Slay is dead. Please sir, call the sh-sh-sh-sheriff and I'll tell him . . . ."

The backhand occurred with such velocity that Calbert could not position to react. He was yet to be in a defensive pose when Henly raised his hand for a second strike.

"No daddy."

Lawrence reached out to capture the arm of his father and after doing so jumped in between his father and friend before anything else might occur.

The aqua eyes of Henly Blackmon narrowed in on Calbert and only him, and were not moved away even while Henly swatted his son from the space Lawrence had forced himself into.

"Boy you button your fucking mouth down properly, and don't ever think again about fixing it in a way to call no one out to this property. The Blackmon name has been drugged into a murder out here tonight . . . and it was a murder that I personally wasn't privy too. Not just this land . . . but this whole got damn town belongs to me. And boy I run it like I good and well want to . . . and don't you ever fucking forget it. If anybody 'round here know how to take care of their own . . . It's me, you don't call no fucking sheriff, I'll take care of him."

Henly looked down from Calbert's face and traced the teenager's eyes to his feet where they were scrapping the top of grass.

"You look a man in his eyes when you talk to him, and if you to yellow to do that, you at the least look into his face and that's what I'm asking of you boy." Henly sniffed while pulling up on his pants at the waist before plowing ahead. "You boys done got squeezed kind of tight out here with a warm body, but I've seen worse. This one is solvable if the right directions are followed correctly. If you don't follow the directions correctly," he stressed the word correctly. "Then trouble finds you that there's no finding a way out of, and that's even with my help. The first direction is to get everybody's mind off of calling anyone else out here until I've got a good handle on some of this mess you boys have made."

Henly stopped abruptly and with a look of fixed aggravation concentrated on Calbert. He clamped a solid hand down on one of the shoulders of Lawrence while still glaring at Calbert and gave these words to his son.

"You take a good look over here at this youngun that you keep calling a friend."

"Daddy, he's just shook up, that's all."

"Shut your mouth down boy and do as directed," Henly replied in a very calm voice.

Lawrence looked first to his father and then as instructed over to Calbert. His friend's focus was still somewhere else. Calbert was not returning eye contact.

"Yes sir, I'm looking."

"The picture you see is what's called gutless. You're looking right in the heart of weakness. This is a being that can stand up straight but don't have a spine. I warned you . . . I warned you good Lawrence when you first brought him around. And I told you then and there exactly who he was. This boy doesn't have that pure blood running through him like you, and I'm not faulting him for who he is because his folks are to blame for that. I'm just stating the obvious so that you'll be able to see that he's worthless, and he is gonna be more trouble out here than worth." After a heavy sigh Henly charged on. "You are in desperate need of my influences right now and that's why you did the right thing and called me. Every moment we got is serious and needed and what we have to set in place ain't up for discussion. I'm gonna give directions, and you follow."

Lawrence was being turned. Before Henly spoke again, his son was almost completely facing him.

"You're going to be what's called the master, the key. Our success will rely heavily on you because I know how you feel about this animal that you call a friend. You're his master, and you've got to be the one to turn his latch and force him to be accountable. He's your friend. You're the one holding his hand, and you're the one that's got to force him to hold onto a secret in his other hand."

Beneath his father's hand, Lawrence shuddered and he could not bring it to an end even though he desperately tried.

"Mastering Calbert? What does that mean daddy . . . I mean . . . I don't know what mastering is?"

Lawrence didn't fight the influence as his father cupped at his shoulders to control his body direction again and this time it was manipulated towards the rear of the cabin.

"I'm about to pour all the understanding you need right down on top of you. Don't let one word cross you. Come on. I'll start directing you on what we're doing while we getting the boats down to the water. You can translate what I tell you in your own way to that mongrel back there because I'm not wasting anymore time on him. I'd just assume punch a nice hole right between his eyes and be done."

Lawrence appeared puny beneath the heavy arm of his father as they walked away from Calbert towards the rear of the cabin.

The moment Henly and Lawrence were out of Calbert's sight for their departure to the rear of the home, he was racing back into the cabin.

He didn't stay inside for very long and when Calbert appeared through the doorway, Clara Freeman was dangling like a lifeless doll from his arms. On his approach to depart, Calbert stopped abruptly and looked down in frustration to Gary Simms like it was his first time seeing him lying there. The distressed young man nearly collapsed in frustration as to how he could carry them both to safety in such a short frame of time. To his surprise, from the rear of the cabin Calbert could overhear shouting, and it was coming from not only Henly but Lawrence also was expressing his thoughts and doing so forcefully. The fragment of the confrontation that Calbert managed to listen in upon settled him in even more disdain and blankness covered his face that twinned the way Calbert felt in his core as he held to Clara Freeman and continued to look down from the steps to Gary Simms. For a few moments more, Calbert stayed locked at this position before slowly turning and trudging back inside the cabin, and when he re-exited, Clara Freeman was no longer in his arms. Calbert was greeted again by a booming voice coming over the cabin from its rear and this time he didn't hear the voice of Lawrence in protest up against it. The voice of Mayor Henly Blackmon was the only one Calbert could hear shouting.

Getting away from the cabin and as far away as he could with both Clara Freeman and Gary Simms was all Calbert really wanted to do. Both of his friends were being unknowingly challenged with a form of danger that they would never be allowed to recover and Calbert wanted to deliver them in a rush to wherever safety was available. It was a daunting task with odds that were stacked against him. It was a struggle to accomplish which made Calbert feel like a failure for not being able to do more. Within the scope of time there was to operate and being all alone, the options were few for Calbert. He could not carry Clara and Gary away from the peril they faced but Calbert desperately needed to get away to himself if only for a few moments. The slope was incredibly steep that led down to Sunken Lake. Calbert inhaled deeply into the night air and headed in its direction.

TWELVE FEET in length was the dock that was built by Lawrence's grandfather many years ago when he designed the cabin. Calbert's feet were large and wide at a size fourteen. Walking heavily he plodded out to the end of the small dock. Calbert needed to sit down and once he did, he allowed legs that felt like meaty anchors to plunge into the cold waters of the Lake.

Even the thought of calling Henly Blackmon out to Sunken Lake stabbed at Calbert Davis. The older man was the most public official in Rix and on that platform alone it would appear to be a wise thing to do, but Henly Blackmon was not your ordinary civic representative. Everyone that had come across him for any amount of time has developed an opinion of some kind and that included Calbert. With the arrival of the mayor, Calbert may not have known exactly what was to take place, but he knew enough about Henly that it wouldn't be pretty and in the direction where the night was headed, Calbert also knew that there was very little he could do to exact change.

Sitting, but not at rest, Calbert's heart raced with a bit of pain to every beat. An unimaginable ache that he had never experienced and he did not like it invading him now.

Up the slope behind Calbert and headed in his direction were Henly and Lawrence Blackmon. Both were being very careful to secure their footing as they eased down towards the dock. Between father and son, they carried a paddle boat that was eventually dropped down in a splash onto the lake.

Calbert heard the splatter that interrupted the otherwise quietness of the lake but didn't turn in its direction as no one said a word to him. The next thing he heard was grunting coming from Lawrence as he dragged back up the hill behind his father. The two were not gone for very long before returning with another boat. Henly Blackmon tied the second boat down and then shoved Lawrence forward to depart the small dock again. On their return from their next trip up the slopes, Lawrence hit the dock first with a handful of clothing and moments later Clara Freeman was over the shoulder of Henly Blackmon as he made it down securely. The two Blackmon's went up again and when they returned they were struggling with Gary Simms in between them.

Sitting with his legs still in the lake up to the shins, Calbert had cried so much that his tears had dampen the top portion of the burgundy pullover he wore. He did not actually witness it take place but Calbert knew that both Clara and Gary had been placed into those boats or they would not have been brought there in the first place.

A hand came down to press against his shoulder, Calbert did not turn to face it but he was very tense and on the edge of loosing it all.

Lawrence was standing at the small space to the left of Calbert and with his hand still in contact with his friend's huge shoulder, Lawrence lowered to a seat. The verbal fight he had picked with his father had become animated again during their frequent trips to and from the lake from the cabin but it appeared now to be totally over. Some very strangling words ended it after Lawrence's refusal to join Henly in one of the boats.

Prior to Lawrence joining him, Calbert had stopped crying. He was now mouthing a prayer. At that moment, his only want in the world was for Clara Freeman and Gary Simms to regain their awareness. It was a desperate need, but the only desire Calbert had remaining was to have his best friend alert and standing next to him. With Big Simms by his side, it would give Calbert the courage needed to confront Henly Blackmon in the manner they should and put an exact end to this night of sadness. Calbert had little confidence in executing this act alone and had even less confidence in Lawrence.

No wooden board had creaked and there wasn't any other movement to alert the boys that someone was lurking over them. Calbert was still praying and Lawrence sit still and his focus was transfixed on the water below them. It wasn't until a voice blasted instructions for them to come to their feet did Henly Blackmon's presence immediately behind them become completely noticed.

His centered on Lawrence first.

"You ain't realized it just yet and it's most likely because you've gotten caught up in sentiment for god knows why, but what I'm doing is for your own good and the future I want you to have. This youngun out here with us needs mastering, and I'm taking it for granted that you've got a strong desire to stay behind to start up on that instead of going out with me to clean this part of your mess up."

If Lawrence Blackmon stood six feet it was barely. The top of his head came right up to the summit of his father's nose. The jacket to the running suit he wore was unzipped.

In the face of his father's statement, Lawrence zipped his jacket all the way up and folded the collar down so that it would not brush against the bottom tip of his chin. Like Calbert, Lawrence's legs were wet all the way up to the shins after pulling them out of the lake. This added to a shiver that had only moments ago attached to him after loosing his shudder earlier. Lawrence bent forward to roll down his pants and then stood again to the top of his height to look into his father's eyes.

By nature Henly Blackmon owned a growling voice. It was also the seasoned voice of a small town politician in which he was. When

Henly spoke his voice carried as if he was always in conversation with clusters and as he spoke, Henly's shoulders bounced continuously as if he was trying to shake something away. His focus shifted away from Lawrence to Calbert.

"Youngun, you best face it, you've killed someone back up there which is against the law of this great state. From the way I was raised, what you did is just fine with me. As a matter of fact, in my eyes it ain't even murder when one of ya'll kill another, but the state looks on it differently. I personally believe that you did what you had to do to help out my boy and from this moment forward if you can handle what needs to be done then it don't matter no more because I'm about to make it all disappear. I got that kind of power. What's needed from you is to snap up out of that daze because we could use some help from you." With an arm outstretched, he pointed. "In the bedroom where that boy is laid up, there's a rug beneath the bed. While I'm gone, I need you boys to roll him up in it and put him in the back of that old truck they came out in. After that, you boys start cleaning the place up and make sure that everything of his is with him and I'll take care of it from there, I've got a place to get rid of him too when I . . . ."

Henly Blackmon's face twisted in disbelief as he stopped speaking. For the second time in the night the older man stood in silence just to study Calbert Davis who introduced mannerism totally foreign to the mayor.

"Youngun, are you hearing anything at all that I'm saying?"

The shouting he had overheard earlier while still at the cabin had given Calbert knowledge that Henly Blackmon had no intention of allowing any of his friends to live, but hearing the actual verbalization spoken specifically for his ears was more than anything he could handle. Calbert's eyes were no longer scrubbing over the top of his wet sneakers, they were holding firmly to those of the man willing and ready to take away innocent lives.

"Ma-ma-ma-m-m-mayor Blackmon, I'm the one that hurt Slay, Law-Lawrence didn't have nothing to do with it. We-we-we won't suppose to but-but we were outside the window watching Slay and Clara. Big Simms tried to stop it all from happening bu-bu-but we didn't listen. Other than me, nobody else has done anything really wrong. Why do they have to be hurt for nothing? An accident, that's all it was sir, and I'll take the full blame for it. If we had just listened to Big Simms we would probably all be home already and nothing would have even happen inside of the cabin."

It appeared to take forever, but Calbert did finally get some of his feelings out. After having done so, he waited for Lawrence to add weight to what he had said but his friend never did. Lawrence father's spoke instead.

"But Youngun you boys didn't listen to what nobody else had to say. To begin with, Lawrence wouldn't have had any of you out here if he had listened to what was told to him. You speak in facts and I'll give you that, and here is some more we need to deal with. Fact number one is there's a boy lying dead on my property that you boys killed and it don't make no difference whether you swung at him with something or Lawrence did, you both were involved. Fact number two, with a murder taking place after he was knocked unconscious, this Simms boy is gonna tell what was really going on out here and I know it's not what I've been told. Fact number three, the little girl is the key to all of this mess and you don't know whether she will remember something or not. You can't take back murder, and in order for me to save the both of your asses, we've got to get rid of anybody that was out here that might know what ya'll was really doing. If it was an accident like you say, fine, call it an accident, but it doesn't change one single thing." Henly moved a step closer to Calbert and when he got there pushed a finger down on to the black stitching that read Reebok stretching across his chest.

"Youngun, you best start getting a better understanding on what's going on out here because it's for your own good and not mine. You look as white as me but I know your history and know that you ain't. Let me tell you, boys that look as white as you don't last a good week in the type of Georgia prisons that you're headed for before some big greasy nigger like the one laying back there in that boat splits you open wide and makes you his woman. And to prison is exactly where you're headed if you keep talking the talk like you've been about what went on out here tonight. Now is there finally some understanding to what I've been trying to say to you boy?"

Calbert started to cry again, but this time his tears fell slowly within. Pained in his effort, he turned towards Lawrence hoping for any kind of help to save their friends. None came his way. With major struggles, Calbert then offered up his reply.

"Yes sir."

"Good. Take Lawrence and get back up and get that filthy body out of my house, and then go around back to the storage and get a dirt pick and those two shovels with the round heads. You boys got the strong backs. Ya'll a do the digging and there's a lot to it to do before day breaks."

When Henly stepped to one side of the dock to give clearance for the two teenagers to move in order to follow his instructions, Lawrence passed by him quickly but Calbert remained. He twisted there in the same spot, eyes dragging low again. Right at the point when he was about to take a step, a heavy palm belonging to Henly rose to block his path.

"Youngun, if you've got any thoughts running through that thick head of yours about fucking with me and the business at hand out here tonight then you'd best fuck me right now or you best forever forget about it. You're just a little simple boy and I don't expect you to know anything much about what I'm about to say to you but I'm gonna lay it your way anyway. I'm a Blackmon," Henly paused for a brief moment to wring his jaw before punctuating, "and around here that name means a hell of a lot. In one way or the other there's been someone by the name of Blackmon running this little town way before there was even a thought given about shitting you out to live here. Right up to this point, you've given me every reason I need to stick a knife in your fucking belly and gut you out real slow. It's time you redeem yourself and start giving me a reason to not believe that you plan on fucking me because that's what I believe." He allowed the statement to season into Calbert before shouting, "You either fuck me right now or run the risk of me fucking you later by getting your ass up there and catching up to Lawrence."

Calbert did not hesitate. He took six long strides and was where he had been directed to go.

Where land touched dock and went up on a vertical incline Lawrence had been there awaiting him. The teenagers looked into one another's eyes but didn't exchange their thoughts before setting out to manage the slope. When they had safely overtook it they began to walk at a normal pace to do as they had been instructed, but when they were sure that Henly Blackmon had disappeared with the boats to somewhere out over Sunken Lake, both boys stopped in their tracks and returned to the dock. They sat back down in the places they had before and remained there quiet as seconds turn into minutes that passed between them. Neither teenager had any idea how far the mayor had paddled the boats out but to them it appeared he had been gone for most of the night. All things remained quiet until suddenly, the night exploded.

"No . . . please no!"

It was horrific. It was heart dropping. It was life changing. It was Clara Freeman. She had awakened and was screaming out for her life. And although her scream was muffled some by distance, her panicked voice rammed into the conscious of Calbert and Lawrence as though she were being drowned right there in front of them.

This exact moment was a pivotal one for young Lawrence Blackmon, for also at that precise instant he shrunk just a little from out of existence as a total human being. It would be his first experience with this deficient feeling invaded down into him to clutch at his very foundation, but this foreign feeling that had grabbed at him would revisit Lawrence several times more throughout his life. Lawrence felt as if he had died himself a little bit as he sit slumped from head to toe next to Calbert over Sunken Lake.

When the night fell back to silent, neither boy heard another word come from anywhere off of lake again, and neither of them wanted too.

It had passed three in the morning but neither boy had any idea of the time. They had long ago stopped keeping tabs on it.

Without indication, Calbert got up to his feet and at a hurried pace returned to the cabin followed closely by Lawrence. The teenagers went in and out of each room, and after having done so they walked straight through the home and opened the door leading outside to the back. Calbert stopped when they were standing near the storage shed. Inside of the storage were the shovels and dirt pick they had been instructed to retrieve. They were standing right there when Henly Blackmon began shouting out for Lawrence.

Lawrence looked to Calbert first who was making a hasty approach towards him but it was not long afterwards before he was racing around the home like he was running in a nightmare.

"He's gone daddy . . . he's gone. Slay's gone!"

After leaving the dock and maneuvering the slope, Henly Blackmon had taken a short walk over to his car. He had closed the door on the passenger side and was in a fast walk for the cabin when he caught Lawrence charging at him in an almost spinning run.

"What the hell do you mean that the boy is gone . . . didn't you say that you were sure that he was dead?"

"I was sure. I mean he had to be! You checked him yourself daddy and he wasn't breathing or nothing."

Lawrence was being held up by both shoulders by his father who released him only long enough to gather up a fistful of the front of his running jacket to pull him back towards the cabin.

"Bring your ass this away."

Calbert had at first remained in the area in rear of the cabin where Lawrence had left him, but he was now circling his way back around to the front. After taking the steps, Calbert re-entered the home through the front door before stepping back into the bedroom where all hell had broken loose earlier. On entrance, he was immediately rough collard and pushed hard enough to the floor that his bald head bounced off the flooring.

"Boy, I'm feed up with being fucked with by you . . . now what did you do with that nigger's body?"

Frighten almost out of his mind Calbert managed, "D-d-don't hit me. I . . . ."

A burst of light painted one wall of the room. They were from the headlights of a vehicle and it demanded the attention of everyone.

Calbert had raised his arms up near his face in an attempt to block any ill will forthcoming in his direction but no more arrived.

Henly Blackmon pressed down into Calbert's arms and used the resistance to lift his body weight away from the frighten teenager.

On his knees and stomach, the large man moved along the floor until he was beneath the lone window in the room.

Crawling over to the opposite side of the window from his father, Lawrence whispered, "Who do you think it is daddy?"

For all the crawling the mayor had done to keep from being seen, the action Henly took next went completely against its logic. He grabbed the seal of the window to pull up and then stood up straight and allowed his large body to block the entire window.

"I don't recognize the car and from here I can't make out much but a figure. It's a female though, and whoever she is, she's getting out." He half spun away from the window and looked directly at Calbert.

"Get up Youngun. Both you boys are coming with me, and you keep that damn flap of yours closed and don't open it for nothing or I'll be closing it for good."

With the commotion taking place, Calbert had already half rose to his feet but stopped altogether to inhale the last strangling instructions thrown his way.

Henly Blackmon looked to his son but pointed down to Calbert. "Do you remember what we talked about earlier in regards to him?"

Although Lawrence nodded an answer, his father was not waiting for his reply. "Well, your job of mastering starts up right now . . . and you the one that better make sure that he keeps his fucking mouth shut."

Henly gave Calbert another look of disgust before he started walking. He then made a circling movement with one arm for them to follow, but then stopped abruptly and scuffed. "The last one of you out, pull this door up closed behind you."

Calbert fell behind Lawrence who was almost in the footsteps of his father when they emptied out onto the porch of the cabin and all three looked immediately over to the area where the vehicles were all parked side by side. Befuddled by what they did not see, Calbert, Henly and Lawrence began to suddenly look in every direction.

The car that Latosha Williams had earlier driven away in with both teenagers' girlfriends was back in the parking area with its drivers door open, but no one was inside or anywhere around it, and there was no one on approach for the cabin.

Calbert pushed by Lawrence to the edge of the top step before exclaiming, "That's Latosha's car."

"Damn it Lawrence, didn't I tell you to watch over this fool!"

Lawrence was only blistered with words; Calbert on the other hand was blasted with the menacing eyes of Henly Blackmon along with some more of his brisk words.

"Shut your fucking mouth boy!"

Calbert did as he had been told.

Lawrence glanced at Calbert and then twisted to watch his father search the darkness for the young girl who had driven up and left the small car running and its headlights on bright.

On the same side of the cabin but beyond the squared parking area was an enormous open field that led out into the woods and eventually over to Gulleytown.

Out in the distance Calbert picked up a movement. From the edge of the porch, he made one large step backwards in search of the whereabouts of the mayor. This action smashed him into Lawrence. Calbert then located Henly Blackmon who was tracing along the banister while walking and looking out in the direction of the grassy field.

Henly pointed.

"Out there . . . there's somebody out there running." In somewhat of a cautious manner, he took a large step backwards and then turned to literally run back over to the area where the two boys were.

"Go! Get the hell out of here and catch up to who ever that is, and I'll get what we need out of the storage and catch up as soon as I can."

Lawrence had twisted past an attempt by Calbert to grab him before bursting from the porch like he had been pushed by someone and by the forth stride, Lawrence was already up to full running speed.

Other than a lunging attempt to stop Lawrence, Calbert hadn't moved, but with assured suddenness, he stepped directly towards Henly Blackmon.

"I d-d-don't care what you say, I'm not hurting Latosha."

From Calbert's vantage point, it appeared as if Henly Blackmon's wide brow had dropped in line with his eyes as he smashed his wide palms into the boy's chest and then tighten them into hard fist.

Calbert had been snatched up so fast that his eyes didn't begin to bulge from alarm until Henly was almost finished with what he had to say.

"You get your ass off this porch and out there after that damn girl right now or so help me god I'll slice open that old witch that's raising you in four different ways. And that's a promise Youngun that I'll make happen tonight right before your fucking eyes."

Calbert was shoved away with so much force that he missed the steps and landed in a bruising fashion on his upper back in almost the same spot where he had laid Gary Simms down earlier. Looking up over his body, Calbert saw the blade of a knife in Henly's hand and they both were coming towards him. Defeating a small struggle, he made it back to his feet and only stumbled once before finding a running rhythm that would take him off wildly in the direction Lawrence had exploded towards.

Calbert never looked back for the mayor. He didn't dare.

UP AHEAD OF CALBERT, Lawrence Blackmon ran mindlessly chasing not one, but two shadowy figures. He appeared to be bounding as he ran through the wide, ankle-high, grassy, flat field on his fathers' property in the direction of some very tall trees that marked the beginning of some incredibly dense woods.

Behind Lawrence and Calbert, Henly Blackmon had torn open the small storage shed that was behind the log cabin and tugged on a string dropping from its ceiling to be given the light needed to see the two shovels and earth pick he had requested earlier. With a jolting kick, the door to the shed was reopened and Henly was instantly a party of the chase also. But before making entry into the lengthy field, he tried first to get a visual on Calbert's whereabouts. Henly couldn't find the large boy in the darkness and couldn't make out much of anything else besides an illuminated logo dancing in the night. It was the back of Lawrence's wind jacket and he was very far up ahead of him.

Henly Blackmon entered the field running as fast as he could but had not traveled very far before his lungs had caught fire and his legs were heavy from exhaustion. He was already too tired to even stand up straight any longer and decided to utilize most of the energy he had remaining to yell out. "Lawrence," he bellowed. "Hold up boy. Stop where you're at."

Henly sucked for air while folding over to rest on knees that throbbed. Henly remain there for several moments before kneeling to pick up the digging tools he had allowed to plummet from his hands and struggled onwards without knowing whether his son had adhered to his request or not.

Most of the heavily foliage woods that he was slowly approaching was also apart of the expansive property of Henly Blackmon. Under the night sky, the forest appeared to grow up and out in different angles like a lightless city. There was nothing picturesque or beautiful about them but these woods were indeed a sight to take in after darkness fell. When Henly had made it close to the point where they began, he had to drastically alter his final couple of steps as to not run up the back of Calbert Davis.

Alone and at the very edge of the field, the teenager appeared staring straight ahead into the thick darkness that to him had much too many shadows to it. There was a wheezing sound that came up from deep within Calbert and he reeked of the smell of cheap alcohol. Calbert had thrown up and some of the remains partially covered sections of his sneakers.

Without introducing his presence, Henly Blackmon drew even with Calbert and traced the line of his eyes as they held with steadiness on the dark trees before them. It took less than three seconds for Henly to analyze that young Calbert Davis had established a heart-felt belief that his presence was not welcome into those woods.

Henly was still attempting to catch his breath when he finally addressed the young man.

"What the hell do you call yourself doing boy? I damn near slammed right into you . . . and where's Lawrence?"

Calbert was lathered in sweat when Henly rumbled up next to his side and he never turned to face his questioner. His vision and total focus instead remained straight forward. But having to be asked again, Calbert tilted his head frontward to indicate what his answer would be.

"Lawrence went in there."

Stress that wasn't concealable appeared over Henly Blackmon when he asked incredulously, "Didn't he hear me yelling up for him to stop?"

"Don't know I didn't," was the grave reply.

"Damn it," frustrated, Henly twisted in a slow circle while finishing. "He should of fucking heard me."

His response was gruff, filled with agitation and mumbled and it was one that Henly didn't expect Calbert to hear. But the boy had.

"Lawrence," his father yelled.

The shout was vibrating and loud, but it sounded to Calbert like it had deaden right there in front of them at the particular point where it had beginning. The voice of Henly never made it out into the woods.

If any of the behavior Calbert had exhibit prior to chasing out into the night was considered strange then the display he was putting on now for Henly had moved on past there to something much more unbecoming than outlandish as he stood in a wide stance but inching forever backward from the edge of the woods. It was a movement Calbert had been unknowingly demonstrating even before being encountered again by Henly Blackmon and it was one he continued as they appeared there together.

Henly continued to yell out for Lawrence and then he suddenly cut his voice off right in the middle of one of his shouts and went into complete silence.

Calbert's silence had remained uninterrupted and he and Lawrence's father just stood there without even observing the other as if they were under some unwritten decree to not speak or forge any further. A small sum of time had elapsed before Henly finally withdrew his concentration from the woods and directed to the location that Calbert had stood next to him in. To his dismay, the boy was no longer there. Henly centered on the teenager who was now two full feet to the rear of him and shivering noticeably as though he was freezing.

In glaring frustration, Henly hurled the digging tools to the ground near Calbert's feet, which didn't frighten the befuddled boy any more than he already was. But what Henly said to Calbert while displaying a deceitful smile simply terrified the teenager.

"Where the fuck are you going? If Lawrence went in there, then little boy we're going after him and there's no two ways about. Your best bet is to start pulling yourself together."

Pleading and nearly buckling to his knees, Calbert whimpered a response.

"We ca-ca-ca-can't go back in there . . . Ms. Sadie told me to never go into those woods. She said there's hants in 'em, and whites ain't allowed."

Henly Blackmon looked directly into the terror that had washed out on Calbert's face. He then took one long step that allowed him to invade the boy's personal space. Henly had gotten so close that the brim of his hat folded down into Calbert's brow and the young man could almost taste the remnants of spearmint from the gum Henly chewed slowly on.

Hatred invaded down on Calbert from a tongue of brimstone.

"Boy, don't you ever again open up some nonsense to me about what some old nigger has said. I own this property that you're so damn afraid of. And I go where ever I please on it, and you don't get any purer white than me."

There's a distinctive sound that a revolver makes when it is positioned to fire. Calbert never actually saw the handgun produced but he felt its cold barrel behind one of his ears and in the other ear, he heard the voice of Henly.

"You most definitely need to find Lawrence because he's the only reason that you're still alive. He talked me into letting you live but in every passing second I'm regretting the decision because I'm sick of you. Last chance, no more double telling you to do something. The next time it happens, I'll be burying that old woman you care so much about in these very woods that she's got you so spooked of." Henly snarled before stepping away but allowing the gun to remain pointed at Calbert's face.

"Now let's go, and don't make me look around once to find you."

Seventeen years old was all Calbert was but because of his size he looked a little older. If there was ever one thing that had been branded into his conscious over those short years of his life, it was that he was forbidden to go into the woods near Sunken Lake towards Gulleytown.

It would be an understatement to say that Calbert was disturbed when he made his first strides into the woods behind Sunken Lake. There was absolutely no light so he couldn't see a thing. As they moved forward Calbert struggled against shrub and vines entangling his feet and tilting him into constant stumbles.

Following closely behind the lead of the older man, Calbert's eyesight eventually adjusted to their new surroundings and it immediately awarded the bothered teenager a rush of frightening images.

Very large trees were in these woods, some so large that Henly and Calbert had to alter their course to get around, and it was especially in these trees where Calbert first began to get a visual on some very disturbing sights.

On limbs above them, Calbert saw people dangling from ropes after having died in horrific ways. A vacant feeling that had no freedom attached to it that he had never felt before invaded down into him. Calbert Davis was dying. And he felt it when it began to burrow down into him when he took his first step into the woods behind Henly. He could do nothing about.

Everything Calbert had ever been told about these woods was showing to have been the truth and he quickly learned to keep his eyes low and away from the trees, and that went especially for the tall ones as he continued his pace following Henly Blackmon in a search for Lawrence that was only ten minutes old but felt more to Calbert like it had been an entire winter. It would only be a couple of minutes later when the man walking out in front of Calbert would come to a hard stop that not even an earthmover could bulge him from.

Calbert stopped also, but he did not continue to stand like Henly Blackmon. The traumatized young man dropped fast to the ground and snatched his hands up to cover his face.

TALYLORSVILLE

IT WAS A CRISP night in October. Heavy-sweater weather is how we refer to it in this area. It was plenty good for sleeping but not for me, I hadn't slept a wink. In fact, I had not even closed my eyes for more than a moment. It was nearing four o'clock in the morning and my grandchild was yet to make it home to me. It was not his character to be still out at this ungodly hour and I knew something had to be terribly wrong.

Hung over my nightgown was a light blanket to keep me warm. I was sitting right here beneath it rocking away when it happened.

I TOLD YOU that there was something about Rix, Georgia that made it extra special and unimaginable from any other place.

From out of the heavens, showering down came a light that was so bright that it looked as though a tiny peace of the kingdom had made its way down and landed in this little county. The sight of it pulled me up from this chair like I was a rag doll puppet. All I could say when I was standing straight up was.

"Good lord almighty."

I knew instantly that what I was looking upon was truly unexplainable and godly. The bursting stream of light just appeared from out of nowhere to exist. If allowed, I would have stood there for a thousand years and watched. It was a wonder to this world and had the magical feel of one and after admiring it my life would be forever changed.

That was the one and only time that I've been blessed to look upon such a creation, and when this magnificent glow extinguished, it left my vision stained to be able to only view the world in the vision that I have explained.

CALBERT REMAINED FACE DOWN on the hard soil where he had thrown himself but eventually gathered at least enough necessary composure to fight back to his feet. After Calbert stood again he was near the side of Henly Blackmon and they both were shielding beneath arms against the arrival of an incredible blinding light that was born through the night and clearer than any the light of day had ever given. The illumination had settled just up ahead of them and as their eyes traveled back down to the forest from attempting to capture where it initiated, Lawrence came available to their focus. He was no more than twenty feet ahead of them and if Lawrence had been there all long he most certainly had to have heard the constant calls of his father.

Walking in silence, there was an added carefulness to every step that Calbert and Henly took as they pushed further into the woods, inching closer to Lawrence's position. What became noticeable instantly to them both as they got closer to Lawrence was his trance-like appearance. His clothing was almost completely covered in blood and they were not before he sat out on the chase.

The hands of Lawrence Blackmon were in a constant tremble down next to his side and his feet were set close together. Lawrence stood arrow straight, very similar to military like posture and his face was complex and totally unreadable. From his rear, Lawrence never felt a presence and didn't turn to acknowledge any. It wasn't until Henly and Calbert had advance to be touchingly close to him did they realized that Lawrence was speaking softly.

"Am I dead? Am I dead," Lawrence mumble recurrently.

If it was at all possible, Lawrence Blackmon appeared to be levels more terrified than Calbert and the inquiry he continued to mutter was replied to by neither Calbert nor his father.

Calbert Davis came to a stop at the rear of Lawrence's shoulder and then immediately began inching backwards in the manner that he had before entering the woods. His dying continued as Calbert wanted to gain more distance from this completely foreign new world that seemed to have just been given birth before him. What Calbert looked out and saw before all of them forcefully verified every single warning that he had been given over his life to stay completely clear of these woods. It was beyond obvious to him that they had trespassed onto something incredible and unfamiliar to this world and they didn't belong anywhere near it.

Calbert felt himself being rustled as Henly shoved around him to get to Lawrence. Henly thrust a hand against one of his son's shoulder for his focus but was given more of the boy's whispered inquiries instead.

"Where are we . . . and what is this place?"

Unimaginable and flawless light beamed down directly in front of Lawrence and beneath the radiance were hundreds of perfect mounds. Each flawlessly rounded and exact in comparison. They all climbed to precisely five feet in height and were made of the simple red clay found all over Rix County. Many hours ago, when the night had began, a half moon was revealed but somehow it had been displaced and was not around anymore to witness this truly incredible setting.

Aglow, as if there was a north star present right above them, each small hill was lit up. The luminosity holding above them reached forever upwards like a hole had been dug in the celestial heavens and pristine light had built a path down through the night.

The stillness of the place was incredible that Lawrence, Calbert and Henly stood bewildered before. It had the look of being untouched by human or nature and it was ear-deafening silent.

It was in a hushed voice that Lawrence had spoken to his father but his words exploded out over the silence like a cannon blast. Henly had offered up a reply to him but Lawrence was too unnerved. He didn't know his father had even opened his words up to him. The mystery before them had him captured.

"You're on our land son. On this side of the lake, most of it belongs to us. It's been in this family for generations. Growing up around these parts, you hear all kinds of foolishness about curses and what's back here in these woods and what ain't. They've been rolling out the nonsense since way before I was even born. It's a bunch of foolishness and wild stories from ignorant folks. You standing back here now and can see for yourself that nothing's back here but lots of red dirt. We'll find out about what this light is all about later when we check the news to see what came over the county to night. It maybe some kind of meteor shower or whatever they call it, but it's something natural, I can tell you that. I learned a long time ago that you've got people that will tell you anything to get your mind where they want it. It's a way of controlling the illiterate to believe what you tell them."

Calbert had slid far enough backwards to be a solid foot behind them now. He stopped sliding suddenly to offer some words of his own.

"We should've ne-never come back in here Lawrence. This place is forbidden." He pointed, "Those little hills out there sw-sw-swallow people up."

Calbert stopped pointing and looked straight up, and it felt to him that the light showering down through the night was also burning down into his soul.

The blood within Henly Blackmon had begun to boil. His salty skin shined under the glow of the bright light and it infuriated him to hear what Calbert had said to his son. There was an effort made by Henly to curtail Calbert from making any further statements but Henly was prevented from doing so by something not under his control. And as Henly had attempted to do with his explanation on there whereabouts, he couldn't explain to even himself why he couldn't reach out and attack Calbert.

Calbert spoke freely again and this time he offered a voice that was unshaken.

"That light is not coming from where he just said. It's a light that belongs to the angels. And it's only shining down because of the people out here and the hatred in their heart." Calbert pointed again. "Those little hills out there look like they go on forever but they don't. They come to an end over in Gulleytown." He reached up to touch Lawrence's shoulder, but his effort never got his friend's attention. "Didn't you see all of that stuff going on up in those strange looking trees coming back here?"

Lawrence thought for a second, and then offered. "No. I didn't see anything at all."

Calbert wasn't deterred by the answer.

"I did. I saw it all. Most of these trees out here, they got souls in them. A whole lot of people have been hurt out here Lawrence . . . they in them trees."

Henly Blackmon continued to be held in bondage by something, he could do nothing but watch and listen as Calbert pointed again. The teenager used his thumb to indicate nothing in particular behind them.

"All these trees on this side of the woods are on the death side. And I'm talking about the death side for black people."

"What are you talking about Calbert", Lawrence interrupted. "I don't understand."

53

"Lots of black people have died up in those trees Lawrence." Without stuttering once, Calbert continued to explain what he had been taught.

"This place is called Sacred Hills. Ms. Sadie says that if the devil is ever chasing you and you make it out here to those hills you'll be safe."

"Devil . . . I don't get it," Lawrence gave, but he still was yet to move.

"That part I don't know. You got to ask Ms. Sadie. But that's exactly what she said. She says that on the other side of those hills is the life side of the woods. One side leads out to the lake and the other side leads out into Dead Man's curve. That's why all those old people say that Dead Man's curve is haunted. Ms. Sadie says that this place out here is too."

Either Henly Blackmon had been given a reprieve or he had simply fought his way past whatever it was that had kept him wordless and away from Calbert because his rage was given a forum again.

He drove the handle of one of the shovels into the boy's stomach so hard that the Calbert was already spitting up blood before he felt any of the shrubs growing up out from the hard ground as he fell to his knees first and then over to his back.

The mayor flipped the shovel so that the handle was back in his hands before he kicked Calbert out of a curl and then dug the round tip of the tool beneath the chin of the terrified boy.

"You need to be killed right now for telling my youngun all those wild nigger stories," Henly screamed. "Ain't a damn thing haunted about that curve over in Gulleytown and ain't nothing sacred about that dirt out yonder and nothing else back here."

The attack against Calbert was vicious and life threatening but Lawrence didn't react to it alarmingly like he had previously. From where his focus remained centered, he was not able to observe his father although Lawrence wished that he could. For the very first time in his life, Lawrence sensed fear filtering from the man who had never shown it before in any form.

What Lawrence did do however, without rotating to examine his father, was quiz into this new fear.

"If what you say is true Daddy and there's nothing to this place . . . then why can't I move?"

This inquiry almost floated from Lawrence. And he spoke beneath his normal voice, in one so light that it sounded more like one of his inner thoughts.

The voice and the inquiry corralled his father and chased him away from Calbert, pulling Henly back over near him.

When Henly arrived, Lawrence continued to float out his thoughts.

"I don't know how he was able to get up, but I was chasing Slay. Where I'm standing right now is probably about where I caught up to him. I mean we were tussling with each other but he got away from me and went out there behind Latosha into all that light. And I'm telling you daddy . . . those hills won't out there when I was chasing them. I mean couldn't see too much of nothing but I believe I would a saw what's out there now if they were there when I got here. I think they came up out of the ground when all this light came shining down." Lawrence's hands had blood all over them as they trembled uncontrollably until he made two fists and somehow calmed them.

"Slay pushed away from me but he didn't go far Daddy. He doesn't have enough strength to run no more. This row of hills in front of me, on the other side of the second one is where he's at with Latosha. I'm pretty sure their able to hear everything we saying." Lawrence sniffled and for the first time was given the authority to look away from the light. His eyes appeared ablaze and all the blood had flushed from his face when Lawrence delivered his father his full concentration.

"He's all yours daddy if you want. You can go get him . . . but I'm not going out there with you. Sorry daddy, I'll rather you kill me right here instead."

Lawrence could not remember a time when his father didn't look an individual directly into their eyes as they shared conversation and he was certain that it had never happened with conversions between them. Apparently things had changed.

Lawrence captured the dislodge look on his father's face as Henly's center of attention went immediately away from him. There was no attempt forthcoming where Henly would try to recapture the searching eyes of his son and Lawrence was aware of this and for the very first time felt a bit of pity for his father. Henly's focus was down below waist level into the darkness in back of them all.

The Mayor of Rix, the self proclaimed overseer of the entire county had tarnished and lost a fragment of luster in how his son viewed him all in that tiny space of time.

Silence had fallen over them all and it lasted for a while until Lawrence parted it and finally spoke again.

'You're not going out there to get him are you daddy? What Calbert's saying about this place is right isn't it? The way you're acting says so. Things are kind of strange back here daddy because when I was chasing after Slay and Latosha, I didn't stop myself from running out there behind them."

Lawrence suddenly appeared much more boyish than his age and his eyes had lost the blaze when he inquired of his father.

"I need to know what it was that stopped me from chasing them daddy. If you give me that answer, I'll do whatever you ask me for the rest of my life."

Henly Blackmon kept his eyes away from Lawrence and Calbert Davis, who had begun to pick himself up from another physical attack. Henly couldn't even look in the direction of the studying eyes of his son. And he couldn't give Lawrence the needed answer to his question, and not only did Lawrence know this, Calbert knew it also.

Some very uncomfortable moments passed, and it was time that allowed Calbert to almost fully regain his strength. Out in front of them all in the middle of the woods a light incomparable to any they had ever witnessed continued its blinding illumination, and from the point where Lawrence remained and everything in back of him continued to be pitch dark. An electrifying slash of lightning ripped into the sky beyond the tall bending trees over their shoulders. Calbert and Henly looked back in its direction and then after a booming rattle of thunder, Henly Blackmon attempted to stir the thoughts circulating around Sacred Hills towards conversational material he could better control.

"I for one ain't quite sold yet that it was the same boy running out in these woods." He gave a quick glare over to Calbert. "It may have been somebody else that drove back out with the girl. Kids come out and park around the lake late at night all the time to do all kinds of things."

"As dark as it was I couldn't swear to anything, but blood is all over me and it has to be Slays. And I know it was Latosha because she was still wearing Big Simms's letterman jacket that she had on earlier. She in the same car daddy, who else could it of been but them? I mean why would anyone just drive up and start running away? I know who it was. If you don't believe it, find out for yourself. Go out there and get 'em," Lawrence encouraged in a matter of fact manner.

"For what? It's fucking nonsense!"

The reply came to Lawrence as cold as the first rain drop did that tapped downed against his forehead.

"We're not wasting another minute out here on that stupid nigger. He's not a worry of mine anymore, and if he ain't dead already, he's got to be pretty close to it by now. Nobody is ever coming back here. Nature will eat up the rest of him over time. We've got some more work to do, let's get back to the cabin and finish up."

"Wh-wh-what about Latosha," Calbert inquired?

"Boy you don't got to worry about that little girl, she belongs to me now."

It happened just that quickly, Henly Blackmon had gained his swagger back.

He squinted up towards the bursting light momentarily and then took a couple of quick steps that placed him right next to his son to boastfully shout.

"I see we're playing the game of hide and seek Latosha." Henly looked over to Lawrence, "Give me her full name?"

"Latosha Williams."

Lawrence didn't say a word. The reply came from Calbert Davis.

"Miss Latosha Williams, two of your friends got into a fight that got a little out of hand earlier tonight after you left my cabin. Despite what all of this looks and sounds like, that's all that's happen. Nothing at all can be done about what happen to the young boy Slay. I'm going to allow him to rest in peace in the spot he's at. And if you don't want to end up in a shallow grave somewhere too, then you best get your behind over here to me right now and let me help you through this like I'm helping Lawrence and this other youngun."

Henly waited for a response but none came. The only sound available was rain falling harder and harder. And there was something miraculous about it coming down, Calbert, Henly and Lawrence were getting drenched, but not a single drop of rain fell where any of the light appeared. Rain fell only where it wasn't.

After sniffling hard enough to flare neck muscles, Henly Blackmon gave his reply to the response he never received from Sacred Hills.

"There's not going to be any begging little girl. I was fair enough to give you a chance to save your own life."

Henly smiled wryly and then half chuckled.

"I want to take that last statement back because I lied to you and I consider myself an honest man. It's good that you didn't come out here. I would have probably got a little violent and killed you on the spot. I've had a rough night. I won't chase you anymore Ms. Latosha Williams, where can you go other than where you live. Let me get this hot temper of mine back under control while your butt gets back over to Gulleytown. There's no where to run to and no one to tell. Just keep your mouth shut and be there when I get there so we can figure what we're gonna do about what's happened tonight." Henly paused to sniffle again. "Don't you tie my hands little girl because I can make your entire family disappear and I know you don't want that. Be waiting for me when I get over to Gulleytown, and keep your mouth shut and you'll have nothing to worry about."

And with that, Henly Blackmon looked over to his son who was ingesting a look of disgust from Calbert and said, "Let's go boy."

As several more drops of hard rain punched through the night at his skin, Lawrence turned beneath his own power to follow the command of his father.

Calbert Davis was frozen by an over the shoulder glare from Henly Blackmon. His only crime was holding too long to his position after the older man and Lawrence had begun to walk back in the direction of Sunken Lake.

Calbert used the sleeve from his sweat top to wipe at blood that had formed at the corner of his mouth. His focus went away from Henly and back to the amazing small hills that existed under an unending paranormal light.

In a voice below a whisper, Calbert gave, "Bye Slay . . . bye Latosha. Don't you guys worry about him . . . he's afraid."

Calbert made his first step away from where they all had been standing, and all at once, the cold rain ended. Calbert never looked back and he never stopped walking but he shivered from fright and wonder as total darkness fell completely over all that had been so blindly illuminated.

TAYLORSVILLE

AS I MENTIONED earlier, Rix is a southern town, one where some of its residents continue to hold to old southern ways that should have long been left behind. Deplorable events that had occurred in the past of this settlement helped it earn the label of a place that was not always very friendly to its darker skin residents. This occurrence of this most recent tragedy around Sunken Lake was separate but very much like others that had found an origin here. This heartbreaking event served only to further damage the relationships of people and sink the communities into further divide. The entire county had to find some way to try and pull itself up from a new chapter of deaths. Lives that ended much too young and deaths that rivaled with the many others, disappearances, and unexplained events that had come about within the community of Gulleytown or somewhere close to Sunken Lake.

Before sunrise would welcome Rix to a new day Henly Blackmon would find Latosha Williams and would deliver home his promise by dealing her a troubling death along with every one else inside of the home she shared with her mother and two younger sisters. The entire families in two other homes next to the Williams family would be killed also. Their homes were all burned to the ground and the people in them all found dead.

Little Rix County had paved a gory history but that particular Friday in October proved to be its bloodiest. Gulleytown lost many precious young lives that night. The loss was so many for such a small area that its older residents believed that with so many children dead in such a short period of time, the neighborhood had lost not only their lives, but also the beating heart of the community. And up to this very day, many people within the Gulleytown area swear that at certain times of the night they can hear the voices from the souls of the children that lost their lives in the fires, and they declare that those children souls will not lay down for rest for anyone.

CHAPTER 2

MARCH 1991 CAMP NOHA, KUWAIT

Enduring temperatures he had never experienced before Private First Class Calbert Davis was in an unfamiliar setting another world away from Rix County on the perimeter of Camp Noha. The assigned duty of Private Davis was to protect the post from any unfriendly or advancing Iraqi troops in a camp set up three miles within the borders of the Middle Eastern Country of Kuwait.

Calbert's arrival to Fort Sill, Oklahoma for army basic training right out of high school was his first trip out of North Georgia and his assignment to the Middle East was his first out of the country. Prior to arrival, he had been equipped and outfitted with the most up to date military gear available to deal with the expected environment, but Calbert was in the heart of an unforgiving desert sandstorm where even the most proficient night goggles limited visibility to only what was directly in front of him. He was on his third night in the Middle East and his first out on scout patrol securing the perimeters.

The first ninety minutes of surveillance Calbert had done in a stationary defensive position one hundred yards out from the camp. He gave that position up to Private First Class Benny Addison from Philadelphia, Pennsylvania who was the other lone member along with Calbert ordered out on the scout surveillance team for the late morning patrol that begin at three and ended three hours later at six A.M. Calbert took over the patrol of Private Addison and he surrendered his which meant Calbert was now rotating around the perimeter of Camp Noha.

Since the Fall of his senior year of high school and specifically the night around Sunken Lake when his close friends were murdered, Calbert Davis had experienced and assortment of personal difficulties. The difficulties affected him inward and outward and at times Calbert would become so unstable that people back in his hometown wondered how he could get accepted into the armed services. Calbert had somehow made it however, and was now in service for his country, a true American soldier.

Seventy minutes into the final ninety of his surveillance, an arsenal of the difficulties of Private Davis came calling upon him again and calling strong.

Following the murders of Gary Simms and Carla Freeman at the point where Calbert had stepped into the woods that backed Sunken Lake he had began to experience troubling sights in his thoughts. The mental images came to visit him on many occasions but never like this, and never before in this foreign part of the world. To escape this incident of haunting, Private Davis ended his patrol and pushed down into the earth to become a part of the sand while clawing for his radio to break open contact with Private Addison but delirium had Calbert calling for someone else.

"Lawrence, help me!" In the howling wind Calbert's voice cracked like a whispering cry.

A response came instantly.

"Lawrence! Who's Lawrence? What's going on Davis, over?"

"He-he he's over here Lawrence. I see him. Slay's here."

"Davis what's wrong out there? This is Benny from Philly. Who the hell is Slay, and why do you keep calling me Lawrence, over?"

"He . . . he's not leaving me alone this time Lawrence. Help, please?"

Calbert dropped his radio and it became lost beneath him while Calbert scrambled for it he was unknowingly kneeling on its call button which made his voice sound even more strained as Private Benny Addison struggled to hear him.

"I swear Slay . . . I didn't mean it. I never meant for it to happen!"

"What the fuck. Davis . . . Davis! What's your location?"

Nothing was heard from Calbert in reply but after several moments he spoke again and this time very plainly.

"I love you Ms. Sadie."

Calbert located the butt of his assault riffle into the sand and positioned so that the barrel of the gun would be against the top of his mouth. As the harsh winds of the dessert tore into him from every direction, Calbert bit down onto the weapon with so much force that that several of his teeth chipped.

On the day of his arrival in Kuwait, Calbert had taken a marker and written the name of one of his oldest friends on the inside of his helmet. When he tightened his finger on the trigger, the blast tore through the entire S-L-A-Y. The large bullet opened the back of the enlisted man's skull to every swirling element of the desert and delivered an immediate end to the many demons that had come alive inside of the life of Calbert Davis.

ASLEEP, THOUSANDS of miles away inside of a college dormitory, Lawrence Blackmon shook awake.

"Calbert!"

His entire body was soaked in sweat like he had been running for hours. Lawrence flung away his bedding and was up peering out from a window in his dorm room as if he had seen someone there, but when he arrived no one was. Lawrence stared into the night at nothing in particular. He felt troubled and damage inside. His movements were stiff and his skin felt unusual. The sweat hugging at his body was coarse and tingled unnaturally up against his skin. Lawrence felt burnt. And all these abnormal things were troubling for him, but what stressed at him more than anything else was this other dry and very empty feeling he was experiencing. This sensation originated from deep down inside where everything about an individual really counts. It was at the core of Lawrence Blackmon, where for the second time in his life, a tiny fraction of him shrunk away. Lawrence actually died away a little again from the complete individual that he really was.

TAYLORSVILLE

AT THAT VERY MOMENT that Calbert Davis committed the act, I died away a little bit also up here in Taylorsville. Calbert was dead, and even though he was another world away from us in Kuwait, Lawrence knew it over in Athens, and I knew it up here long before anyone could inform us.

CHAPTER 3

TUESDAY, JUNE 11, 1999

TAYLORSVILLE

It's been almost ten years and my travels have taken no place other than to Gulleytown, Stansburg and back up here to my home in Taylorsville. From a physical perspective alone I have not been beyond Rix County for any reason but my spirit has traveled greatly and gone to almost everywhere I've placed my thoughts and they've been to a wide variety of places. It appears that when you set your mind to something it's truly amazing what one is capable of accomplishing.

There have been many tragedies that have taken place in this county since I was given an opportunity to live and I have paid particular mind to all of them. The reasoning is not because I'm in the business of everyone, I just happen to be the type personality that leans a keen eye to this type of thing. It's been nine years, eight months, a couple of days and some desperate hours since the last senseless slayings that took place in Gulleytown and around Sunken Lake. All the individuals involved and responsible had gotten on with their lives almost like it never happen except for Calbert Davis, whom

I believe looks down consistently over all of us in Rix and that goes especially for Gulleytown.

Henly Blackmon remains an active resident although retired from politics at least on the surface anyway. He still can stir a boiling pot with the best of them, but now spends the better part of his time alone fishing and hunting. Henly's son Lawrence relocated forty miles west of Rix to Athens after high school. Of late he's been operating a tiny veterinarian practice after fulfilling the necessary requirements and completing post graduate studies from the big university there.

This tale is centered mostly on Lawrence Blackmon for it was him and his actions where it really took birth. From this point forward, he will mainly be where the focus is laid.

The young man to his credit had evolved and went through a lifetime of changes since the night he cowardly stood by and did nothing as his friends were slain one after the other by his father.

Lawrence sought removal from beneath the hateful presence of Henly Blackmon and there was indeed a healthy price to pay to accomplish his wishes. He was driven out of Rix and forbidden to return. There would be no further contact with anyone there and his death would be the penalty if it was found that Lawrence had broken the agreement in any manner. A little over two years back when his mother passed, Lawrence had set his mind to challenging the warning to return for her funeral but like he had done on numerous occasions, Lawrence turned the vehicle around before entering the county. He regretted it. Lawrence knew that his presence should have been there for the services even if he had to watch from the woods. Living own his on had been tougher than he had imagined, especially in the beginning, but the future as of late started to look much brighter. Lawrence Blackmon had fallen in love and fallen hard. Whitney Connors was the beautiful young woman that had met his every desire and Lawrence had proposed marriage to her. Their first acquaintance was more than eight years earlier while attending the university. They were instantly attracted and dated on and off throughout college but were more committed to their studies than one another. After graduating the two simply lost touch but found one another again by pure coincidence. Whitney entered a clinic one rainy day with a malnourished puppy she had found outside her apartment. The facility was the one Lawrence was at practice, and from that point on they have never lost one another again and the love between them blooms openly. The couple practically lives together in one or the others home.

The tale picks up on this particular day within the kitchen of Whitney's apartment where Lawrence is sitting across from her at a small table after enjoying a nice dinner.

There was a big smile on Lawrence's face. It was something he had formed a habit of doing while looking into the eyes of Whitney and reflecting on how lucky he was to have her in his life again and how incredible their future would be.

With her hands open, Whitney forced them halfway across the table to gather his before speaking.

"You are aware of what today represents, aren't you?"

With a smile ever widening, Lawrence gave back, "Yeah, it's Tuesday, the day after Monday."

"That's very funny mister, try again. And this time forget about what calendar week day it is."

In a defeated gesture, Lawrence shrugged his shoulders while turning up his palms.

"Alright Whitney, you've got me. What's today because I have no idea?"

"Our six month anniversary you silly man, you don't remember proposing to me six months ago? I can't believe that you don't remember that."

"Come on babe, you know I could never forget that."

"I don't know. It doesn't seem like you really remember."

"I was just playing. How could I ever forget that moment and the way that you answered and that afterwards part?"

Whitney smiled.

"I know you'll never forget that afterwards part, and me neither. But it seems like you really forgot your other promise that you made to me."

There was a look of confusion offered by Lawrence, and this time he wasn't faking.

"What promise . . . I mean which promise?"

"Your promise you made to take me to your hometown."

Whitney tightened her fingers on Lawrence's hands after feeling them stiffen and hurried forward with her thoughts before he began resisting.

"We've been to visit my family so much that you're practically already part of it already and you've even won over my uncle David and we both know how socially militant he can be. I know you're tired of me bringing this up but Lawrence you promised, and on top of that, it's beginning to bother me more and more that you've shut me completely out of your past. We're getting married in two months and not one single person in your family even knows it."

Whitney's eyes were big black and beautiful like wet olives, her disappointment showed through them as she continued.

"Your father wouldn't approve of me, you've made that perfectly plain on more than one occasion, ok, I got that, but we're adults. What we share is certainly beyond ignorant points of view. Sometimes when I think about how inflexible you are about taking me to Rix, it makes me feel like you're the one that really has a problem and you're using your father as a crutch."

Whitney was breathtaking in her delicate dark brown skin. Gorgeous in every manner imaginable, her face was angelic and her hair was soft and silky to the touch. Whitney's lips were full and plump. There was not an angle to view her from that didn't prove picturesque. Lawrence knew and loved every inch of her but what mattered more than anything to him about Whitney, was that she was the most thoughtful and intelligent woman he had ever met. He recognized the disappointment in her face and could feel it in her touch. He had become captured up in it while responding.

"Never have I been more proud about anything than the opportunity you've given me to marry you. Your answer built me up into a complete man." Pressing harder through her hands, Lawrence willed his desire.

"I love you in a way that there are no words for and my father and no one else will be able to touch that with any form of hatred. You are me . . . you're every part of my heart."

Whitney tingled inside after his brief sharing but stood her ground.

"That's not what I'm after Lawrence. Your love for me is not a concern. You've shown that in countless ways. What I need from you is what you're hiding from me. You're hiding yourself from your past and now that means that you're hiding me also. You grew up less than fifty miles from here and haven't been home since you came to college, and if I'm remembering correctly, you even moved away from home prior to even coming to Athens," she sighed. "We've got an August wedding planned; you know all there is to know about me, my parents and grandparents, and all of the people in my life. Don't you think it would be fair that I knew something about what you've cut yourself off from before we take such a large step? How would you feel if the shoe was on the other foot and I was offering you the little you've offered me?"

Very handsome under a blonde head of hair is was who Lawrence Blackmon had matured to be. He wore his slender weight well on a six foot frame that hadn't grown very much since leaving high school.

Before Whitney could pour out another word he was out of his chair and immediately over to her. Lawrence allowed the tip of his nose and forehead to rest against hers before placing his thin lips against hers.

Where was he to hide now, Lawrence thought while holding to his precious Whitney? From him, she needed what he couldn't give to anyone. There was too much hurt and disgust in what Whitney demanded. Lawrence never had a woman with enough confidence in him to seek out all of who he was and be ready to accept whatever the outcome might be. Whitney did this because she loved him enough for the both of them and was most definitely the key to any future that Lawrence cared about. She was one of the valued few people still alive that gave his life any real meaning.

Although she was not aware of it, Whitney Connors was a major part in what kept Lawrence surviving. She was already in a vice-chair position in underwriting for a national insurance company that recruited her right out of the University of Georgia. Her performance and talents within the firm's Athens satellite office had earned an offer to a very rewarding senior position at its California headquarters. It was Whitney's for the taking and she had been given a month to consider it, and it was not the first time such an offer had come across her desk.

Lawrence was well aware of all of the advancement offers that she received because Whitney kept him informed about all aspects of her life. On profession alone, he knew that a small college town like the one they lived in would not be able to harness forever the talents Whitney possessed. Lawrence also knew that he played the most pivotal role in her remaining in Athens for awhile longer.

Purposefully excluding her from a great deal of his past had finally torn a path large enough to where he could no longer allow it to remain open without it possibly ending their relationship, or at the very least cause harm to it enough that his soothing words were not sufficient. Whitney had given all of who she was to him and was deserving of much more than equal treatment.

Gathering both of her hands again, Lawrence kneeled next to her and waited as Whitney twisted her shapely but tiny body from beneath the dining table to face him completely.

"First of all, I'm sorry for ever allowing a doubting thought to enter your mind as it regards my feelings for you. What we share should never be subject to question by anyone." Clear rimless spectacles had been added to Lawrence's persona during the second semester of his sophomore year of college, he pushed the glasses up towards the top of his nose before charging on. "I know longer look upon him as my father but the man that gave me life belongs to whatever the world has that represents separatism and hate. He's not alone in his opinion and he will never understand or respect what you and I share." He paused again but it was to reflect this time. "I dated the same girl in high school all the way into my senior year. We broke up at some point. Senior prom was coming up, and here was this other girl, we liked each other enough to want to go to our prom together. My dad found out about it. The night before we were set to go, he had some of his associates go by her home. They did some serious hurt to her father. You see this man that gave me life has a natural way of turning a little piece of innocence into something uglier than you can imagine. It may not be the best thing to do, but I just try to forget most of the repulsive things he's done that I know about. That incident was one of the final ones before I just had to get away from him. He's been a racist all his life. People back home know it because it's always been rumored. My mother, who was nothing like him but was there for him lived in hell. She even left him before she was killed. This is a cruel man that I'd rather keep as far as possible away from the person I love more than anything else in this world. I have no more ties to him, they've all been severed."

Blinking continuously, Whitney had listened intently and it could be easily told that she gained in understanding from Lawrence's sharing. She immediately inquired of him.

"What's the name of the place where you said your mother passed?"

"My grandfather died there also . . . it's called Dead-Man's curve."

Lawrence couldn't hold Whitney's eyes any longer after the reply. He closed his.

Nodding her remembrance, Whitney remained quiet until she saw that Lawrence was again watching her.

"Yes, that's exactly what you called it. I've never shared this with you, but I've heard you shout that place out in your sleep before. Explain it to me . . . I guess I want to know what's it like and why has it captured so much of you that it causes you nightmares?"

The uneasiness was noticeable as it reared in Lawrence. Whitney also felt it in his touch.

"That's a real tough question to give you an answer to Whitney. And I say that simply because you're not from Rix. However I answer probably will sound a bit absurd."

"Sweetie, I promise, if it does, you'll never know it."

"I doubt that."

"Come on, you're opening up. Just keep right on talking and don't worry about how what you say sounds."

"That's easy for you to say."

"And it's even easier to do, especially when you're being honest."

With a groan, Lawrence gave, "Dead-Man's curve, well, I guess the simplest answer to give is to say that it's just a sharp curve, but I know that you want much more than that, right?"

Whitney didn't bat a lash. She sat expressionless and latched onto Lawrence whose voice suddenly had become unsettled.

"The place that you're asking about probably means a little something different to anyone you ask. You'll be hard pressed to get identical answers from any two people but I guarantee that whatever answer is forthcoming; it'll be cut along one of two different ideas and nothing else. One belief is that it's a place where the spirits of the dead emerge from the woods and come out into the curve."

Lawrence studied Whitney for several moments before adding, "The other belief is that what I just told you is total nonsense, and that it's just an insanely sharp curve that some people misjudge even though they've been rounding through it for most of their lives. You've got one curve and two contrasting beliefs. But there's no denying one fact and that's irregardless to which belief is held . . .

people die in that curve. There's never been an accident there where a person involved lived to tell about it."

What Lawrence had revealed and the dreary manner in which he spoke seemed to have done its part to shake Whitney up. Her expression had gone even further blank. But somewhere deep within, she found the desire to search for more.

"Of the two theories, which do you believe in Sweetie?"

Lawrence offered her a half smile that really didn't belong on his face at that moment. He ended it before responding.

"I pretty much expected that to be your next question. These two theories as you call them, pretty much run along racial lines. Talk to most anybody in Gulleytown about this and they would probably mention something about spirits or something they've seen in the woods that line the back of the curve. The people over there are solidly behind those spiritual sightings. Everyone else in Rix doesn't really believe a word of that. Nonsense is what they call it."

Whitney interjected, "Gulleytown is where you say all the blacks live, right?"

"Yes. I guess for the most part you can say that."

"Ok. I just wanted to make sure that I remembered that correctly. You can go on about your belief."

"As you know, I grew up in Stansburg, and I certainly can not speak for the community, but I personally believe that there's a little truth to both sets of beliefs."

"Why Sweetie, explain why you've taken on some of both theories?"

"Whitney, if we could, can we end the topic of Dead Man's curve here? I believe I've given you my answer and I don't want to go much deeper into it right now. But I will say this though, I don't ever remember a black person being killed in that curve, and most of them live right there where it is."

Whitney released his hands to reach for Lawrence's somewhat pronounced cheeks and then kissed him where strands of his hair had dropped past his hairline and into his face.

"That's a kiss for the spirits and the people that believe in them." She was smiling but allowed it to fade to add, "Skin color and race have always been problematic for individuals looking for an excuse to place themselves above someone else. My father taught me that as a little girl and it holds very true. In our marriage we're not going to hide from individuals like that. I know I'm certainly not. I love this dark skin that I've been blessed with, and I'd love it if it was as white as yours. I will face down ignorance for what I believe in. And that includes your father's hatred. It doesn't frighten me at all, and if that's what concerns you then it shouldn't frighten you. But if you're that apprehensive of what his reaction to me might be, don't take me to places that there's a high likelihood he may be . . . like beneath a white sheet."

Whitney laughed and so did Lawrence.

"He's not on our list of people and places to visit. I want to be introduced to some of the friends you grew up with . . . that little bit will satisfy little old me."

"But there's no one there Whitney. Remember me telling you about Sunken Lake and all my friends drowning there and Calbert killing himself during our freshman year of college? I mean, don't get me wrong, I had a steady girlfriend at one time and a few other people I hung around with a little, but as far as I know they've all left Rix and are living in other areas."

Distancing himself from his past had become common for Lawrence and it was something he was very good at.

The look on the face of Whitney suggested that he was doing another commendable job at it, but she flipped her expression to combativeness in a hurry to counter his move.

"This is your weekend to be out of the clinic . . . right?

"Yes Whitney. You know my schedule better than I do."

"I most certainly do, and I also know that you're aware that all of my weekends are free." She paused in a curious manner to examine his facial expression as he watched her before continuing. "Before even entering this conversation I had decided to drive to your hometown this weekend. The way I look at it, you've got two choices, you can take me there, or you can decide not too, but one thing is for certain, I'm going to Rix irregardless of which decision you choose."

To illustrate the seriousness of her intentions, Whitney's expression turn rigid, yet she remained a picture of beauty even in sternness.

Lawrence framed the smoothness of her face before pushing back strands of Whitney's hair that had fallen off her shoulders to cling at her tighten jaws.

"Would you really go there without me?"

"I shouldn't have too." Knowing her battle was won, Whitney faded her fight. "I shouldn't have too because you're the man I love, and I expect you too."

"Why do you always have to make so much sense?"

There was an attempt at a reply but Lawrence headed it off.

"Don't Answer. And please forgive me for being so inconsiderate for so long. Of course you shouldn't have to drive there by yourself . . . we'll go together Saturday."

While Whitney broadens a smile, Lawrence quickly added, "My father's home is one place we won't be going anywhere near and that's not debatable. But we're definitely going by to visit my mother's grave, and after that it probably won't take more than five or ten minutes to get through the rest of town and we're getting out of there and coming back home, deal?"

Whitney matched the intense concentration Lawrence centered her with before adding, "It's a deal as long as you throw in Dead Man's curve. I want to experience some of those spirits from Gulleytown."

The demand lowered Lawrence's blood temperature to near frigid and forced him into realization. He was on his way back to Rix Georgia.

An intolerable father had forced his departure and Lawrence had carried away with him his own fair share of some of the horrors the tiny town held. He would be returning, and not alone. There were no outward effects displayed by him that Whitney could see, but Lawrence was coming apart at the seams. Everything he had run away from was close again, entirely too close.

Whitney was awaiting his response.

His silence was prolonged but as fast as he could offer it up, Lawrence offered, "You really want to go by that curve Whitney?"

"Why yes. And I mean that with all my heart."

It was a slight tremor that suddenly grew in severity, Lawrence was crumpling but before he could plummet, Whitney pushed forward out of her seat. The action surprised him and proved to stabilize Lawrence as he allowed her to force him to the floor with her landing squarely on top of him. His tremors escaped to live down deep inside of him again.

"Well, what's this all about?"

Whitney was undoing the buckle to his belt.

"I'm all excited now."

The belt came easily free.

"Relax . . . and not another word."

On the kitchen floor, Lawrence Blackmon lay flat on his back with the woman of his dreams all over him but he was never relaxed. His thoughts were all over Rix County, and they were at the height of nightmarish.

MANY EVILS HAD TAKEN form around Sunken Lake and most occurred long before the one that involved Lawrence Blackmon. Social differences between the communities were what most of the difficulties were all about and this tragedy continued them along the already existed path in an even more disturbing pattern after the water-blotted bodies of Clara Freeman, Gary Simms and Latosha Williams were drug up out of the lake and placed next to each other atop its step banks. Adding a strange twist of complications was the whereabouts of Solomon Builder. He had been with the party of teenagers and officially declared dead as having drowned also but his body had never been found.

The distressing deaths of so many of its young nearly destroyed Rix and especially the community of Gulleytown and it set the area on pause for a while until residents could find adjustment to what had been taken away from their lives. As time passed, mysteries surrounding the tragedy anchored to the small community and blended to folklore. These legends took on a haunting life of their own almost immediately following the discovery of the bodies of the teenagers. Rumors produced beliefs and before long there was no longer any credence given to the official statement of the events that the authorities had reported. Stories circulated of sightings of residents who had reportedly lost their lives that night back from the dead, and these sightings increased tremendously within the small area where Dead Man's curve elbowed its path.

The woods and undergrowth that backed the dangerous curve grew so thick that it was impossible to even look past what was in the immediate tree-line and it continued in denseness for nearly a half mile to where it ended in perfect fashion at a tract of hard earth redder than any eyes had ever seen. It was shaped like an oval. Under the bright sun the area is loomed over by a dark haze forbidding natural light. When nightfall arrives and it is cast beneath the glow of the moon, the deepest darkness imaginable occurs and covers this region. Residents on the side of the tracks where Gulleytown is refer to this large clear area of Georgia clay as Sacred Hills. There is no origin on the title to describe it and no query on the inclusion of hills even though there were none there. Throughout Rix, there was practically no discussion of even the existence of Sacred Hills. The place was revered and forbidden and only a precious few had ever maneuvered back behind the woods in Gulleytown to come near its presence. Residents were frightened of this setting and it was a natural fear because this place was unnatural.

Beyond the area known as Sacred Hills were more dense woods which eventually led out to a elongated field and finally to Sunken Lake. Within this general area, many people with one thing in common had lost their lives; they all lived some where within the squared half mile area of Rix called Gulleytown.

If any name fit perfect to its community it would be Gulleytown. To its immediate rear, a natural gulley sinks deeper down into the pit of the earth than any other place in the entire state. The giant gulley made Gulleytown look extracted from its surroundings. To the west of the gigantic earth divot, beyond the thick entrapping woods, on further past the clearing known as Sacred Hills is property that belongs to retired Rix Mayor and cold blooded murder Henly Blackmon. And right there in front of his cabin lays the dark and suspicious waters of Sunken Lake.

RIX COUNTY

TUESDAY NIGHT, JUNE 11, 1999

FOR A SMALL percentage of some of the residents of Gulleytown with little else to do to escape time, public intoxication was indeed a problem. It was a charge that one of the individuals from the community had been taken in to custody for at 11:10 in the night and secured eventually into a one bed cell. Cleveland Banks sat alone in his cell. He was ten years into middle age but looked years older thanks to heavy and consistent drinking. Cleveland was arrested after a sheriff deputy had witnessed him urinating between parked cars in an area known as Front Street in Gulleytown. The arrest of Cleveland Banks had become an expected one by not only Cleveland but whichever deputy it was patrolling the area to assist him into the back seat of their county vehicle. Cleveland's arrest was a weekly occurrence. It happened every Tuesday around the same hour after the short, light-complexion, balding habitual violator had finished spending most of the paycheck earned honestly from his job of collecting the city's trash. Cleveland was usually out early enough the following morning to be ready for the next day's work. With the arrest of Cleveland, it brought the number up to two inmates detained in the nine cell county jail. The other inmate had been there almost three months awaiting a murder trial after not being able to establish a bond behind stabbing his wife with and ice pick. His tiny cell was separated from the one that held Cleveland Banks by a cylinder block wall and a thick metal door that closed with the jolting vibration of a mule kick.

When he wasn't drunk beyond consciousness, Cleveland had always proven to be a very entertaining inmate within his cold grey cell although at times, irritating. Sitting still was almost impossible and he challenged with a vociferous spit-flying rant about any and everything. He would get so worked up that on occasion he fielded questions from someone that no one else but him could apparently see. This warm Tuesday night, Cleveland Banks owned his consciousness and the entertainment was on full eruption.

Pete Crance was Sheriff of the county and most people said he looked the part. He billowed up in height to a hair below six foot-seven. The sheriff was in possession of a long nose that stayed beet-red all the time and it hooked over a bit more towards his lips as each one of his fifty-seven years had passed. Pete Crance was over half way into serving his third four-year term as Sheriff and was known as the kind of law official that had a kind word stored away for mostly everyone he came across, and a talking friendliness with the populace he served.

At 11:20, the Sheriff was making his final security walk through to get a visual on his two inmates before leaving the jail for the night. The large door separating the two prisoners vibrated the walls as it rattled closed behind his departure from one cell area to the next. After two back surgeries, Pete Crance walked stiffly and his carefully placed strides indicated obvious pain. In the manner he had always done on most Tuesday nights, the sheriff tipped his head while eyeing Cleveland as he walked by the prisoner's cell on his way out of the cell-house area to deliver the turn-keys to one of his deputies.

Pete Crance wanted to get home for as much rest as possible and be well prepared for a trip to a South Georgia the following morning to pick up a prisoner who had been given permission by the state's correctional department to attend a family member's funeral.

Cleveland Banks zigzagged on his approach through a cell that reeked of corn liquor and made it to the bars that separated him from the sheriff. Most of his teeth had been lost years ago in various battles, but the two fangs were holdovers and fronted the corners of the top of Cleveland's mouth. His lips were large and alcohol discolored and the bottom one stuck out with a scaly peel. He sucked it in and then back out of his mouth continuously like he was some kind of giant insect. Cleveland was loud and bothersome even if there was no one else in his cell to annoy and on the occasion when someone was in his presence, his every statement was followed up by a pause as he slurped at his bottom lip to gauge the affects of what he had said.

In a winded breath, Cleveland huffed at Pete Crance as the Sheriff took strides to pass his cell.

"Sheriff, you're in some mighty big trouble."

The hard slurring of his words made the appearance of Cleveland Banks more disturbing than it actually was.

"I got a message for you." Slurp, slurp. "You shouldna never killed them babies. You show shouldna." Slurp.

Not only tall, Pete Crance was slender also, with only a small belly that had slid down below his belt to correctly indicate his age.

The statement by his overnight inmate had stopped the sheriff in mid stride. He removed his thick plastic glasses and wiped at the lenses with a pocket napkin before sitting them back to rest on his nose again. The Sheriff then stepped a little closer to the cell to draw a better focus on the round almost elf-like man begging at his attention.

"What in the world are you rambling on about tonight Cleveland? Last week you slept on the floor because you were up in arms about somebody coming through the walls and sleeping under your bed. Come on with it. What you got for me this week and make it quick so I can get and try to catch some of the late news with my wife."

The eyes of Cleveland Banks were dancing around the uniformed Sheriff. He leaned back for a moment but didn't fall because he had the presence of mind to clutch to the bars before speaking again.

"There's little children out there hollering all over Gulleytown for you." Cleveland let out a hiccup loud and jerking, and it momentarily steadied his ever swaying movements.

"You don't believe me, do you Sheriff?" Slurp, slurp. "None of you murdering sumbitches believe nothing. It's built up in you that you think we all stupid or something. Them babies still on fire out on Front Street and they crying just like they was the night you sumbitches burned them up." Slurp. Cleveland had small but bugged eyes and he concentrated them around the lower areas of the sheriff's uniform as he continued.

"Look at 'em. Don't act like you don't see them babies down there around your legs."

The uniform of Pete Crance was dark brown with a lighter brown stripe down the side of both legs. Cleveland's attention came up and he caught a glimpse of the rotating eyes of the Sheriff. The small man then pushed an angry finger up.

"I got a message for you Sheriff . . . ." Slurp, slurp. "Slay Builder says that you a dead man."

Five minutes earlier, Pete Crance had emptied a full bladder. It had just filled again. He had been a picture of composure also, but not anymore. Pete stood as unsteady as the man before him and was fighting hard to keep what had rattled him within.

"What did you just say," the Sheriff mumbled.

"Slay!"

The name was rushed back in a half yell.

"You heard exactly what I said." Slurp. "The Preacher Builder's boy, the one you sumbitches tried to kill over by that stinking lake."

The name stabbed into the thoughts of the sheriff. He knew the father, and he definitely could never forget Solomon Builder.

The color drained from the sheriff, even from his nose, and it took place with such quickness that Cleveland Banks looked away. But an instance after he had looked up to him again, Cleveland would have sworn that something evil had found its way into the tall man's face at almost the same rate it refilled with color again.

A reply was forthcoming from the Sheriff, and with it was a tiny portion of the unsettledness brewing within him.

"Where the hell did you get that pack of lies from? Slay Builder died out on the lake with all of them other kids and you know good and damn well he did. We pulled up personal belongings that his own folks said were his and that he was wearing that day. And we drug that lake a week looking for him. Just couldn't find his body, but he's in there somewhere and I know it. You're drunk and way overboard Cleveland, but most of all, you're walking in some dangerous territory. You'd be best served to get your ass over there on the bunk, and start sleeping this off so that you can make it out of here in the morning."

"I ain't going no got damn sleep and what you drug out of that stinking lake was what you put in there. Slay was never in there. Folks from Gulleytown know all about what you and old Mayor Blackmon did to them children over on that stinking lake." Slurp, slurp.

"Hic."

The body twitching hiccup startled the Sheriff and the damning accusation almost sent him to an early grave.

Closing the distances, Pete Crance stepped further towards his prisoner, stopping as he came right up on the bars to clasp his fingers around the rough hands of Cleveland Banks. From there, he manifested his anger.

"What is it with your kind over there in Gulleytown? What will it take for you animals to stop making up lies about that boy? You see what you're doing is stirring yourself up a bunch of mess that might cause someone you care about like maybe that little grandbaby of yours some real hurt."

A grimace held to the face of the Sheriff as he lowered to gain an almost level view to the eyes of Cleveland Banks.

"You listen here . . . as far as I ever saw . . . Slay Builder was a good kid. The best all sport athlete I ever saw come through these parts, and he come from decent hard working folks. I even believe if he had lived, he would have had a decent future somewhere away from Gulleytown, and that's saying plenty for anybody that comes out of that cesspool." The sheriff studied his suddenly quiet prisoner for a moment before boring forward.

"It's a shame that when you get all liquored up like this that you can only babble nonsense and foolishness. You clean overlook who it was out there still dragging the lake another whole week after the official search had been called off. I was all alone under that cold water looking for that kid. I was the only one still trying to return his body to his folks. What did you do other than stand by and watch me like most of the rest of Gulleytown? You maggots need to do like decent folks around here done long ago . . . let the boy rest in peace . . . and stop all this foolishness about seeing him every . . . ."

"Look . . . down there around your legs Sheriff? What about them babies down there playing that you burnt up?" Slurp, slurp.

The eyes of Cleveland Banks darted low in all directions after he had cut the sheriff off. He focused again on his tall nemesis before adding, "What about them Sheriff? Killing them grown folks and teenagers is awful, but ya'll shouldna killed them babies . . . you shouldna."

For an instance, the sheriff's attention diverted from Cleveland and shifted lower to the area around where he carried his revolver which is where his prisoner focus was also.

The lips of Pete Crance quivered ever slightly as more of what Cleveland Banks had to say sent his eyes racing up again.

"Yeah, you see 'em alright Sheriff, and guess what else? It won't no drowned man I seen walking over by Gulleytown tonight. It was Slay Builder. You know it, and I know it. I saw him just as clear as I'm seeing you." Slurp. Pause.

"The message is . . . he's going to kill you dead for pouring gas on them babies."

Cleveland paused again but it was not his intention to do so on this occasion. He had to in order to adjust to more of his wicked hiccups. Once settled, he watched as something evil flushed the blood away from the tall man's face who was still attempting to crush through the bones in his hands.

"That was the message he told me to give you."

He tucked his lower lip in and out from the space between his teeth before allowing words to pounce again.

"You a dead sumbitch."

"You're about to be given the hugest favor a man in my position can give a man in yours, and for your sake, you had better recognize it as that and do as told. I'm walking away from this shitty cell and I'm going to act like when I passed by you were on that bunk over there sound asleep." He clawed more pain using his nails into his prisoner's hands before continuing, "You had best take this kindness I'm offering as a pass and fall out over there for some rest, and if I ever hear you mention the name of Slay Builder again in this county, I promise you that the best bloodhounds in the state won't be able to find where I stuff your rotten ass."

Behind Cleveland, the thin mattress that was to be a part of his bedding for the night hung half on and half off of the steel bunk. The Sheriff let go of his hands and without saying another word Cleveland made his way towards it, but right before he could, the sheriff had one last piece of advice for him.

"After they let you out of here in the morning, don't go right off to work. You go find that dead nigger in and tell him that I'll see him in hell."

Cleveland finally got to his bunk, allowing the mattress to remain as it was. He shifted his weight until he lay completely on one side and then sent laser vision over in the vicinity of the Sheriff, but he never looked directly up at him. Instead, Cleveland focused again on the area around the tall man's legs.

Pete Crance was watching Cleveland Banks and he did so with an unblinkingly eye for several moments before taking a tinder step that took him away from the cell. He followed the original step with more purposeful ones. The way Pete Crance stalked away, one would have never thought that he had even stopped for a chat. And before Cleveland could blast out another disturbing hiccup, the Sheriff had exited the cell area through another heavy gray metal door. It wasn't five minutes after his encounter with Cleveland Banks did the shaken Sheriff have an edgy Henly Blackmon on a phone connect engaged in a heated discussion.

OCTOBER 1989

The lake front property owned by Henly Blackmon was expansive. The nearest neighbor was further than a half mile away and in the opposite direction of the grassy land that was more than three football fields in length from the lake to the woods. Where land owned by Henly continued but the tract of earth referred to as Sacred Hills was not his property even though he claimed ownership. Henly had never before laid eyes on those mystifying hills nor the blinding light they existed beneath, and those small hills had never before been under the scrutiny of any white individual who had lived to tell about them.

After the chase for Solomon Builder had come to an end, the struggling walk back through the woods was a manipulative one for both Calbert and Lawrence. Henly Blackmon went on a strangling tirade that was based purely on supremacy and how it would factor into all the decisions he had made over the course of the night. The teenagers were still shaken from the encounter with Sacred Hills and had never regrouped from all the events that had taken place prior to their venture out in to the woods. Neither knew what to say and both remained absolutely quiet and willed themselves through Henly's tirade that didn't end until Pete Crance arrived in his Sheriff vehicle twenty minutes behind their return to the cabin.

Sheriff Crance parked with his tail lights to his vehicle facing the lake, like all the other vehicles filling the squared gravel parking area. Elbowing out of his car, the sheriff made a tight loop to get past a small blue car that he gave a fleeting look before setting his sights squarely on the new town car of Henly Blackmon. In the area also was a beat up and rusted old pick up truck and a shiny red mustang that gained very little of the Sheriff's attention.

Pete Crance had been elected Sheriff of Rix County over the incumbent less than twelve months earlier with a ton of assistance from Mayor Henly Blackmon. It was an elected position he had waited his entire life for and was extremely proud to have. He approached the cabin with long purposeful strides and was accosted prior to arriving by a hard shove from an obvious discomposed Henly Blackmon.

Clutching at the arms of the sheriff, Henly maneuvered him backward before scorching.

"It's fucking 3:45 . . . what took you so damn long to get here?!"

Sheriff Crance was initially startled for he had not observed Henly advancing from the side of the cabin, but his resistance set in almost immediately. His attempt to free himself failed miserably however. Nonetheless, he huffed back.

"What the hell is so damn important that you've got to drag me out of the bed at this hour? Damn it Henly, I was . . . ."

"I'm in no mood for any of your lip tonight Pete! Just shut up so that I can explain this as fast as I can." He released one of the Sheriff's arms but maintained a pull on the other one. "Let's go, we need your car for this."

The statement cast silence over the Sheriff as he allowed a more thoughtful view of the flustered individual who had been best man at his wedding. Pete Crance appeared now to be easily giving in to being guided back towards his county vehicle but as soon as they had reached the parking area, the Sheriff engaged Henly Blackmon in a profanity laced confrontation that almost sent the two men to blows.

Bursting from within the cabin was Lawrence, and moments later Calbert appeared on its porch. Both were given a colorful view of the shouting match. Their hearts heavy, the teenagers could only look on as the Henly crammed down into the small car belonging to Latosha Williams. Trailing Henly was Sheriff Pete Crance in his cruiser as they gunned away from Sunken Lake and into the lightless night.

"We're on our way to Gulleytown to make sure everybody stays silent."

Calbert remembered the last hate filled statement spoken by Henly Blackmon before he drove away.

MIDNIGHT TUESDAY, JUNE 11, 1999

Front Street was the perfect name for the two lane road that fronted the Gulleytown community. The line-straight street ran parallel to railroad tracks and it ended abruptly at the beginning edges of Stansburg where Gulleytown came to an end.

Beginning at a flashing light off of Maplely Street which was the street the town square was located on, Front Street stretched for twelve country blocks. With no other traffic signals, Front Street continues and comes to an end at the point where it nose dives with no mercy into an unforgiving bend in the road called Dead Man's curve.

From the well-educated to the best street hustler, if they were black, you were likely to find them residing on one of the many streets slashing through the neighborhood behind Front Street. Single family homes were abundant. And there were large residences also, but most of the homes were small and constructed almost right on top of one another, four to an acre lot. With so many homes there was hardly any breakage for any open space but there was this gapping openness. It was right in the perfect center of Front Street. The grass was flawless and green and without blight and the opening appeared out of place for its entire surroundings. Missing from this beautiful tract of land were three homes that belonged to unsuspecting families who were burned alive inside of them almost ten years earlier. Seven children and five adults lost their lives in the flames. Of the three families, one belonged to Latosha Williams.

SHERIFF PETE CRANCE had been on a phone call with former Rix Mayor Henly Blackmon. Moments after hanging up he exited the county jail on his way home for the night to his wife of seventeen year and Jasper, an old bloodhound they had raised from a puppy. The Crances had parented no children in their residence on the northern tip of Stansburg.

A normal ride home from the jail never took more than eight or nine minutes at any time of the day or night, but the sheriff would not be making his normal commute. Over the past several months, the sheriff had been getting more and more tangled in a drawing need to enter Gulleytown. He did this at least once a week and late at night after he knew the streets would be practically clear. Pete Crance had been at odds with himself for many years over some horrible mistakes he had made in his rookie year under the influencing forces of then Mayor Henly Blackmon. It had become a common occurrence for the sheriff to deviate from his normal route. Instead of turning left from Maplely at the flashing signal and heading directly for his home, the sheriff turned right and went over the rail tracks and then made an immediate left to Front Street and into Gulleytown. There was no question about the decision tonight after the smothering conversation that Cleveland Banks had drugged him into.

Until becoming Sheriff, Pete Crance had never been much of a leader at anything but he would oftentimes race far over the top in being the top follower of whom ever the individual in charge was, and for Pete, that character was mostly Henly Blackmon. Under Henly's guidance, the Sheriff had been somewhat of a crippling individual, but he had mellowed considerably since the final tragedy that had taken place in Gulleytown and around Sunken Lake. Under his title of Sheriff, Pete Crance had not served his constituents well and failed his office for the revolting acts he gave life to nearly ten years earlier in this very community. If it were any way possible the sheriff would reverse his morally reprehensible actions and return every life to Gulleytown his hands had destroyed. Such an act was not feasible, and even if it were, Henly Blackmon would somehow find a way to not allow it to occur.

What Pete Crance was badly in need of was someone that could help him or at the very least an individual to confess his prominent role in murdering so many young lives.

Life was rotting right out of the sheriff, and it was not because of any illness he had encountered. There was hardly a day that passed where he did not feel watched or followed but had no idea of who.

This experience kept him challenged and on edge. When alone, Pete often screamed out his pain but he never sought any relief for his turmoil. It had gotten tremendously difficult for him to continue suppressing the dark images always spinning through his thoughts from a cool night a decade earlier. His conscience would no longer allow the form of evil he had taken part in to lay at peace within him. Cleveland Banks had been perfectly right earlier, Pete Crance constantly heard the suffering voices of small children he had killed begging out for him to save them. The fire he set was very vivid in his memory. He remembered how angry the flames were and how they killed indiscriminately as they jumped from home to home.

With his entrance into Gulleytown and an assist from Cleveland Banks, the Sheriff encountered a new era of personal suffering. The images of the deaths his hands had caused were clearer. He could visualize exactly what the drunken man was speaking of. The small children that his hands had burned were all over the cell area of his jail. They were even behind his eyelids when he blinked. His sins were too terrible. The Sheriff was in need of the kind of help not found walking around on earth, but he never sought it and there was none coming. Pete Crance entered Gulleytown at the very least once a week to express his regrets and sorrows and to ask forgiveness from everyone his actions had harmed. This act in itself haunted him, but he continued it anyway. It was how the Sheriff sought relief from his many demons, and also believing that he was in some manner helping his own soul.

It was only minutes after midnight when the Sheriff made his way down Front Street. He knew that it would only be a matter of moments before the first tiny voice would come alive in his conscious and add more burden to his world. Pete Crance had expected it and it was delivered without mercy. Crying voices came rushing harshly into his thoughts and their screams were of a horrendous nature. The Sheriff cringed as he came along side the empty space where they all had lost their lives. The children were all there and as burned as they always were while he drove past.

Sheriff Pete Crance did not slow down but was fixated on their faces as he whispered his relief.

"I'm sorry to you all."

Directly ahead of the vehicle, something big lay in the roadway. The Sheriff would not have seen it even if he had been turned in that direction. There were far too many demons being active for him to have seen anything clearly. Striking the object solidly, the sheriff shifted violently as he traveled right over it with front and rear wheels. Clutching at the steering column, Pete Crance veered right until he was up against the sidewalk, where he parked his car directly in front of a small unlit home.

Front Street was empty and dark as the Sheriff uplifted from his vehicle carrying only a flashlight to search the street where all of the street lights had burned out years ago and were yet to be replaced.

Standing tall beneath his hat, Sheriff Crance grimaced as he began the first of several footsteps to get a close up look at the rotted log lying out of place near the center line of the street.

Images continued to challenge the sheriff from particularly back up the street a few homes where only the open space appeared. It was only a blur, but from over his left shoulder Pete Crance saw someone approaching him and coming fast. Whoever it was must not have appeared any more unusual to the sheriff than any of the other bizarre activities that took place during his trips at night into Gulleytown. The sheriff had grown strangely accustom to observing things out of the norm.

The blur drew much closer and the sheriff could plainly see who his stalker was but Pete reacted as if the individual was just another haunting image his thoughts would deal with. It would prove to be a grave mistake and it would also be the very last time that the Sheriff would ever stand tall. A clubbing blow twisted him down to the ground fast, and it was the force behind the twelve-inch knife blade that kept him there. The sharp knife entered through one side of the sheriff's neck and was ripped viciously enough downward that it lodged against the chest plate and was being inched downwards, diving for the heart.

"Sorry."

It was the last word of Pete Crance.

A hissing gurgle could be heard as his body jerked twice before stiffening. Blood overfilled the opening to his mouth.

While kneeling down next to the sheriff, his killer dug the long murder weapon from its cavity while taking a long moment to look up towards the empty space centering Front Street where houses once stood. There was relief taking place there as the cries of the burned unattended children begin to fade while traveling celestial.

The killer began to run back past the sheriff's vehicle. The strides were bursting an became and all out sprint all the way down to the end of Front Street, where the pace slowed for a leap to clear the small gulley that signaled the end of the community.

The killer of Sheriff Pete Crance was eaten up almost immediately by the dark woods that grew thickly behind Dead Man's curve. A dead Sheriff had been the only one to see the set angry face of the killer.

WEDNESDAY JUNE 12, 1999

The murder of a southern sheriff on a skin dark street in a small segregated town had the makings of simmering Rix County into a broil. From both sides of the railroad tracks distrust, dislike and in some cases down right hate emanated and it lingered over all of Rix. Residents from Gulleytown and Stansburg had always lived separately but the communities were at all times were sociable. The day that followed the murder of Pete Crance, they weren't even that any longer. People were in the streets early expressing strong viewpoints. Factories and plants shutdown before noon and they forced employees from the premises in an effort to diffuse some of the tension following the unsolved death. Rix County was smoldering, and by nightfall, it was in total disarray.

DANDLER

NORTH WEST OF THE town seat is another unincorporated portion of the county called Dandler. It's a tiny setting, smaller than Taylorsville. Georgia Highway 44 splits right through it in less than a half mile as it continues on through Fandale from Rix. The presence of Sixty-two-year-old former Mayor Henly Blackmon had been demanded out to this community to a private residence. When first asked, Henly had sworn against coming but eventually obliged and was now resting a discomforting hip that was in need of replacing like he had done for the other one four years back. Henly appeared large and to a great degree very dumpy in the night air outside of a ranch home in a sheet metal chair built strong enough to hold his expansive girth beneath a car-less carport. He nursed a glass of dry scotch in one hand as his other pulled at a slow burning cigar rotating between two very pink lips. Over the years, the age gods had cursed him unfairly. Puffy purplish rings circled reddened dry eyes. His skin was even more pinkish than his lips where there weren't ugly patches from a deteriorating liver. Gout caused him an uncomfortable limp and he was oftentimes swollen over most of his body. But what caused Henly the most outward discomfort was neither of those ailments. It was violent body heaving coughs that he emptied out almost endlessly that tortured him the most, and it turned his pink skin towards devilish red.

It had been a day fixed in turmoil but a bright sun had shined over it that saw Henly spending most of it paying his respects to the widow of Pete Crance. Nightfall found him on the boundary of the county at the home of his lifetime friend Dennis Jacobs and his wife Fanny. With Henly's arrival and at the behest of her husband, Fanny Jacobs departed the home to visit with friends and other community leaders who were meeting for a prayer service in honor of the slain Sheriff. They gathered at a small church that was right off highway 44 also and not very far from her home. Her departure meant that the two men were alone as they had wished to talk.

Big Dennis Jacobs as he was known around Rix was even a larger man than Henly but he wasn't as solidly built. His weight was uncontrolled obesity and it was especially pronounced in a hanging abdomen. The sheer mass of it slanted his shoulders and pulled the huge man over into a lumbering walk that looked more like a slow slide. His stance was always an unbalanced one on incredibly wide size seventeen feet. Dennis was wrinkled through his scalp and bald except for stray bristles on the sides and each of his facial features were small and that went especially for his lips, and it all looked totally out of place when compared with the rest of his body.

The home of the Jacobs was all red brick and the outside door to the kitchen was made of glass and gave entry from the carport. It was two steps up and several away from where Dennis Jacobs had left his old friend sitting outside alone only seconds ago as he returned inside.

No more than two minutes had passed before Dennis made a return wheezing and sucking having lost half his breath just by walking into his home to add several more splashes of scotch to his glass. His seat was close to where Henly's was and it faced him, and while inside, Dennis flipped on a light that dove out from within the home to cast him and his guest into sitting, shadowy bear-like figures.

Earlier in the spring, Fanny Jacobs had purchased spray cans and painted the metal chairs that they sat in into a darker shade of green. Dennis Jacobs made one of the chairs cry out beneath his weight as he angled it forward and within only a foot from the chair straining beneath Henly Blackmon. Using a paper napkin, he wiped perspiration away from his forehead and then patted at the abundance of soft skin hanging beneath his chin before attempting a reply to a scolding remark from Henly that had pushed him inside his home for another drink.

"Henly, I'm telling you, the Builder boy killed Pete. I know you think that's crazy but it's the truth. I'm worried and I'm about to loose my mind with all this stuff happening around here . . . and now he's got to Pete. With him dead, it only leaves the two of us, and Slay Builder is not just going to stop at killing Pete. He's out to kill us too Henly. We're the only ones left that knows about what happened on the lake." He wiped at more sweat accumulating about his face. "There's a lot of stuff happening around my property Henly and I'm tired of telling you about it and you paying me no damn attention. My patience is thin now because I've started loosing a grip on life over this mess we're in. I keep asking you over and over again to bring your ass out here so that you can see for yourself that this boy is still very much alive but you're to damn pig-headed to listen to anything anymore. Well, he's killed Pete now . . . and I'm tired enough to let him kill me too because I can't stomach any more of this or you."

Rising up to the edge of his chair, Henly exploded back.

"You son of a bitch . . . you better tame that damn tongue of yours when you talking to me!"

Henly held up his hands to cough but it didn't materialize and he wanted badly to continue his statement but he was experiencing some swelling in his throat which pushed at him to wait for several moments.

"What happen to Pete last night was that he let his guards down and some sick bastard running wild in that mess-hole took the opportunity to kill him. Those darkies in Gulleytown started playing on his conscious and it wore him down to death, and according to what I just heard out of your mouth, your weak ass is next."

Before he could remove the cigar from his lips a dreadful cough ravaged him. A cough that concerned Dennis Jacobs to the point where he covered his own mouth while attempting to hand over a pocket handkerchief. The effort was waved off and at the very opportunity Henly was able to speak again came forth these words.

"Since you want to go back in time and talk about the night on lake, I'll oblige you, let's talk about. It was the night after everything happened; remember I came out here after they drugged the body of the last girl from the lake? Remember what I told you? I looked you straight in your fucking eyes and told you that the Builder kid died in the woods." He pointed. "With these eyes I saw the inside of head spread all over the floor and I keep the iron poker that did it on the back seat of my car for a reminder. There's nothing that you can tell me about seeing him, or him killing anybody? The boy is dead. No way in hell he could of lived from the kind of wound that dumb Davis boy put on him without some kind of medical attention almost on the spot, and I know for a fact that he didn't get none of that. Now the boy did get up and run . . . I didn't lie to you about that, but as sure as I'm sitting here, he's dressed in dry bones somewhere in the woods in back of my property. And that I'd pretty much stake my life on." Gritting his teeth, Henly snarled, "Nigger-loving Lawrence probably had something to do with hiding him because his story never added up, and we would have got to the truth of it all with the little girl if Pete hadn't . . . ."

"Don't say it Henly! I don't want to hear it again about what Pete did to Latosha Williams. He's dead and has paid for those sins now, and doesn't have to deal with all this craziness anymore and on top of that, he's probably glad that he's finally gotten away from you too."

Dennis fell suddenly quiet but only because Henly was almost coughing himself into a convulsion again as his eyes watered from the strain.

After seeing that he would be fine, Dennis picked up again.

"Slay Builder killed Pete Crance, Henly, and I don't care what you say about what you seen with your own two eyes. I'm telling you that I've seen the boy in my house standing right above Fanny and I while we were in bed and I saw him with these fucking two eyes that I own. He's not dead. He's not even close to being dead. At least two nights a week I can see him. He lets me see him standing outside of this house somewhere watching me."

Very nervously, Dennis emptied the contents of his glass into his mouth and then held the glass upside down while looking over into the hard eyes of his friend.

Henly's entire body tightened, rigidness could be seen all over his face and the cigar he had held between his lips had all but been bitten in half and was folded and still flaming below his chin.

For the better part of his life, Dennis Jacobs had feared Henly Blackmon and what he could do to a man with his abilities to control the actions of others and with his own bare hands, but at this point in his life, Dennis wasn't biting his tongue.

"The word crazy really didn't apply to me until here of late so I never paid much attention to it. But I must have been out of my fucking mind ten years ago to let you snag me into this kind of mess. I should have never allowed you to push me into covering up all of what you and Pete did to that Williams girl. It was fucking disgusting. Drowning my ass . . . if I could do the report over right now I would and it would serve you murdering mortherfuckers right. Something is haunting me and I don't just mean Slay Builder. And if you weren't so thick headed you'd listen when I keep telling you that I'm seeing things out at this house that I'm not suppose to be seeing and I'm tired of it Henly . . . I'm fucking tired."

The statement in its entirety was the harshest Henly could ever recall anyone hurling his way and he didn't respond immediately for he couldn't. He was slumped over again in a ragged cough and attempting to will his body back into a normal breathing pattern. The discomfort passed slowly as it always did and once it was over Henly didn't bully out his anger in the manner Dennis Jacobs had expected. The unsettledness in the former mayor's demeanor was glaringly noticeable but the response he offered was tilted more towards calming then anything his host would have ever imagined possible for him.

A buzzing fly ended its buzz and landed on the rim of the banana straw hat that Henly was never without. He swiped it away before saying anything.

"The death of Latosha Williams ain't the first that you covered up." There was a pause which was for affect only before the next statement was added with a bit more of snapping hostility.

"And don't for one millisecond forget what I know about what you do to little boys when they're laid up in the morgue with you." Henly coughed wildly again but smothered it quicker this time.

"You've been coroner around here for more years than I can count and I ain't never heard you say nothing about being haunted for all the filthy shit you've been doing to dead little boys. What you've done is gone soft like Pete and bought into the craziness that those Gulleytown animals been feeding you. The Builder boy ain't haunting you . . . you haunting yourself, and you need to stop before what happened to Pete happens to you."

Dennis Jacobs had not expected Henly to dive into his own personal demons and the coroner reddened behind it almost to pigmentation as disturbing as the man that had given it.

"Damn it I'm sick of you and all of your callous responses to everything that doesn't hold well with you." The large man rocked and then slid forward in the chair to place his empty glass bottoms up next to his bare feet, and then leaned on one of his giant forearms towards his guest.

"Calbert Davis is dead and he's been that way now for a long time. Pete got torn open last night which leaves you and I and your boy still breathing as the only people that know the truth as it relates to what you bastards really did out on your property to those kids. You're either going to come by here tomorrow night like I've been asking you to see whether what I've been telling you is true or not, or you go get your hacking, self-serving-ass back into that fancy white town car and don't ever let me see you on this property again. And I mean that pretty much in the same respects as how you banished your own fucking flesh and blood from this county way back." Dennis huffed hard once before adding, "And so help me Henly, if you show up out here again, one of us will die behind it. And I'm at the point where it really makes little difference to me which option you choose."

Over fifty years of friendship had been shared between the men, never before had Dennis Jacobs been so forcefully convincing. From somewhere he had found the courage to release the most meaningful words he had ever spoken to Henly Blackmon, and he spoke them with very little care towards repercussions.

The hidden sounds that crepe out only under the hours of darkness was the only sounds that could be heard as those fiery words hung low beneath the car port and over both men. Neither lost contact with the others weathered eyes.

Tossing away half of his cigar, Henly Blackmon fingered a matchbox from a pocket on his shirt. From the tip of a match stick, he added fire to the cigar and drew hard on what remained of it. He then drained his own whiskey dry before uplifting from his chair.

A look of fury corned his eyes when he set a pace with barely a limp towards his car. Away from the carport, Henly didn't turn back in the direction of Dennis until he was standing beneath the bright stars and inside the open door of his long vehicle.

With certainty, Dennis Jacobs knew that Henly always kept a handgun inside of his car. Watching him walk away, Dennis's breath rushed right up out of him and he found it nearly impossible to breath until he finally heard the voice again of his old friend and knew he was not about to catch an angry bullet.

"What time do you need me out here?"

Finally, Dennis thought. After trying for so long he had finally been given confirmation that Henly was giving credence to what he had been trying to tell him.

"He comes at different times of the night, but the young man has never showed up before eleven o'clock."

There was a single nod that wasn't noticeable by Dennis Jacobs because of the type of darkness the night held, but there was indication of it by the movement of the cigar that Henly held between his lips. And not another word was spoken as Henly folded into his vehicle, and instead of turning the car around in the space that was provided in the driveway, he backed away from the home slowly.

As he wondered what in the world his old friend might be thinking of, Dennis remained perfectly still and looked on as the headlights of the car sprayed the top of trees while it descended the rise in the middle of his stretchy drive. When the lights had disappeared and only darkness remained, Dennis scanned his property from one end to the other. More cries screeched up from his chair as he pushed away to stand and to whisper.

"I know you're out there somewhere Slay Builder. You always are. And from what you did to Pete, I know that you know that townsfolk are going to be looking for you."

Fear had angled into the face of Dennis Jacobs as he moved towards his home and stepped inside.

"God is going to have to step in to help us. We're all in trouble here."

The light carrying out from the house onto the carport was extinguished as the glass door leading into the home was latched and the heavy door behind it was closed also. Dennis Jacobs slid a deadbolt across the door and checked it twice. He then maneuvered around the dining table to peer out of a large bay window carved into one of the walls of the kitchen that looked out over a small pond and into the woods in back of his home. He was looking for any early signs of a visitor that night.

CHAPTER 4

THURSDAY, JUNE 13, 1999

Late Spring temperatures in the deep South can burn pretty hot. In Northeast Georgia smothering humidity can be added, plus a pop up rain shower or two to keep things settled down a bit. Minus the rain shower, the day had lived up to history. It had been clear and boiling all the way up to around seven-thirty when the sun settled. At precisely eight that evening a wake for Sheriff Pete Crance began at The Greater Fellowship Church of Rix. This was the same church off Highway 44 that a prayer service had been held the night before that Fanny Jacobs had departed her home early in the night to attend. A large number of residents predominantly from the Stansburg community flowed in and out of the gathering. Services were schedule to last until ten that night but the church would keep the doors open as long as people continue to arrive.

By eight-thirty the church was more than three quarters full, the service was going on as planned and all was normal except for the quiet entrance of one Henly Blackmon who had not ventured into a place of worship since childhood. Henly was out of his usual attire of starched kakis and a white cotton button down and in its place he adorned a wardrobe of all black for the evening, jeans and shirt. On entrance he squirmed into a seat, taking up a generous area of one of the back pews. Henly tilted several times for comfort but did so without causing anymore notice and had successfully positioned where no one else was within two empty rows of where he had lodged. He wasn't bothered and for the most part kept his heaving coughs at bay or squashed them within. For the better part of a half hour, Henly remained planted to his pew like a large sweet potato before making a quiet an unnoticed exit.

It had all went as planned so far. After exiting the church, Henly strung a straight line for his car to gather items he would need for the nights occasion. He pushed back a full head of gray hair before pulling on a solid black cap that fitted elastically to his head and then with as much suddenness as he had been shoved, Henly doubled over into a coughing spasm that would eventually push him to one knee. He recovered slowly but once he had, Henly moved away from his car and stepped with assuredness towards the high brush that filled the area in the back left of the church. These woods would take him in the direction of the next county to the place where he had been summoned the previous night, to the Jacobs' home.

In total darkness and in a larger than life manner, Henly Blackmon had marched away, and as he had planned, his trek into the woods went unnoticed by anyone coming or leaving the wake of Pete Crance.

ATHENS, GA

THURSDAY NIGHT JUNE 13, 1999

ON THE INSIDE, Lawrence Blackmon was tangled and twisted and on the outside he had not stopped quivering or slept for a solid moment since watching a breaking news report early Wednesday morning describe the grisly murder of the small town sheriff he had once idolized when being coached by Pete Crance in his introduction to pee wee football. At that time in their life, Lawrence referred to him as Uncle Pete. That was apart of their good history. He and the sheriff shared sordid history also. History that was disturbing and it bonded them more so than the good. It was this bond between the two men that had Lawrence soaked in sweat through his clothing and freezing at the same time while entertaining nightmarish thoughts of what might have truly happened to the sheriff in Gulleytown. A summer cold, one of sudden and harsh nature was the reason he was not making himself available to operate his clinic and remained locked inside of his home. As he had done on the previous day, Lawrence had begged clear of the concerns of Whitney to offer him care. Horrible images from the past were forcing their way back into his thoughts again and they were advancing mercilessly to where Lawrence was watching the murders of his high school friends over and over again without the escaping disguise that his sleep had always provided.

The second Thursday night of each month had become a night that breathed life back into Lawrence. His life needed it. It was purposeful, one that he now based his life around. Lawrence Blackmon was trying as best he could to put perspective on the murder of Pete Crance but it was layering him with difficulties that he couldn't find a way to shake. Lawrence knew that he needed to leave his home on this night irregardless of his troubles but since becoming aware of the murder, he had not taken more than a dozen steps and none were anywhere near the direction of his securely bolted doors. In bed with his bed sheets beneath his chin, Lawrence attempted to push aside a bone-chilling image of the sheriff firing a shot and Latosha Williams' head exploding as her small body bounced against the trunk of his issued vehicle. Lying inside of his bedroom with his back to the door, Lawrence needed to conquer his fear and find a way to leave his home, but at the moment the murder of Pete Crance and memories from Sunken Lake had him captured.

Lawrence forced away another thought of leaving to fumble over his bed in search of the remote that controlled the television. Lawrence Blackmon could not muster enough courage to simply leave his home but he wanted to make sure that the cheering from the crowd of the baseball game being played would drown out the on going blast from the gun ringing through his ears that stopped all of the pleading of Latosha Williams, and ended her movements forever.

DANDLER

IT HAD TAKEN right at an hour and a half for Henly Blackmon to fight through brier patches and maneuver through vines and spider webs to finally reach an area that he thought was perfect to handle the business he needed to attend to. It was a spot that was naturally sunken within six feet of the tree line of the woods behind the catfish pond in the rear of the Jacobs' property. Henly made his appearance even smaller by perching down on a folding chair that he had carried along with other items out into the woods. The small chair was backless but would serve its purpose admirably to provide Henly as much comfort as possible while he awaited the ghost haunting Dennis Jacobs.

All had gone well up to this point, Henly had accounted for everything he had anticipated needing for his night venture in to the woods except for the rain. A clear night had turned cloudy and grumpy and within ten minutes of his arrival, the rain provided unwelcome company in large flopping drops that dove hard into the muddy waters of the catfish pond.

For close to two hours Henly sat quietly with barely a cough, he had neither heard nor observed anyone other than the rain, thunder rattling the air, and lightning slashing it. The flashes of lightning were powerfully illuminating and easily highlighted the fearful antics of the enormous figure of Dennis Jacobs in a window looking out over the rear of his property. He carried on like he was actually seeing some form of ghost for real.

The legs of Henly Blackmon had stiffened after having sat so long in such a heavy down pour. In fact, he ached all over but much more than that, Henly was totally frustrated. He was angry and felt foolish for allowing himself to be cornered into such nonsense to wait in the woods for a dead man to appear. Gathering himself took a few moments but after several large rocks Henly was on his feet again and contemplating the manner he would deal with his old friend for dragging him into such humiliation. With his arms up high above his body in a long stretch, Henly stiffen again and strained to smother a yawn while his heart skipped from rhythm at a sight that came into view. Standing within the sunken area where he had been perched enabled Henly a view to his immediate left that had previously been denied by a huge cedar tree he had leaned against for better comfort. Less than five feet away from him and close enough to the breaking edge of the woods to be seen clearly by anyone in the home through the constant slashes of lightning was the ghost that haunted Dennis Jacobs.

With quickness but very carefully Henly leaned for the tree again but this time he did so for cover and peered around it to make double sure that he was actually seeing what he thought was there. In the lonely environment they were in and in appearance alone what Henly saw would indeed strike fear in the heart of a man and most definitely one of the caliber of Dennis Jacobs.

At a couple of inches above six feet, standing wide and powerfully in the pouring rain was a full shouldered almost beastly looking man. The rain appeared to blast away from his back and shoulders as it found its way down to the earth.

Captured by what he saw, Henly was shocked and transfixed against the cedar tree.

There is a life that the wild gives to the wilderness that is foreign to any human but this man possessed it. In giant intakes through his nostrils he breathed in the rhythm of the trees and all the rest of the woods. With his every exhale his entire back expanded, it was intimidating when couple with his extremely large hands that tighten in and out of fist. Like it was his very own possession, he just stood in the openness to the woods. He was confident while watching the humorous antics of Dennis Jacobs. It was obvious that he owned not a fear in the world.

Henly realized that his mouth was still open from either yawning or awe as he looked down and noticed that he had been balancing on his toes. He came down and as far as he knew took his first breath since his sighting of this strange looking man and with it came a different rhythm to his heartbeat. It raced up and down as though it was about to pole vault out of his body. Henly also felt faint until he finally closed his mouth, and then in an instance, his emotions went from shock and fascination to total destruction. He sized over the imposingly built younger man again but this time with total malice at the control of his heart.

Henly observed brown combat boots and camouflage pants caked in mud up to around the knees. A tan belt had been taken from the pants and hugged at his waist to pull down tightly on a matching camouflage fleece and it made it appear several sizes to small and him to appear even larger than he actually was. Henly tried to imagine but there was no way that he could actually tell how long this man had been standing out there only feet away from him and peering across the pond at the hysterics of Dennis Jacobs, but he did feel fairly certain that his own large presence had not registered notice.

With his adrenaline pumping, Henly fingered for another object he had carried out into the woods. He had rested a tire iron below his knees against the same tree he had moments ago unbolted from. High above the trees lightning slashed with jaggedness again. Henly readied for the blasting of thunder that he was sure would follow. Only seconds passed before it began its rumble and as it did Henly lunged with the quickness of a man thirty years younger, and with immobilizing force bloodied the unsuspecting man. Henly actually smiled as he acted and watched as his prey dropped in a boneless manner to the soggy earth.

OCTOBER 1989

AS SOON AS the news spread about the drowning on Sunken Lake and the fires that leapt through Gulleytown, people came from both large and small places that were miles away. Many of them just wanted to see where such tragedy could happen and others came to offer any assistance they could to help the residents of Rix. The county and state agencies searched and drug all of Sunken Lake but the body of Solomon Builder was never discovered by the sheriff office of Pete Crance who led the search and rescue efforts. Found under the water were all of the teenager's personal belongings but not him. Residents of the communities wanted answers to this mystery but county officials had very little to offer. Officially, the reports stated Solomon Builder as presumed dead by accidental drowning. This conclusion was written up in entirety from eyewitness statements given by both Calbert Davis and Lawrence Blackmon. The teenagers swore to have last seen all four of their friends and that included Solomon out on Sunken Lakes in one of the paddle boats drinking and partying. Rumors of Solomon Builder being still alive and reports of sightings began coming in to the Sheriff's office almost immediately after the official announcement of his death but there had never been any serious investigation into these reports. The investigations off the entire tragedy that occurred over the night when so many of the young lost their lives were never thorough and gaps were filled in by individuals under the influence of Henly Blackmon. It was all a part of the mayor's overall plan to protect his way of life. The inactivity by the office of the sheriff and other Rix leaders to follow up on the allegations that Solomon was still alive only added fuel to a fire already out of control. This coupled with other strange occurrences help birth the folklore in Gulleytown as it relates to Solomon Builder. Deaths continue to occur in Dead Man's curve and tales surrounding Solomon grew more intriguing with each lost of life because after his supposed drowning all of the deaths that took place in the curve came with reported sightings of a rugged dark individual seen somewhere near the scene.

AFTER MIDNIGHT, FRIDAY MORNING

JUNE 14, 1999

IT WAS APPROACHING four in the morning, a time in Rix where no one was out and about and even stray cats had stopped crossing over streets and found a place to curl up for sleep. The rain that came late in the evening had been heavy and constant but even it had bid its goodbyes an hour earlier leaving the entire county saturated and in puddles. Mud formed a thick mess around shoes in the dark woods that were on Henly Blackmon's property across the long field from his cabin. They were two very large men but Dennis Jacobs and Henly Blackmon had one of the toughest struggles in their lives hauling the dead weight of Solomon Builder from one man's property to the other in the condition the rain had left the soil.

After arriving at Henly's cabin, they walked across the field and then a good distance back into the woods, further than Dennis ever wanted to go and even further than Henly had expected they would.

Slay Builder was laid out flat on his back and his clothes cut away. A run over pair of size fourteen service boots, his filthy military fatigues and a large knife were tossed against the eroded bark of a dogwood tree that had fallen to its death years ago.

Like the bark on the trees surrounding them in the woods, the skin of Slay Builder was rough and as dark as the rich soil. He was attired in only dark green boxers and an undershirt that matched which clung to his skin because of the rain. Slay was laid stretched out long only a few feet away from his discarded clothing.

With an odor of wild rankness, Slay Builder lay perfectly still. There was an untamed bushiness about him that existed without regulation. Coarse dark hair grew long and tangled from his face and head. His entire body was incredibly hardened, a muscle lay beneath every muscle and each of his facial features were large and defined. All had been expected over thoroughly by one Henly Blackmon. From this inspection, nothing about this face or this man reminded Henly of Slay Builder or identified him to be the individual he had once sought because time had changed the young man so drastically over the years. Henly found nothing familiar until he massaged his fish hook-damaged fingers into Slay Builder's bushy maim and two fingered the puncture his skull had withstood from an iron spike swung by Calbert Davis. It was Solomon 'Slay' Builder for sure, the recognition almost stopped Henly's breathing as he whizzed and coughed himself close to a seizure.

The tire iron that Henly had swung had broken open a three-inch wound that half circled the right eye of Slay Builder. It was a clear wound that the rain had found its way down to and washed most of the remnants of the bleeding into the soil beneath him, leaving a pink crack that had swollen considerably. Other than the violent transgression from Henly and the resulting unconscious, Slay Builder appeared well. Slung over a tree limb directly above was a rope with a noose at the end of it. This sight was the first thing that Slay focused in on as he regained alertness. He put up a slight struggle but gave it up almost immediately as if expecting this faith and then with calmness attempted to gain his feet but was hindered by a tangling of duct tape wrapping his ankles and more binding his wrists that had been pulled beneath his back.

Perched nervously on the fallen tree next to Henly Blackmon were all four hundred-pounds of Dennis Jacobs. At the first sight of movement from the restrained man he practically leapt away from the tree and in the process nearly toppled over a rusted can filled with gasoline that he and Henly had also carried into the woods. It was his constant complaints and threatening actions that had initiated the evenings events but the Rix County Coroner was in no way thrilled about what was to take place and was having a great deal of problems with where Henly had chosen to relocate Slay Builder too. Dennis Jacobs had made no attempts to hide his insecurities.

Aside from his old friend's odd behavior, the entire night for Henly Blackmon could not have gone better if he had written it out. He had long doubted the insistence of Dennis of having seen anyone on his property and had pretty much believed him to be an old fool for even mentioning such nonsense but that was all history now.

Beneath the mercy of Henly was the ghost of Gulleytown and life couldn't get any better for him.

Dennis and Henly were the best of friends but held contrasting views on how to handle the outcome of finding Slay Builder. For the better part of two hours while awaiting his nemesis to awaken, Dennis Jacobs danced about nervously with the surprisingly agility of a man half his size. Just by being in the presence of Slay Builder gave him troubles and he found even more by where they were located with him. They were much too far back in the woods for his sanity and it filled him with fright that manifested in everything he did. Dennis Jacobs wanted absolutely no part of the woods they were in.

With Slay Builder roused, Henly pushed away from his seat also and in a cautious manner drew closer until he was a half of foot in front of Dennis Jacobs. Both had sought and obtained a less obstructed view of Slay now that he was finally awake. The look of desperation that Henly expected and wanted was not there. Instead, there was somewhat of a strange glow emitting from his eyes that escorted a coy smile. What they looked down upon served to further unnerve Dennis Jacobs and for all intended purposes practically infuriated Henly Blackmon.

HENLY BLACKMON HAD always believed that Slay Builder was no longer alive despite of all the rumors circulating to the contrary and the beliefs of some of his closes friends. The fact that he really had survived Sunken Lake only fed the desires of the former mayor to make sure of his death this time. It was only the strong and persistent opposition of an emotionally charged Dennis Jacobs to not have the murder take place on the fringes of his property as the reason Slay Builder had not already been beaten to death. Dennis had found success in persuading Henly to move the unconscious man but he never imagined ending up where they were. Henly Blackmon was in complete control and the life of Slay Builder was at his mercy now that he had regained full consciousness which was exactly what Henly had waited hours for.

A PAIR OF snake skin cowboy boots ultra black in color tightly gripped Henly's feet. Dennis Jacobs came up closer to Henly's back and was immediately bumped aside and he watched as a mud-wrapped boot heel came down on the chest of Slay Builder.

The act of aggression was sudden, but no reaction came from the man below it. It was if the transgression never took place.

Henly scuffed, and with the toe of his boot lifted the chin of the prone man to discard a disgusting ball of the bile he had coughed up. Thick and yellow, it landed in a bushy corner of the rugged mustache shaped around the smiling lips of Slay and soaked slowly down to his skin.

The response to the vile act was an eerie chuckle that exploded upwards and attached to Henly. It pin-balled to affect all of his pressure points, forcing him to almost slip to the ground while adjusting his weight so that much more of it would be driven down onto Slay Builder. Henly broke the fall by using a shoulder of Dennis Jacobs who was then shoved away again.

Henly lowered and was rewarded a clear unmistakable view of supreme confidence gazing up from eyes that shined like glassy black pearls. Something inside of them captured Henly and a calmness he had never felt before began eating away at his hostility. He felt pleasant and peace but not for any noticeable time before shaking it away with tenacity and Henly replaced it with an imaginative thought of how fulfilling he would soon be as he killed this animal. Before his imagination could take him any further, Henly first had to recover from another bitter cough that burst through his insides.

Henly settled and was finally steady enough to address Slay Builder for the first time.

"Well, well, well, I finally get the pleasure to meet the ghost of Gulleytown." Henly paused to smile rather confidently in his own right.

"The funny thing is, you don't look like much of a ghost to me, truth be told, you look like every other creature running about over there in niggertown."

For all the bravado displayed by Henly, Dennis Jacobs had none to match. He was terrified and it was obvious. The confidence and the smile that was locked on the face of Slay Builder held him on the verge of delirious. He at first sought to get a closer look at the man but now he had to practically force himself closer. With a lean that was more of a push, he was up against Henly again and rewarded with the attention he sought.

"What the hell is it Dennis?"

"Henly let's not get into any of your little games, just get on with your business and let's hightail it from back here."

Dennis Jacobs realized that he had more than invaded the space of his friend, he was literally up against Henly but he didn't back away as he glanced over their surroundings.

"Henly, there's something not right about us being back here like this. I can feel it . . . I feel it in my bones. It feels like he's the one that brought us back here, not us. We shouldn't be back here with him."

These beliefs were whispered to Henly Blackmon, but Slay Builder had heard them with clarity.

His smile evolved into full laughter and the mere sound of it dove into Dennis Jacobs and rash at his skin.

"Big man, it's far too late to be thinking about doing any running."

Slay Builder had finally spoken.

His voice was strong but somewhat strangled and carried and emphasizing quality soaked in surety. His words simmered the former mayor for they were not towards him. His brief statement also served to push more fear into the county coroner who believed the words emanated from out of the soil and not the person of flesh on top of it.

"There's no where to run Big man, the spirits will find you wherever you are."

Each word and every sound of laughter made by Slay was lobbed and exploded up between Henly and Dennis as if intended for the ears of someone else. And Slay Builder had yet to look into the eyes of either of his captors, instead, his focus linger above them in the branches.

Fear mixed with paranoia is dangerous and it was affixed to Dennis Jacobs on the instant his focus drifted upwards to the trees where Slay concentrated. He would never overcome what he saw and life would never again be the same.

When Dennis delivered his focus back down again, the smile was no longer there and neither was the face of Slay Builder. The beautiful face of Latosha Williams was there in its place. Appearing next were faces of the young boys Dennis had had his way with after they were cold, dead and locked behind a steel door inside of his county morgue. The impossible all of a sudden seemed possible as Dennis Jacobs stood motionless while being haunted.

As he continued to follow the eyes of the ever changing faces on Slay Builder, Dennis locked on to images screaming out of the darkness all around them. He dislodged from Henly and abruptly dropped to one knee and offered an unnerving request.

"Get down Henly!"

Tucking his head, Dennis cowered beneath one of his forearms.

"Get them away from me."

Up until that very moment Henly Blackmon had remained relatively quiet and even unbothered throughout the entire night by some of the nonsense displayed by Dennis, but the latest antics had crossed the line and he wasted no time in showing his disgust.

With a snarl, he shoved the tree of a man over from one knee into a flop to his back.

"If you gonna be a fucking coward, be the lowest one you can, but keep the fuck away from me with it."

Moving away from his friend's outlandish behavior, Henly refocused on Slay Builder, and with all the strength he could will, kicked the defenseless man where his ribs were exposed and challenged.

"What are you doing to him, nigger!?"

The impact of the assault was gut-wrenching yet Slay barely budged and protected his words from the inquiry while continuing to only concentrate on the tree branches high above him.

Once more the heel from one of the boots of Henly was pressed onto the chest of Slay as the angry man lowered again while smothering a cough.

"I see that you've learned a few monkey tricks over the years. They got poor Dennis in a world of fix but they won't be working on me. All you doing is making it worse on yourself boy."

From his back, Dennis rolled over to his stomach and snatched up his arms to cover his head. He shouted out from his new position.

"Henly . . . you piece of shit . . . just ask him your damn question and let's get the fuck from back here!"

Henly never looked in the direction of Dennis, instead, he coughed his color red again and once settled, got back to inquiring of Slay Builder.

"Boy that rope hanging up there that you keep gawking at is for you. It's gonna hold your death and that's a promise as sure as I'm breathing. The situation you're in here will not get any better for you, but you can make it a whole lot easier on your people over there in Gulleytown. In order to do that, all you have to do is give me the name of whoever it is whose been hiding you for all these years. How you been surviving boy?"

Engaged in an animated struggle against something that only he could see, Dennis Jacobs screamed out his fright while rolling back over to his back again.

The laughter of Slay Builder cracked through the night as Dennis clutched at one of his sides. It appeared that he had been released from one futile struggle and was now fighting for his life against another haunting image that had escaped from the dangling noose hanging from the tree above them. In a brief passage of freedom from his struggles, the large man sloshed to his feet and hurried to the side of an infuriated Henly Blackmon who was attempting to stand firmly after breaking a jaw of Slay Builder with a thunderous kick. Henly followed with an assortment of kicks and stomps using the tip and heel of his boots and the results left the young man's face hard to look upon.

Laughter ended the attack and Slay followed the mocking gesture up with a long howl that sent shivers racking through both the men looking down on him. And at that point it finally happened, Slay Builder centered his focus and directed it squarely on Henly Blackmon and in silence he kept it there for so long that it pushed Dennis Jacobs a half foot to the side of him.

Slay strained to tilt his head a tiny bit and then spoke again.

"Been watching you for years . . . and I mean watching you good on every opportunity you gave me. From all that watching, I learned a lot about your habits Mayor Blackmon. I know what time you like to get home by, how you like your food cooked and the time you like eating it. I know when you go see your doctor and even the time you usually cough your way to sleep at night. You a real easy kill Mayor Blackmon. I could have done it at anytime a long time ago. Made you disappear, I could have."

Hours earlier in the night for nearly thirty minutes, Slay Builder had stood several feet in back of Henly Blackmon in the woods in back of the catfish pond of Dennis Jacobs, while Henly sat heavy and wet awaiting the younger man's arrival. While blinking continuously Slay paused and pondered including Henly on this fact as the two men above him remained quiet. A decision was made that Slay knew he would pay his life for when he maneuvered past the position of Henly and eventually placed himself out in the open to be at the mercy of the man he knew would do him the greatest of harm.

Resting his head on the ground, Slay decided against including Henly. Instead, he believed it would be more meaningful to give him something else.

"You asked the question whose been hiding me, but I really don't think you want to know Mayor Blackmon, it might just bust open that old hateful heart of yours.

"Henly watch out," Dennis screamed while ducking, swatting and spinning clumsily. "How the hell are we supposed to get from back here? We surrounded Henly . . . they got us surrounded"

With the help of the likes of Slay Builder, Dennis had been working his way up to becoming insane for some time. He now finally possessed the look.

Despairingly Henly eyed the frighten man but not for long, the words of Slay Builder drew his attention more.

"Is that rope up there for Lawrence? It better be if you want the person that's been keeping me hid from you for so long."

Slay emitted more laughter and it forced Dennis Jacobs to tighten at the core of his soft body. He was convinced that it was the entire woods laughing out instead.

"Hard to believe isn't it Mayor Blackmon? You raise a son hoping he'd be just like you and he turns out not wanting to have anything to do with you or all your twisted beliefs."

Slay wanted to stop and enjoy the affects his words were having but didn't dare for he had no idea how much more time did he have remaining before Henly got desperate and sought to kill him.

"Remember running back here? Before you and all your hate could get far enough back into the woods, Lawrence got to me and hid me." Straining, Slay twisted his neck and shoulders in order for some of the blood pooling inside of his mouth to spill. It did into the soil in a band-like strand. He then looked back to Henly and hurried to speak again.

"If it had of been Lawrence on top of me, Calbert would've hit him too. I knew his heart. He didn't mean it. He hit me pretty good. Hard enough to kill me, but I didn't die. It wasn't my time yet. I woke up, and when I did there was no one around and that gave me a chance to run. I went out the back of the cabin but my head was spinning and I was in so much pain that I just kept falling. I tried to hide but I knew it had to be somewhere far away after I heard your voice. I was running as hard as I could but Lawrence still caught up to me. I couldn't make it one more step. I knew he was chasing me, I could hear him calling. I didn't have a whole lot of life left in me, so I pretty much gave up to him. I guess it's sort of like I did to you earlier on the big man's property, but for a different reason."

In an instance Henly poured out sweat like never before, his blood pressure leapt into the danger zone as he remembered a moment earlier in the night. Something had tapped harder at one of his shoulders that he believed the rain alone had the ability too. As Henly trembled in pure anger, he was certain now that it wasn't rain at all.

Slay spilled more blood from his mouth while watching in satisfaction as Henly came to realization that he had been toyed with.

With a small smile settled over him, Slay continued.

"Lawrence is not a killer like you are Mayor Blackmon. He's got plenty of faults . . . but he's not a killer. All of that running and chasing must have sobered him some and got him back to thinking correctly because when he caught me back here, he was there to save my life. And that's just what he did."

Trying desperately not to display any hurt, especially none to this man, Henly spun away.

The moments of silence provided a small window of opportunity for the disturbing antics of Dennis Jacobs to take center stage again. Muddied all over from rolling about the ground, Dennis cupped at his ears before pointing and screaming out.

"Henly look!"

Turning slowly, Henly faced the hand gesture and saw absolutely nothing. He then looked back to Dennis who had much more to offer him.

"For god's sake Henly, they're going to allow us to leave. They're opening up a path between them to let us go. This is it . . . it's our chance. Let's get the hell from back here while we still can."

"Dennis shut up all of that fucking nonsense," Henly shouted. "We're the only people out here. I don't know what you think you're seeing but it's not real."

"Lord almighty Henly, you've gone mad. Everything is real you dumb bastard, and none of these folks out here are going to allow you to kill this boy."

Uncalculated and very calmly, Henly pulled a handgun from one of his pants pockets. At the instant that Dennis caught sight of it, the large man coward beneath his forearms again.

"I'm gonna put this on the cross Dennis."

He stopped abruptly to cough up something that looked awful but was back at Dennis Jacobs immediately.

"On the cross and everything I hold fucking worthy, if they next word that comes out of your got damn mouth is something stupid, it'll be the last."

Blood sprayed from Slay's mouth and nose as he snickered at the events unfolding between to old friends. He continued to press down on a nerve he knew was exposed and sensitive.

"Silver with a bone colored handle, it's just like Lawrence described it. That's the same gun he told me that you pulled on him. Is it the one you and the sheriff killed Latosha with too . . . huh Mayor Blackmon?"

Words of death delivered all the focus back to Slay Builder.

"You raped Latosha before you killed her didn't you Mayor Blackmon? How many little girls like her did you have to rape and kill to earn your title as the master?"

"Shut up you lying nigger," Henly snarled at the laughing man as his finger circled the trigger of the weapon.

With little regard to the threat, Slay continued his laughter and expounded on the facts as he knew them.

"There is truth in everything I've said. Tell him Lawrence," Slay shouted. "He should be out here somewhere by now looking for me. You ask him if I'm lying."

Slay twisted his focus away from Henly and briefly affixed it on a specific tree before looking directly into the face of Dennis Jacobs to exclaim, "Look in the right place and you might just see my old buddy. He could be out here to save his friend's life again from the killer in you Mayor Blackmon."

The night sky was almost completely hidden from view by large leafy limbs. Dennis scanned the top of several trees and he didn't have to say a word for his expression revealed everything that need to be said. The trees appeared human and there was gruesome murder being committed in all of them.

Henly's fury cascaded from the trees to land on his friend. Slay Builder had found a way to capture the imagination of Dennis Jacobs.

There was nothing Henly could do to help him, but what he could execute was to get rid of the individual responsible.

"Time to burn this nigger," he shouted. "Help me get him up on the rope Dennis."

Dennis Jacobs had other ideas. He took a frightened step backwards and followed it with another larger one that took him stumbling over a small bush. He kick-slid further backwards while seated on his wide behind and proclaimed, "Are you seriously insane? Why would you dare touch him again?"

While attempting to stand, Dennis lost his footing and flopped again and after finally regaining balance, Dennis delivered the bush he had tripped over an expression of apology as though it was human. He then began scrambling away.

"Fucking coward," Henly mumbled before stepping to straddle Slay Builder. The gun in his hand was pointing down in his direction.

With his laughter still on display, Slay yelled out, "Your time is up big man, running can't help you now."

Henly reached to secure the can of gasoline. While holding it in his hands he jumped as high as he could and crushed into Slay's chest. The snapping of ribs cut through the early morning air. Henly smiled as he emptied the contents from the can and made sure to stand far enough away from Slay to not splash any of the gasoline on to his own clothing. The match sparked easily and the flames leapt up to greet the darkness with the expected death of Slay Builder in their burn.

Running full out in the opposite direction behind Henly was Dennis Jacobs. He stopped to look back and what he saw sickened him and forced Dennis to yell out in anger filled with disgust.

"Henly . . . you fuck . . . you fucking crazy bastard. You've just killed the both of us!"

Dennis Jacobs picked up his run again in the thick woods but this time he ran as if he was being shoved forward. He glanced back twice more and on each occasion was captured by a frightening image appearing to be closing in on him.

Two slugs from the handgun Henly fired entered the right temple of Solomon 'Slay' Builder. Up until that point he had continued to laugh even as he burned. The gunshots deaden the night except for the popping and sizzle of human flesh burning down to bones.

The sound of gunfire behind Dennis forced him lower as he ran. He stumbled once more but was to terrified too look back again into all the death that was chasing him. Dennis ran and kept running even after the woods behind Sunken Lake had released him. He had fled and by doing so kept his life, but he would soon find out that he had not escaped at all. Dennis Jacobs knew all too well from experience that his haunting was nowhere near over.

ALMOST FORTY MILES to the west of Rix County and the dark woods that separate Gulleytown from Sunken Lake was Lawrence Blackmon inside of his own small home in Athens. He was shaking in violent trembles and fully drenched in sweat. He had every light in his home burning as he lay awake in bed, eyes bulging while experiencing a conscious dream.

Lawrence had not left his home since he learned of the death of Pete Crance. He had finally done so around midnight Thursday and was hoping his departure would provide some form of relief from a hollowed pain that had overtaken him. Leaving had not. In fact, Lawrence felt even worse.

At exactly seven minutes after four early Friday morning, Lawrence was racked with a harrowing feeling that he had experienced before. He remembered the carved out feeling of pain he felt when Calbert Davis had died. It felt as if a part of his soul and everything that provided him inner peace had been dug from in him and there would be no replacing it irregardless to his attempts. Lawrence did not want to believe it. He didn't want to face it but he could feel it . . . Slay Builder was dead.

CHAPTER 5

SATURDAY, JUNE 15, 1999

IN ATHENS EARLY on Saturday there was a twinge of coolness arriving with the morning that was most uncommon for the time of the year. A heavy fog accompanied it that closed visibility down to only car lengths.

After having denied himself sleep for several days, it finally found Lawrence Blackmon and held to him for most of the day on Friday which was also the day his fiancée Whitney enforced her will and earned a presence back into his company. She had arrived at his home at noon to awaken him from a dream filled sleep and would not accept another of his excuses that had kept them apart. She forced Lawrence to finish off a container of soup before joining him in bed and didn't stray far from his touch until after six that evening when she went to the kitchen to prepare dinner. Later that Friday night when Lawrence finally did leave his bed, he never returned. He sat close to Whitney through the remainder of the night, holding hands and talking about matters of a serious nature regarding his experiences while growing up in Rix County. What Whitney didn't know and what Lawrence hadn't included her in on was the true reason he could not get back to sleep and it had everything to do with him being deeply troubled about returning to Rix.

The fog had completely uncovered the college town by ten and a beautiful day had made its way through when Lawrence forced the passenger door to his jeep closed after securing Whitney. They both dressed summery, she in white denim shorts and a white t-shirt that barred most of her shoulders. Lawrence wore faded jeans and a white pullover of the lightest fabric of cotton that three-button down to his chest. They were a happy couple that was in love and it showed in everything they did together, and that went especially for Whitney. The visit to Lawrence's hometown meant she finally was about to be given the opportunity to view his past, the one part of him he had shielded from her.

Outwardly, Lawrence illustrated happiness but within, he was a wreck, wondering whom he might run across from a past he sought distance from and how it might affect his fiancée. They yielded into sporadic traffic on highway 78 that two-lane them through Athens Clarke County and would eventually land them with out a single turn into his hometown of Rix County.

ON FRIDAY IN a service open to the public, a representative from the office of the Governors of Georgia was one of the dignitaries included in a group of notable individuals that had come to pay last respects to Sheriff Pete Crance who was laid to rest later the same day. The representative left behind a check totaling twenty-five thousand dollars for information leading to the arrest and prosecution of his murderer. Eight deputies had worked under the slain sheriff, one of them had been appointed to fill the responsibilities until a special election could be held to elect a new lead officer of the county. The newly appointed sheriff had ordered several individuals with lengthy criminal backgrounds from the Gulleytown area in for questioning regarding the slaying. It served little purpose in solving the crime for they all had strong alibis. The effort however was not a total waste, more than one of the men questioned gave pertinent information. They spoke of an individual they had seen walking about in the woods earlier in the evening, but irregardless to the consistency in the stories, the officials questioning them gave those statements no credence to investigate further. It appeared no rational officer in Rix County would. There was no solid lead for an arrest for Pete Crance's murderer that didn't find a dead end into Dead Man's curve.

RIX COUNTY UNFOLDED to Whitney just as Lawrence had described it. It was green, spacey and unmistakably homey, and split almost down the middle into two sections, Gulleytown and Stansburg. Textile churned the town with a handful of manufacturing plants located there that made clothing, plastics, zippers and buttons. Two large sawmills picked up the employment where the factories left off. Three family-owned and operated groceries along with one national chain pretty much fed and supplied the entire county. Two of the local grocers were in the heart of Rix on separate corners of the town square. The other local market was a strong mile away down highway 78 past the forth of five red lights that backed each other in a separated row through the main artery of town.

Lawrence Blackmon had not been born in Rix, his birth took place sixty miles further east in a hospital in Augusta.

The home he was raised in was within an exclusive neighborhood in Stansburg dotted with the counties more affluent residents. Henly Blackmon is sole owner but the home was passed down from his grandfather through Henly's father and had been in the Blackmon family since fourteen years before the Civil War.

Lawrence was the second child of Henly and Phyllis Blackmon. He had one sibling, a sister who was five years his elder. Sarah Blackmon had departed the county for the Midwest following high school. She is a Mormon and lives in a small town in Montana.

Whitney never much pressured Lawrence for any information about his sister, whom he professed much love, she however struggled with the fact that he had refused to reach out to her in any way.

Right before eleven Saturday morning, Lawrence and Whitney arrived in Rix. Three tear-filled hours were spent at the gravesite of his mother. From where Phyllis Blackmon had been laid to rest, it was only a short drive to a loose board that preceded the rail tracks that led over to Front Street and Gulleytown. Away from Front Street, Lawrence steered immediately to the right off of the pedestrian friendly street and onto the first narrow side street that had come fast upon them.

While sitting up with Lawrence on the previous night, Whitney had listen intently as he explained in detail the history behind the family orientated community where his mother had allowed him to spend so much of his time as a child. Whitney visualized some of what she thought his childhood was like as she rolled down the tinted window of the jeep to be better included on the sounds and smells of Gulleytown as they traveled through.

After arriving at his home on the previous day, Whitney realized that Lawrence was not even close to being his normal assuring self and though he offered much in his efforts to shield this fact, she saw right through to the worried unsettledness of his heart. She carried concern but kept her worries within and was finally given a ray of hope that his spirits were uplifting the second they crossed over the tracks and entered Gulleytown. His smiles were no longer performance-based and they lasted. His voice grew with vibrancy. He was even more animated and his eyes even had a shine to them. The suddenness of the change was a bit of surprise to Whitney but she welcomed it because it appeared that whatever it was that had been worrying Lawrence had magically disappeared.

Gulleytown and the way that it had been described to Whitney seemed almost like a make believe place, but now that she was actually there it wasn't hard to tell that something was indeed totally different about the place then anywhere she had ever visited. The community seemed to have a shielding spirit covering it from end to end like an invisible bubble. Whitney felt the difference the moment they entered onto Front Street. Her smile was a radiant one and it went from Lawrence and out into the community and the faces of the happy children at play in front of homes that for the most part were built only feet apart; small homes and larger ones made of brick and wood. There was evidence of abandoned properties and others that were rundown, but overall the community seemed to be one that cared warmly for its neighbor.

Along the side streets, there wasn't much in the form of vehicle traffic, so Lawrence drove slowly up and down each street without missing one. He drove even slower and with much more excitement when explaining in vivid detail one of the many stories he had experienced somewhere along every street. But there were three separate occasions where Lawrence appeared to shrivel right before Whitney's eyes like he was someplace deep within himself in a trapping daze. The first of those occurrences came after they had been crawling through the streets for about twenty minutes. It happened without warning and suddenness.

The car salesman like chatter Lawrence had delivered to describe every single home they past ended. The vehicle lurched as it stopped.

Lawrence didn't shift to a position of park and allowed the vehicle to roll a bit before bringing it to a lurching stop a second time. In a dragging drawl of someone emotionally winded, Lawrence spoke.

"That's where my friend Gary Simms lived."

His eyes barely lifted towards the home and not another word was said as Lawrence drove slowly away.

Gary Simms never got to know his mother. She died when he was only an infant. Two weeks following the tragedy that took his life, his father and younger brother uprooted and moved away from Gulleytown to Saluda, South Carolina, leaving Rix County behind forever.

On another street not more than two minutes later, Lawrence jerked to a stop again when the small brick home of the parents of Clara Freeman appeared. Lawrence didn't drive directly off this time. He allowed his eyes to linger over the home. Clara, like her boyfriend Slay Builder, was the only child of her parents and had been spoiled with love just as he had. At the time of her death, both her parents were letter carriers employed by the small post office.

Watching Lawrence closely, Whitney remained quiet while they sat there as she had done when they were before the old home of Gary Simms.

Lawrence focused on the home but his thoughts billowed into the past to an encounter he'd had with Arnold Freeman, Clara's father. It had taken place on the first day the normally cheerful man had returned to his postal position after burying his only child. While at the Blackmon's home to deliver the family's mail, the small suffering man made an inquiry that simply paralyzed Lawrence and he could remember it like it was yesterday.

ARNOLD FREEMAN first nodded as he encountered Lawrence standing in the doorway of his parent's home.

"Here's your folks mail son."

He invented a semblance of a smile before continuing.

"The wife and I have been pretty twisted around by all that's happened over the last couple of weeks and I want to apologize that I ain't shown the decency to come by and tell you how much it meant to us that you went as far as fighting one of the boys to try and stop them from taking that small boat out. They had no business being out on the water after drinking like ya'll had. The sheriff spoke mighty highly of you and said that you and Calbert both did all you could to stop them." His eyes had watered and a hand was out in an offering to Lawrence.

"Thank you son . . . we appreciate everything you had in mind to do."

Arnold Freeman was deeply focused on Lawrence's eyes and he never looked away and even traveled deeper into them as if searching for a light.

"Son if I may, I need to ask something of you. I know that the sheriff and all those investigators done probably ask you this over a hundred times, but is there anything you could have forgot and didn't get to tell Sheriff Crance about what my baby was doing before she went out . . . ? I mean it could be anything, little stuff like, was she happy out there? Was she smiling at everything like she usually did?"

Spiritually from within, Lawrence had developed a habit of lessening from being whole. While being pressed into confronting the misery and harm his actions had caused he shrunk a little at that moment. The wounded man was searching, and his search had pulled up an infested memory from Lawrence's inner beings. It was the memory of Clara Freeman inside of the bedroom before Slay had re-entered and Lawrence with her there trying to force his way into her. It was an act of cruelty, and it presented itself in the forefront of Lawrence's thoughts like a land mind going off.

Without noticing it escaping his hands, Lawrence dropped the mail that Arnold Freeman had given him as the horrible scream he had heard from Clara coming off the lake advanced in his memory to place a hard freeze over his body and stained his reflections.

A battered man that desperately needed the truth stood in wait before him but Lawrence did not offer it up to him. He knew then just as much as he does now that he should have but couldn't bring himself to do it. Instead, his reply allowed the lie that had been invented to stand and continue.

"Yes sir, Mr. Freeman, Clara was laughing and smiling, she was being the same person she always was."

With inner hate for himself, Lawrence could not look the hurt man in his eyes anymore. He found the small space in between them to concentrate his focus while finishing off his lie.

"Seems kind of funny, but what I remember most was she and Slay both seem to be having the time of their lives."

Fighting harder to keep his emotions together, Arnold Freeman kneeled down for the mail and handed it back to Lawrence before turning and walking away to gain some distance. He whispered, "Thank you for that son."

In his hasty departure, Arnold Freeman had given himself enough separation that the teenager would not be exposed to the eruption his emotions were about to produce.

By creating distance, Arnold Freeman was not in hearing range when a reply came in a whisper back to him.

"I'm sorry sir," Lawrence said with his eyes closed, "I didn't mean to hurt anyone."

THERE WAS A small window with sheer curtains centering the upper portion of the front door, they parted momentarily and the face of a person out of place for this world appeared and directed a concentrated focus inside of the vehicle and specifically towards the expanding eyes of one Lawrence Blackmon.

"Did you see that?" Lawrence murmured.

All at once he had no more breath, and almost broke through the seat belt in an effort to be released.

"My god . . . I can't believe what I just saw."

The attention of Whitney had been for an instance drawn away from Lawrence. She had glanced to the other side of the street to a shady tree where two older men were playing a game of cards. She turned her attention to him and then the home instantly. "What babe?"

Lawrence yelled, "Don't get out."

Before waiting for a reply, Lawrence was out of the jeep in a cautious hurry and on the front yard approaching the home. Within seconds he was pressing hard against the light on the doorbell.

The face had disappeared from the small window in a fraction of a moment, long before Lawrence had exited the vehicle. He assaulted the door bell and frustration became evident as he pounded heavily against the door with his fist.

"Lawrence. Lawrence."

When Whitney called out for him the second time, she did so much louder, loud enough that the men across the street turned in their direction.

"Come on back babe . . . no one appears to be home."

After several more bursting bangs against the door and beneath a banner of suspicion, Lawrence began to back away. He walked mostly backwards all the way until he was no longer on the property of the parents of Clara Freeman.

Whitney had leaned over to his seat awaiting.

"Who did you think you saw in there?"

Lawrence had directed the vehicle into the drive gear before answering.

"To be completely honest, I'm really not sure but someone was there."

He pulled away from the home hesitantly and stared back in its direction from over his shoulder which induced Whitney to also turn in curiosity. She looked back as long as he did but never exposed him to another inquiry of whom he had believed he had seen. In turn, Lawrence never offered up another word about the face of a person appearing before him that he was positive had been dead for ten years. He knew it to be a fact for he had stood within a very saddened gathering of mourners attending the heart breaking funeral.

As Whitney looked on, Lawrence delivered the vehicle to a hard stop for the third and final time. They were in the deepest section of the community and in the specific area where Gulleytown had derived its name. Jaggedly, the red earth dropped away into pits sixty to one-hundred feet deep in some places. They were dangerous drop-offs that could vacuum a life away with one slip.

A small yellow home is what Lawrence had stopped in front of. It was shaped like a box with sunny white trimming rounding the door and all windows. Almost in isolation from all the other homes in Gulleytown, this home sits on a parcel of land at the very back of the community. From the street the home appeared to sit in a cul-de-sac but it wasn't. Similar to a cul-de-sac it was a closed passageway but the entry wasn't big enough to circle a vehicle around in and only one home sat behind it.

Bright red paint sparkled from a swing set that was perfectly positioned below a window that watched out over it from one side of the home.

Other than how the land disappeared from sight behind it, there was not anything about the home anymore drawing in interest than any of the others they had seen but she knew that there was something particularly interesting about it for Lawrence because they had stopped again. She waited quietly for him to include her.

The home belonged to the son and daughter-in-law of Cleveland Banks and the couple's two year old son. They had lived there for eight years after rebuilding the home from the ground after Edward and Thomasina Builder had died in the flames of a house fire. They had lost their lives only months after the tragedy that had taken their son.

An explosion of memories pounced through the thoughts of Lawrence. They were mostly moments of enjoyment from the childhood he had spent on this exact property. A temptation to unbuckle his seatbelt and canvass the uneven yard all the way to its end pushed hard at him. He felt pulled to venture over the spotty grass to peer down into the giant earth cavities that he played above along with his friend almost every day of his youth. From the backyard beyond the unusable land there was a clear look from over the top of distant trees into a portion on Sunken Lake.

Lawrence had taken the look on so many occasions while standing shoulder to shoulder with the best friend he had since elementary school.

Whitney had broken her silence. She had made an inquiry that had pushed right past Lawrence.

Lawrence sits there physically in her presence, but mentally he was far away from her and everything else to a time when life was much simpler for him. He remained there until one of Whitney's hands found a place on his arm and eased him back into the present with her.

His focus was delivered first to Whitney, and then Lawrence broke open his words seconds later.

"I'm sorry Whitney . . . did you say something?"

"Babe, I asked if you were ok, you were concentrating so hard I thought I'd lost you?"

He joined their hands and then said, "Of course I'm okay. It's just really strange being back here like this, that's all."

"We've been circling through these narrow streets for over an hour, it isn't hard to tell that we're in a place that means a lot to you."

He nodded in agreement before saying, "Like I told you last night, here in Gulleytown are where all of my friends lived except for Calbert. I feel kind of strangely connected to them all again just by driving through and seeing kids doing some of the same things we use to do."

Whitney threaded their hands and pulled them up next to her face to kiss the back of his.

"You don't have to say it; I can tell that this was the home of your friend Slay."

"Yes. This was where his home was."

"Lawrence, I want to thank you for your courage and opening up your past and allowing me in. All that worrying you were doing, you see this wasn't so bad after all. We got a chance to spend some time with your mom and we're here where so many of your memories are. Not bad for a day in the country, but I do have one complaint."

"What's that?"

"I'm hungry, when are we going to eat? If there ever was a cornbread county, this has to be it. Places like this always have at the minimum one eatery where all the locals go for something they love."

Lawrence took one final look over the property and begins backing the jeep away. He chucked and it ended his trance-like state of mind he had fallen under.

"I don't know about cornbread county but I'm about to introduce you to the best tomato and mayo sandwich you've ever tasted."

"Mayo and tomato . . . no you didn't say a tomato sandwich? By cornbread I was seeking real food like ribs and some form of greens or something along those lines. I know we can do much better than a sandwich babe . . . especially a tomato one."

After repeating his chuckle, Lawrence responded, "trust me on this one Whitney, it may sound a bit bizarre, but it will blow you away."

In silent protest, Whitney folded her arms.

"I promise you'll love it," Lawrence begged as he turned the jeep hard to the left and came up on a stop sign where he turned right and accelerated as they were back of Front Street.

"Oh my God . . . Lawrence slow down!"

Whitney's heart raced, her eyes expanded while her mouth remained open. She unfolded her arms to brace the dashboard as Lawrence pushed down hard on the brakes to slow the vehicle almost to a stop again while rounding into Dead Man's curve.

"Wow! Incredible."

Whitney had yet to catch up to her breathing as she turned to peak back into the deadly curve as Lawrence smiled over to her while speeding the jeep up again to leave Gulleytown behind for good.

TRAVELING FOR the better part of four miles along a two-lane rural logging road, Lawrence had been forbidden to pass other vehicles because of the many winding turns, but before he could reach mile marker five, he navigated the jeep from the road and drove up close to three fuel pumps that looked more like iron dinosaurs. They ranged up to six feet in height and were spaced four feet apart with a fresh coat of white paint except for the bold thick font of red lettering indicating the three brands of fuel. The pumps stood in loose gravel fifteen yards out from an old country store that could fit perfectly on a postcard from a time period all but passed on.

Lawrence had been showing off a smile the entire ride up to Taylorsville which was an unincorporated portion of the county that didn't even show up on most state maps. He ended the engine of the jeep while brushing his lips against Whitney's and then delivered to her the brightest smile she had seen in over a week.

"Go inside and order us up two country specials with extra salt on mine. I'll be in right behind you after I gas up."

"You're kidding right; those things have gas in them?"

"The best, as I remember."

"Hmm."

It was all Whitney offered in reply before she slid away from the vehicle to do as she had been requested. At a normal pace she walked for several steps and then slowed to glance over the surroundings.

The store had an elevated entrance. Whitney stopped and stood at the very top step to take it all in. There were seven wood chairs, three were in no specific order but the remaining four were pushed in around an oak table that had squares painted into the top of it where used pop bottle caps were aligned for a game of checkers. Firewood was cut thick and stacked high against an outer wall in one corner of the porch which was the entire length of the store. There was a chunky ice cooler next to the firewood and a large window over it that offered and easy look out to where Lawrence stood pumping fuel. The establishment had a tin roof and built right above it was a faded white sign proclaiming Ray's Country Store in black lettering. The entrance was almost cornered, to the left of it was an ancient cola machine and on the other side to the right was an even older RC cola machine. They both were buzzing with life as Whitney stepped between them to pull a screen door open wide enough to enter.

Ray's Country Store was open for customers but you wouldn't be able to tell by the business it was doing. There were no customers inside. Only a straw of a man with silvery hair was inside sitting behind a fizzing bottle of cola that had salted peanuts bubbled up to the top. He was perched on a red bar stool fronting the counter with one palm resting around his refreshment and the other one holding his head. Beneath a pair of overalls, he wore a white t-shirt and was wrapped from waist to ankles in a greasy cooking apron. The elderly man spun on his stool in the direction of Whitney as she approached. He lifted a trucker's hat from his head that proclaimed 'gone fishing' and offered her a giant smile before speaking.

"Howdy Youngun. What can I do ya for.?"

Whitney smile also, "Well, howdy right back at you. Is this your place?"

"Why yes it is."

"Well it's been highly recommended . . . and oh my . . . I wonder what my parents would think of it."

Whitney whispered the last portion of her statement beneath her breath while twisting in all directions to open the small inviting store to all of her awareness. Every miscellaneous item imaginable was packed into one of the four tiny isles above wide plank flooring. Net webbing caps and a variety of southern flags and bandanas all for sale hung from strings attached to the low ceiling. Two oak dinner booths backed into each other beneath the window that fronted the store, and in the rear of the establishment a cooler stocked with Pabst Blue Ribbon and Budweiser lined the wall.

Whitney found the slender man again to say, "I forgot my camera, but you don't know how much I wish I had it with me right now. Your entire premises looks like a scene from how my parents have described the places they grew up in."

"Youngun, I hope what you're mentioning means something good. I reckon I never heard those kinda words put together like that to describe my store before."

The reply came while the older man pushed away from the serving counter to circle it and stand facing Whitney with his back to a long grill.

"I assure you it means something very good to them."

"Another deep wrinkled smile was offered up to Whitney.

Raising two fingers, she offered, "I've been advised to place an order for country specials, two of them. Cook one with extra salt please, and I'll take mine with fries if you serve them."

"I think I can accommodate ya."

"Great. What about a public facility, is there one here that I can use? I've been all over the place but haven't stopped anywhere to freshen up some."

"The bathroom door is in the back by the coolers," he pointed using a fryer basket he had just picked up. I cleaned it and put a large roll of wiping napkins in there no more that ten minutes ago. You make sure to watch that door when you fitting your way through it, it's got some kick to it. And Youngun just so you know, taters come with everything you order here. What ya having to drink?"

"My fiancée should be coming in on my heels, as long as it's cold; I'll take whatever he's having."

At the door of the public restroom, Whitney twisted at the handle and leaned hard against the spring heavy door pushing her way inside, the door snatched closed on her entry exactly as she had been warned.

After fueling the vehicle, Lawrence tipped over the porch and eased his way quietly through the doorway. On site of the pole thin man next to the grill cutting tomatoes into halves, he muffled laughter.

"There's arthritis running through these bones Youngun, every move made over these splinter old floors I feel in them. There ain't no sneaking anywhere in here without me knowing."

There was never any eye contact made, the older man didn't even turn from his craft to issue the caution that could be clearly heard over the sizzle of deep frying slice potatoes.

Unable to suppress laughter another moment, Lawrence spilled it out in bunches.

"Uncle Ray, I thought I had you this time but I see you've still got eyes hidden all over this place."

"Well I'll be a plum nickel!"

There was relaxing easy tone to the Ray Blackmon's laughter, and it became a larger part of his expression as he circled the counter again while wiping another grease stain into his apron.

"Will you look at what's been blown in here from some far off mulberry tree." With powerful hands he clutched to Lawrence's shoulders before pulling him into a smashing hug. "You've been gone 'way from here long enough for folks to take you for being part of the dead . . . what done swung you into these sticks again Youngun?"

"You Uncle Ray, I'm here to see you and to eat that special you working hard over back on the grill."

"Plum shoot youngun; it took you all of ten years to get your tail back here to get it?" An open face gold tooth sparkled in a smile that was fully dentures. "Sit yourself down here while I get back 'round to shake some more salt on your 'matas like you like 'em. You look . . . ."

Lawrence had been stirred towards the first of four stools as Ray Blackmon leaned through a low swinging door that provided entrance to the other side of the chrome line countertop, and then he cut his sentence off abruptly.

The giddy smile disappeared and was replaced by a look of agony. A sudden tremble shook at Ray Blackmon and with a blank stare masking his face, the older man seemed to have remembered something that he should never have forgotten.

"Uncle Ray, is there something wrong? Do you need some help?"

The inquiry was given as Lawrence swiveled in concern on the stool and delivered his focus to the rear of the store and the brown door to the restroom where the attention of his uncle was directed. The concerns of Lawrence eased as his smile was back to greet Whitney who reappeared from between cases of Budweiser stacked from the floor to up near her shoulders. Standing, he allowed one of her arms to circle his waist as they turned towards Ray Blackmon who looked as if he had passed out on his feet.

"Uncle Ray, it's with great pleasure that I introduce you to this incredible woman that is about to make me the happiest man alive by becoming my wife. This is Whitney Connors, the woman I love and can't live without." Lawrence placed a soft kiss right at the corner of her lips and another one at the tip of her nose. "Whitney, this old scout represents the only family I have left around here. This is my Uncle Ray Blackmon."

In a powerful blush mixed with her smile, Whitney extended her hand but her actions were erased by the reaction of Ray Blackmon.

The older man stumbled away from balance.

"Uncle Ray!"

Racing for him, Lawrence practically jumped the swing door. He issued a firm hold to the shaken man whose eyes were rolling. Lawrence then pulled him back upwards to attempt to steady him after the fall Ray Blackmon had taken over onto a steel storage freezer beneath the serving counter.

After several moments of not responding to any of the concerns directed towards him by Lawrence, Ray Blackmon indicated with a nod of approval that he had recovered but was yet to offer any verbal reply. His stumble had shifted his dentures. Ray Blackmon pushed them back to a proper fit and eased his mouth closed which had came open with the introduction of Whitney.

"Come on. Let's get you a seat around the counter from this hot grill."

"No Youngun," Ray Blackmon had found strength. "I'm just fine now." He patted away the concerns of Lawrence with a hand across his nephews' and then willfully removed Lawrence from pushing against his waist and chest.

"You know your daddy would set this whole county to blaze if he caught wind of his youngun marrying outside of his race. He'd burn up my house, his, this store and me right along with everybody else. And no doubt would burn you too."

"He's already tried to kill me Uncle Ray, remember. And I don't care what he thinks or what he might think he can do to me. After every thing we've been through I think he knows that there's nothing else he can do to hurt me anymore. Any hurt he had left hanging over me died when mom did."

Having never been informed by Lawrence of the threat against his life by his own father, Whitney would have normally stored away to her memory such unbelievable acts and unveiled them through inquiry at a later time but much was occurring at the moment and she never really gave what she had heard a second thought.

The eyes of Ray Blackmon were much more watered down in concern now then they had been on Whitney's entrance into his establishment but that didn't stop him from not withdrawing them from her even while addressing Lawrence. He finally did to study Lawrence after the remark made by his nephew in regards to Henly Blackmon.

Blinking rapidly, Ray pushed away from the freezer.

"Dab gun it. Move back youngun. Let me get to those taters."

Twisting past Lawrence, he turned his back on the surprise look from his nephew and the blank expression that Whitney offered up.

"You two Younguns grab up a seat, your orders coming right up. These taters might be a little more crisp then I'd a normally cooked 'em, but I guarantee they is just as good."

Most of his body was shaking as Ray Blackmon shook the wire basket in his hand to get the grease away from the sliced potatoes. When he turned around again, there was food scattered all over the two white plates that filled his hands.

Lawrence was seated next to Whitney when Ray Blackmon wiped another grease spot from his hands onto his apron and then presented a strong hand to Whitney.

"Pardon my manners Youngun . . . welcome to the family. You showing up show do add some needed prettiness to it. This boy couldna chose a prettier young woman to latch onto." Continuing his focus on Whitney, he added, "If I'd a known from the beginning I was cooking for family, I'd added in more of my hidden recipe. You shoulda told me you were marrying this youngun instead of raising a fuss about some flash camera and this old place of mind."

His expression changed, Ray Blackmon looked from Whitney to Lawrence and pointed a finger.

"And you shoulda had your tail back her for your momma's passing, and I don't mix words when I say that. I don't care what kind of mess is going on between you and your daddy, it shouldna been allowed to come between what you and Phyllis shared. She loved her children tighter than skin, and I believe she jumped that gully into those trees in Gulleytown on purpose so not to hurt no longer over loosing the two of you and not being able to even talk to you any longer." Standing up from a lean, he continued. "Don't you go taking me saying that as blaming you for her passing because you die when your time come is what I believe and it was Phyllis's time or she wouldna passed."

Feeling his emotions slipping, Lawrence spoke in an attempt to fight back tears.

"You're absolutely right Uncle Ray. Her funeral was something that I never should allow anyone to chase me from. I'm not a runner any longer. It took me awhile and a lot of help from Whitney but I finally have a better handle on the direction I should be seeking instead of worrying about whose after me. I thank her daily for that.

When we drove in earlier we got the opportunity to spend some time at the gravesite which was something I needed. There is no way possible for me to overturn all the mistakes that I've made, especially as it relates to mom, but while at the cemetery I made a promise to her and myself to do better at facing my faults head on."

Ray Blackmon slid into an easy chuckle before saying, "I sure wish this little lady woulda come through these parts years earlier since she's the one who's gotten you to thinking clear headed. I thought I'd be under a dirt ceiling myself before hair or tail of you ever made it through this way again. How's your 'matas youngun?"

After not hearing a reply from Lawrence, Whitney looked up and was surprised the question had been addressed to her. Embarrassed, she took a napkin to swipe at a tiny lump of mayonnaise cornering her mouth and then chewed her food faster before attempting a reply.

"Well," she stammered, "prior to today, if anyone had told me that I'd be depicting a tomato on bread as delicious I'm sure my response would have been they were in some way disturbed." She giggle before giving, "to be totally honest . . . this is absolutely the best thing I've ever tasted between slices of heavily mayo bread. And at the risk of giving off a first impression that I'm small but greedy, I tempted to ask for seconds."

"No need to be bashful in here Youngun, nobodies ever been able to eat just one my 'mata sandwiches."

LAUGHTER CONTINUED to fill the setting as Lawrence and Whitney finished every corner of their meals at Ray Blackmon's establishment that was located less than thirty miles from the line drawn to separate the state of Georgia from the bordering state of South Carolina. Eventually the conversation moved outside under the sunlight where every once in a while a customer or three in passing from one state to the next would interrupt them by stopping by the country store for a variety of items but mostly fuel.

Around the oak table, the old man allowed Whitney to best him three out of five times in a friendly game of country checkers. They played while munching on salted peanuts and sipping cold bottles of pop that left rings of moisture where ever they were place down.

Ray Blackmon had learned or been given the gift of pleasantry and applied it generously to all he came across. He was a true southern gentleman and talented at making people feel right at home in his place of business.

"What in the heck is this world coming to when big city folk like you can come down into the sticks and beat an old pucker like me in a game invented in these parts?"

"I'm not from the city Mr. Ray, at least not anymore. I live in Athens now, and you can hardly call that a big city."

"That's Uncle Ray to you Youngun and its city enough for me. You folks drive too doggun fast, all of you." From a pocket that ran across the top of his overalls, Ray Blackmon pulled a handkerchief, removed his hat and wiped his brow. He replaced his gone fishing hat before asking, "You hear about them burying the Sheriff yesterday? This whole county's been all out of sort since they found him blooding up the streets."

A twinge of uneasiness like he had experienced nights before developed within Lawrence but he managed to keep it covered up. He turned up his bottle of pop and waited for the last peanut to slide into his mouth before placing the empty bottle down on the corner of the checker table before looking to Whitney first and then his uncle.

"Yes I've heard. It's been on the news and I've read about it."

"Everybody in this state shoulda. It's been in all the papers around these parts and that includes the one they drop off here from Atlanta every morning." He looked at Lawrence with a bit more scrutiny before adding, "Your daddy been taking the death of Sheriff Crance kind of hard."

"That figures," Lawrence whispered but Whitney heard and he could tell by her expression.

"Henly and a pick-up load of followers have been chasing up a lil' hell late at night down in Gulleytown, and for the most part this new Sheriff they stuck in there been letting 'em get away with it. It's a bunch of mess and they just making it worse. If they tryna start a war it show ain't going off like they planned. They didn't figure on them Younguns willing to fight them back they have. They ain't like most of their elders were and rightly so. You push one of 'em and a whole bunch of 'em push you right back and a lot harder. Rix County on the verge of blowing its top, and the whole fuse is being carried by your daddy."

Lawrence Blackmon believed every word of what his uncle was explaining to him even though his head shook in disbelief.

"I can't believe anyone in their right frame of mind would still follow his advice. He's not even mayor anymore and hasn't been for a long time."

"It's got nothing to do with being the mayor. Your daddy has always meant plenty more around here to a lot of these crazies than just the mayor. And to a heap more of 'em, it's all the better he ain't. They believe they can get away with more of their foolishness now without it branding his office by association. They out looking for a reason to fight and your daddy will lead them right to one. Last night it was good and quiet for a change, and I'm inspecting it'll be close to the same thing over the night 'cause Henly is pretty much their only leader and ain't none of 'em right smart enough to do nothing without him. He left out of here right after the funeral to go fishing on that little farm he owns up in Toccoa County. He passed through here right before his trip, and I'm telling you Youngun, something had him white-skinned. I'm past him a few years in age and I ain't never seen him act the way he did yesterday. He was all jittery and fast moving like he was running off from somebody. I know my brother like I know my own skin, and yesterday he was tired and had death pushing at his eyes when he pulled away from here. He won't here for long and didn't speak much on nothing in particular. I pressed him about his health and he just pushed right past that. He did say one thing that was strange coming from him. He said he'd seen some puzzling things of late and needed to get away to sort some 'em out. I inquired how long he'd be gone and he said not to look for him back until past the weekend." Stopping for a brief moment to clear his throat, Ray Blackmon continued. "For the folks in Rix sakes, I'm praying he stays away a lot longer then that. Henly's my blood and all and I'll always carry good love for him because I was raised to love your blood no matter what, but he's an evil S.O.B and there's no changing him and I mean none."

"He raised me to despise but I don't. I don't wish harm on anyone, not even those who would wish it on me, but daddy, I don't know. Maybe he shouldn't have left. He keeps going into Gulleytown bothering people; someone is going to show him an end to all that hate."

With astonishment Whitney watched Lawrence but never said a word.

Ray Blackmon eased back on his chair eyeing Lawrence also before giving, "This is a good town Youngun. Ain't but a bucket of no-goods around here about hate and dividing up, most folks I know just wanna see their younguns grow and be left alone, the same as you and me." He glanced to Whitney to take the conversation in a totally different direction.

"Ya'll gonna stay the night or has a day in the sticks been too much for you city folks?"

"Those are exactly my wishes Uncle Ray. We should stay because we don't have to be back for anything but Lawrence has made one excuse after another why we shouldn't. Maybe you can talk some sense into him?"

With one finger pointed, Ray Blackmon did exactly as he had been asked.

"Youngun don't start your marriage off by giving your pretty wife a bunch of cants and shouldas or you'll find yourself alone in a hurry. The first lesson in marriage is that she's always right and you're whatever's left over."

Between laughter, Whitney chimed in, "You tell him Uncle Ray, I've fallen in love with you already."

"I'll tell you what . . . ." Digging into a pocket, he tossed a ring of keys across the table to Lawrence. "The keys to the cabin are on there. I've ran down to his house to feed them dogs of his twice already. That was the main reason he came by here. I know you won't be going by there and I can't rightly blame you after what happened the last time you was there, but if it pleases you, you younguns can sleep over in the cabin. You ain't got to worry about your daddy 'cause from what I seen of him yesterday, he won't be back this way anytime soon, plus he hardly uses that property anymore. If that don't suite you, you can ride on up further to my place. Heaven knows I can sure use the company."

"If it was left up to you we'd be around here forever Uncle Ray."

"You got that one right on the head boy."

"Yeah, I know I did. And thanks for the invite, but we're taking a pass." Checking his watch Lawrence went on. "It's about five thirty and we've still got another stop. I'd planned on being back in Athens before nine if possible." Lawrence stood and smiled before speaking to his uncle again.

"There's a tremendous favor I need to ask of you."

"You bet you son, shoot."

"I want you to put your best pair of overalls in the cleaners and get them heavily starched. The main purpose we stopped by was for me to ask you personally to be my best man in August."

Standing and grabbing for Lawrence's hand, Ray Blackmon eased into his chuckling smile again.

"It'll be my pleasure Youngun. I'd be plum honored too and congratulations for proposing and for becoming a critter doctor too."

"I just need to know if I can get a catering commitment from you for the reception. I want everyone there to taste some of your delicious sandwiches."

"You betcha pretty lady, and in my wedding gift will be my hidden recipes. I'll be passing 'em on to you."

Laughter continued and for another five minutes the great conversation persisted before Ray Blackmon saw the young couple enter their vehicle and drive slowly away.

TAYLORSVILLE

WHAT BECOMES BLATANT and obvious immediately when sitting down for a talk with me is a half-broken dialect. If I'm using it to translate this story, then you must have recognized at some point this tragic tale would eventually come rushing to center directly on me.

Not more than a couple of miles farther than the country store of Ray Blackmon is where my home is located in part of the county we residents call Taylorsville. Although it doesn't officially begin at the country store, most inhabitants of the county include Ray's place when mentioning Taylorsville and explaining how to get out here. It's named Taylorsville for no particular reason that has ever been explained to me and I have lived here all my life. A more suitable name would probably be Lonelyville because of its emptiness; hardly anyone lives here.

My property begins along a spur off of highway 44. When school is in, one bus comes to Taylorsville to make one stop, and that stop is right next to my mail box to pick up the three school age children that belong to one of the seven families scattered about and that number includes Ray Blackmon and me. And as far as my memory serves, seven families are the most that has ever lived in this part of Rix County.

From the center of a narrow road sprouts wild grass and it's lined sporadically on both sides by stretchy sycamore trees. The road leads from the highway and runs on a straight line for a half mile right up to my front door. According to my mother, the home in which I reside is the very same one that I was born in on a pretty spring day in 1925, and as if no other place existed, I've lived right here everyday since. I am the child of a father whose skin was as chalky white as the oldest piece of barn cotton and a mother who was as dark as the shell it burst from. He was six years her senior and they met on her thirteenth birthday which was the first day she had been allowed to accompany her mother to perform housework for wages in the home of his parents.

Now if I sit here and tell you that the union that afforded me life was one agreed upon by both my parents I would only be putting forth a lie. It was most certainly not. At my age there is not much time left available for lying and foolishness, so I certainly won't use any of the opportunities I have left for any of those.

On the first opportunity they were allowed alone together, my father savagely raped my innocent unsuspecting mother. This ugly encounter brought about my birth and amazingly at some point later in those forbidden times, the two of them fell in love which came as a complete shock to me when I was told. Their relationship was so prohibited that his father with the help from some other residents from Stansburg came out to this home and stole away my mother's only brother and their parents. The small mob drove them out to Sunken Lake and forced them into the woods. Their bodies were never discovered, it was to put it simply, the end of their existence.

My father was a part of the mob that delivered death to one-half of my grandparents, and to this day I have convinced myself that his participation was forced. I will make no attempt to paint even a single stroke that presents the man that gave me life as an angel, but he was not a bitter devil either, at least not in the acts that took place before my eyes as I grew up.

I did not get to know him for long because many years back he died in a very grotesque manner and it was somewhat of a copycat of what has come to pass to a great many of whites in this county. My father died in a crumpled car against the un-giving trees that line Dead Man's curve. Given the history of that little stretch of roadway, I don't know why any white citizen of this county would ever drive through that death trap again. That little bend in the road has on its own played the role of equalizer for the many injustices.

On the day of my birth, my father was forced away from their home by his father and he, my mother and I lived here in Taylorsville together until his accident. Following his death, my mother and I lived here alone until she turned thirty one, at that age her heart imploded, ending her life early also. I was their only child and was bestowed at birth with the sharp features, eyes, hair and tone of skin as my fathers. I own skin that has allowed me to pass through the cycle of life as a full-blooded white woman. Very few in this county know of my true ancestral identity and I have not done anything to change that over my years.

Everyone I have really ever come to love has departed from this earth which leaves me mostly alone all the time. I mention that only to segment to what I am about to explain. I was yet to be given birth to when my grandparents were murdered. I can not truly identify with the hurt of loosing members of my family that I never was given an opportunity to meet, and though she showered me with all of her love, my mother was so young and inexperienced when she gave birth to me that until my father's death we practically grew up almost like sisters beneath him. I eventually had a child of my own, whom I named Maggie. She grew up attached to me with love but as an adult she even grew estranged, allowing drugs to replace my love. My daughter married a man that only contributed to her addictions and we were navigating through a period where she had not spoken a thimble of words to me in several years when he placed a gun behind her head. He took her life first and afterwards turned the gun and destruction on him.

At this point in this tale, I feel it is time I share more about who I am and who I represent because I truly want you to fully understand my position and also be aware that even though I have been linked to the pain of loosing loved ones, I had not felt pains harshest regards until I lost my beautiful grandchild. I lost him in the wind blown sands of some desert outside of a place that I had never even heard of before.

My grandchild, Calbert Davis was and still remains the main artery of my heart. He offered me love and it was pure love. The destruction of Calbert saw its beginning before he signed up for the armed services. When his total destruction finally did occur, it left only emptiness where my heart once was. Calbert was the only one that existed there.

Unlike him and the rest of my family, I have lived an aged life that has seen me gray and slowed and watched as a shade of haze has settled over most of my vision which is a direct reflection to how I most often feel since his departure.

The afternoon is over and early evening has arrived. It's almost the time when those busy glowing lightning bugs arrive to add intervals of light to the night. Since the day of Calbert's death and at this exact time I have sat down here on my old porch rocking away in his and my favorite chair. The very chair he and I rocked together in for the precious few years of his early childhood. As his only remaining family member, I was awarded custody of Calbert after the death of his parents.

Four feet of stacked bricks elevate my home from hard Georgia clay. Formidable bricks that I was told were masterly mason by the bare hands of my grandfather. Night after night I've sat here since the passing of Calbert and it seems as though all of my thoughts are of the ghost that haunted him during the final year of his life. I have tried desperately to take my thoughts to other places but they have always been pulled directly back to Calbert and the many difficulties that controlled him until this one evening when the out of the ordinary became ordinary.

It was Saturday the fifteenth of June and growing late in the evening when a white vehicle approached that appeared gray like all things under my eyesight. I recognized the vehicle and had seen it often over the past several years but only under the cover of nightfall. It came traveling across my property beneath the draping trees to stop within feet of the plank boards that lead up onto my porch.

AT TWENTY NINE Lawrence Blackmon was the spitting image of his father when Henly was the same age many years back. He owned a handsome but rough look that could easily fill the cover of a magazine but instead he was hiding behind dark windows on the dusty back roads of Georgia.

It was halfway between six-thirty and seven that Saturday when Lawrence stepped down on my property in open toe sandals, jeans and a pullover penguin shirt. As I remained seated, he circled my rocker and with piercing blue eyes held firmly to the expression of surprise I offered for finally getting an opportunity to observe him under the burn of the sun. As with his practice on the numerous occasions when he has stood before me, Lawrence placed his warm lips against my awaiting cheek for a kiss. We were both wearing infectious smiles when he pulled the small stool beneath him that he usually sat on during his visits to a spot right in front of me and after we had finished our pleasantries, the young man placed his smile to the side. The way it disappeared made me believe that it never really belong there in the first place.

I looked on as his mouth tightened at the corners before he attacked me with his hurt.

"Where is he Mrs. Sadie . . . ? Thursday night I got down here on time like always but he didn't show up. Slay has never not showed up when we were suppose to meet. He's never even been late before. I circled through Gulleytown until almost two in the morning but he never broke the surface of the woods."

The words spoken by Lawrence were charging out at me and the expression on his face showed his deep concern.

"Good lord child, you must be in my thoughts, 'cause after we'd talked a spell I was planning on asking you pretty much the same question, but no sense in me doing that now that I know that you don't know either. But there's no need for either of us to worry 'bout that child because where ever he is, is where he wants to be. It's his nature. He goes and comes by his own choosing and you know that as well as me, but if I had to guess, I'd say Solomon is somewhere out in them woods near Gulleytown keeping his head low to his shoulders. He knows some of your papa's folks been acting out in town over what happened to their sheriff. Last I heard from your Uncle Ray was they riled up down there, riding in bunches with their guns racked up in them big-wheeled trucks they drive. Just to think on it real good . . . it wouldn't surprise me a bit if your poppa don't have some of them fools snooping out in the woods about his property as much as that child's name been on townsfolk's tongues here lately." I sighed but not long or heavy enough to add to the profound worries of Lawrence and then continued. "I've been doing a little worrying over that child myself but only because he can smell rain days before it starts to drop and most of the time he'll leave up out of them woods and come up here to sleep out back in my little shed. It rained buckets a night or two ago and I ain't seen hair nor tail of him."

Sitting almost a perfect foot from off of my right knee, Lawrence slid slightly forward to catch all of my eyes before explaining.

"But that's precisely what's got me worried Mrs. Sadie, his behavior is changing and Slay never changes. The night it rained like that was when we were supposed to meet up."

Nervousness took control of Lawrence briefly and it dictated his loss of eye contact with me, but after fumbling with his hands for a moment he picked up again.

"I haven't been at my best since getting the news on Sheriff Crance being killed. Been stuck up in my house for the most part but I did manage to get out late Thursday to meet up with Slay but couldn't find him. Mrs. Sadie, I've got a bad feeling about all of this and it's dragging me into places that I don't need to be in."

"Bless you child . . . is that what's turned you here in the open light of day knowing what your papa would do if he saw you here?

"No Mrs. Sadie it isn't, but it's what's keeping me here right now. It's been almost ten years; I finally decided to just forget about his threats. I actually came over to show Whitney around, she's been dying to get here to see where I was raised."

"That's the child you thinkin' on marrying?"

"Yes Mam. The one I've been telling you about. I just can't seem to say no to her, not for long anyway. She's most responsible for me being here in broad daylight, and to a lesser degree Slay. I took her by to meet Uncle Ray and he loved her right off and my original plans were to bring her on up to meet you but I thought better of it when I remembered all I needed to talk with you about. Uncle Ray is certain that daddy will be out of town for the entire weekend. Whitney had been begging to see the lake and plus she was a little tired. I tried leaving her at the store but she wanted no part of that when I told her what time it would probably be when I'd be back by to pick her up. I drove her back into town and she'll be at the lake until you and I are finished talking."

His eyes drifted and they went up to capture the sun which was slowly dropping behind the tall pines in the distance. Knowing Lawrence Blackmon in the manner I do, I could easily place vision on his troubles. I've seen them often and that was especially after the tragedy at the lake and after he had run from his father's home to live up here with Calbert and me.

His focus was on me heavy when he began to speak again. He was almost pleading into my hazed over eyes.

"It's been three years since you brought him back into my life after I thought he had died. Every since then we've met at an hour past midnight the second Thursday of every third month. The day and hour have never changed because Slay never changes. He's always been there waiting for me until the other night. I got a feeling that someone else has found out he's still alive and it's killing me. I've been feeling like I felt that morning Calbert died and that's not a feeling I need in me anymore. I don't want to believe it can happen, but I'm worried that someone has really found him out there." His eyes had expanded and Lawrence really was pleading when he paused and then begged.

"Mrs. Sadie I need to know where to go find him . . . and don't tell me you don't know because I know you do. Where is he?"

I had stopped my rocker and Lawrence had taken a hold to both my knees. Strangely, I didn't feel one action or the other for what he had asked of me had me pretty much numb and the look on his face concerned me even more. Lawrence Blackmon was deadly serious.

From resting on the arms of my chair, I dropped my hands onto his. I wanted him to do more than hear my response to him. I needed Lawrence to also feel it.

"Child no, you get your mind from there! Sweetie you can't go where that child is. You get it out your mind, you get it out now and you keep it out for both our sakes."

His disappointment was obvious. Lawrence pulled his hands from beneath mine.

"Why? Why can't I go where he is?"

"You just can't. You take Mrs. Sadie's word on that and leave it be."

I tried to bring his hands back to me but Lawrence would not allow it. He seemed to be in deep thought and his thoughts soon became his words, and some of them I don't believe he intended for me to hear.

"As a kid I remember my mother warning us of a place we should never go. Yeah. And Calbert once said something similar to what you just said when we were in the woods behind the lake chasing after . . . ."

Lawrence ended his words very unevenly and he dropped his eyes right along with his head but not before he had cut a path of similar unevenness through my empty heart.

If it had been anyway possible for him to vanish into thin air, at that very moment poor Lawrence Blackmon would have done so gladly. He was a healthy man, a strong one but right then and right there he appeared neither strong nor healthy. In fact he became lesser of a human sitting on that small stool before me.

His conscious is what made him smaller. It squeezed life from him over the ugly actions he had practically initiated that had cost the lives of so many around Sunken Lake and Gulleytown, and that included the life of my Calbert.

In all the time Lawrence had lived in my home and we had spent together before and after the death of Calbert he had never strung together one sentence about what had taken place over the course of that frightful night. He had admitted to no guilt for his actions, but to Lawrence's credit before being run off from Rix, he had begged for everyone's forgiveness, and he begged and pleaded for it beyond everyone's capacity and threshold to forgive.

I have come to love young Lawrence Blackmon, much in the way I would love my own grandchild if I still had him around in his fleshly body. And it is because I love him in the manner in which I do that I needed to warn him away from his thoughts of roaming the woods of Rix County in search of Solomon Builder. I knew if he did, it would surely deliver him into the hands of a sure death.

"Listen to me child because what you about to hear is important. There's a patch of land near your father's property that he can't touch and you neither. Your presences don't need to be anywhere near it and that's what your momma was rightly warning you about when you was a little one."

I waited and made sure that Lawrence was holding my eyes before I told him anymore.

"Here's a story I learned when I was just a child, and it came straight from the mouth of my momma. Somewhere way on the back of your papa's property is where my grand-folks were pulled up on a rope and killed a long time ago. She said if you keep going past there, closer to Gulleytown, it's some kind of place back there that's guarded. She says it looks like the regular dirt you see in back of Gulleytown except the sky over it is as dark as a stove in plain daylight." I pointed. "Momma said at night that same sky will light up like the sun there that's about to hide in back of those trees yonder if somebody trespasses out there that don't belong. And let me be the one to tell you child, you don't belong. You can't go near back there, and if you do, even the Angel Gabriel can't protect you from what'll happen."

To bring more emphasis to what I was explaining to Lawrence, I waved a strong finger before him while continuing. "For some reason, whites just ain't allowed into this place."

Sitting up straight, Lawrence had listened intently as I told him my mother's tale and he was ready to speak as soon as I finished.

"I was always told by my father that people made that kind of nonsense up to scare whites. I've heard him say that no one knows what's on his property because they've never been back there and . . . ."

And just like that Lawrence stalled out again and his expression indicated hard thought. When he picked up again it was under a hushed tone as if he was only talking to himself.

"My father wants people to believe that it's a bunch of foolishness but Slay doesn't buy it. He believes every word you just said. And I know exactly where this place you described is. I should have known all along that he would hide there if he didn't want to be found."

The eyes of Lawrence had widened again and through them I could see right to his thoughts and good lord what I saw there bothered me to no end as he stood to his feet.

"My father is not right about a lot of things and there is no place in my life for the way he lives his, but he's right about one thing . . . people don't know what's back there on his property. There are some small hills way back there, small and red. I saw them with my own eyes." Lawrence was clouded in trouble when he announced. "I'm sorry Mrs. Sadie but I've got to go. I'll make another trip over here probably next weekend to bring Whitney by so that you two can finally meet. You'll love her and she's definitely going to love you, but right now I've got to get back to her and then I'm going to find Slay."

And without uttering another word, away from me in a rush Lawrence went. He gained freedom from my home and was within reach of his vehicle when he stopped at my mention of the name of Latosha Williams. It lifted him back up to the stool next to me.

"Yes child, I know that babe was raped out there, and I know you and my grandchild lied to cover it all up."

It happened twice within a ten minute time frame, Lawrence Blackmon shrunk away again. There were no tears streaming from his eyes but it was easy to tell that they were falling. They fell down on his inside to his emptiness. His mouth was ajar and I imagined Lawrence releasing a quiet scream from it. Never wavering, my eyes held to him, it was obvious that he had begun to suffer like some animal wounded by a human and I was the only human there, and my presence in itself began to press unbearable pain into every tender nerve in his body.

A tremble entered Lawrence's lips and that is when he closed them without offering a word in denial. He just sat in a slump shaking his head and appearing to be reliving the tragedy he had hidden away for too many years.

A large tear finally appeared and it ran in a slow line down from one of his eyes and was soon followed in like manner by others until open came the flood gates.

With hands bonded over my lap, I sat there in watch only, extending Lawrence no physical support for I have lived long enough to know that what I had to afford would serve little purpose in the pity of self where he had fallen. Instead, I just waited until his crying had eased and his focus was again on me, and then I pressed down a little bit harder into his hurt again.

"Every last thing that happened over on your poppa's property, I know about child . . . and I've known since the morning after it happened. I remember it clear, like it happened this morning 'cause I sit here thinking about it all the time."

No longer right off of my right knee, Lawrence had moved further to my side and a bit behind me pushed back against my home. I don't know if he could ever be ready for what I was about to tell him but he had positioned for it, and to my Lawrence's credit, he was not attempting to leave away from me to search for Solomon Builder any longer. I took a long full look back at him and watched as he gave off a heavy sigh and then began explaining to the young man the depths of my knowledge of his and my grandchild Calbert's ugly sins.

"The weather early Saturday morning after yawl's ball game won't very cold but there was a small wind that nipped at you every once in a while. I remember that 'cause I was out here. My feet had gotten a little cold so I stepped back in for some thicker slippers and to pull a blanket down from the closet to sit under while I waited for Calbert. Right about the time I was ready to come back outside, he almost knocked the door off the handles runnin' in here with no breath in his body and sweating so heavy that his clothes was hanging all raggedy off him. I worked to get him settled down, and when my grandchild got to talking and explainin' all ya'll had done, he couldn't quit."

OVER THE PAST three years I had been getting visits from Lawrence Blackmon, they came after he had visited with Solomon Builder and they were always late at night when hardly anyone was traveling up or down highway 44 but those large transfer trucks carrying overnight cargo to places I have never heard of. Not in one instance over the years or during the short time he had resided with me did I ever let on about all I knew about his drunken actions and the innocent lives that were ended because of it.

For a few moments I stopped explaining what Calbert had included me in on, for the time of the evening had finally arrived for my tarnished eyes to behold beauty. Lawrence and I had a long road to travel and me stopping like I did may have not been at the most appropriate time, but the sun had hidden itself for some other part of the world to marvel over and with that occurrence it was time for my enchanting fireflies to appear.

THE RIX COUGARS had won their ballgame over their rival red devils of Lincoln. They reveled over the victory for a time on the field and then went to listen to a congratulatory speech from their coach before showering and eventually leaving the varsity field house.

Calbert and his girlfriend Kim Hopkins rode in the backseat of a car driven by Lawrence, who was accompanied by the girl he had been dating since the beginning of the football season to a cabin owned by Henly Blackmon above Sunken Lake. Following them and hauling along two cases of beer in his father's truck were teammates Gary Simms and Solomon Builder, who were being trailed to the log cabin by both boys' girlfriends. By eleven that night everyone invited had arrived to the cabin and at some point broken off in couples to separate areas of the home.

By twelve-thirty, Latosha Williams was pulling her cheerleader sweater back over her ponytail and had pushed away from Gary Simms to start gathering her belongings to meet a curfew. The two teenagers had been huddled together in an open den that seem a lot smaller than it actually was because it was crowded with stuffed animals, all trophies of kills made by Henly Blackmon over the years. Beneath the sweater, Latosha wore a long sleeve white shirt and a pleated cheerleader skirt. Hanging over the top of it all was a heavy burgundy letterman's jacket that Gary Simms had given her after they first began dating.

From the sofa they had held one another. Gary Simms stood to be next to her and was tugging at one of the sleeves of the jacket making it difficult for Latosha to comfortably wiggle back into.

"Come on Latosha, why don't you lay back down and be a little late just once for curfew? I've got to be getting back over the tracks myself but I'll be late if you will, or how about we call your mom and tell her you need another hour because you caught a flat, that way you can stick around with me a little longer?"

"Gary, I wasn't raised to straight up lie to my mom and I'm sure you weren't raised that way either." She smiled while love patting his cheek. "And even if I could stay longer, this wouldn't be a good night, Clara and I have to be in Athens in the morning to take the S.A.T. We really shouldn't have stayed this late and we definitely shouldn't have been drinking."

"Forget about the S.A.T, you've got plenty of time to take it. Everybody else in here is taking care of their business and you in here worried about taking a test. I'm tired of always missing out on sex with you."

"Here we go with that again Gary . . . you know I'm not ready for that yet. And you better be glad that I'm even letting you go beneath my bra."

"Latosha, you sound real crazy bragging about a bra. That's called teasing and you been doing it for some months now. At our pace we'll be already graduated before I see if you wear panties or not. How you going to keep doing me that way Latosha, especially when you know there's other girls that wanna do anything I ask?"

"Then you're free to have them. You're drunk Gary and acting stupid again." Pushing away, she defiantly said, "move away from me and go to those girls that want to do it all for you."

Latosha maneuvered and left Gary Simms in the den alone while she called out for Clara Freeman.

From the front door of the cabin, the hallway leads past the living room and the den down to where all of the bedrooms were and eventually into the kitchen. The hallway was narrow, one where an individual would have to stand to one side to allow someone else to pass.

After walking away from Gary Simms, Latosha stood before one of the locked bedroom doors pleading for Clara Freeman to join her attempt to get home. Within a few minutes a drunk and highly agitated Lawrence Blackmon came storming out from behind another door. He went by Clara intentionally brushing against her small hips as he passed.

The unwelcome invasion was given very little of Latosha's attention, she was more interested in seeking his help than anything else.

"Lawrence."

He ignored her and continued walking.

"Lawrence, would you please stop and help me?"

Lawrence sneered back at her but didn't say a word.

"Since we're all your company, can you simply ask Slay to open this door so Clara and I can leave? Would you do that for me please? Nobody is listening to me, and we can't get home past my curfew."

Waving a frustrated hand gesture, Lawrence turned his back on the request, however he did respond.

"Slay open up the door man so they can get the hell out of here . . . and they better take Susan with them because she can walk home if it's left up to me."

The shouted response was scolding to Latosha even though she knew they were intended for Lawrence's girlfriend Susan McCoy.

Not waiting for a reply, Lawrence stormed out of the cabin.

Eyes redden from crying, Susan dashed out of the bedroom door Lawrence had left open and ran past Latosha out of the cabin behind him.

The yelling coupled with the consistent pleading from Latosha pulled Calbert from behind another closed bedroom door. He tugged into a sweat top as his girlfriend followed him out and ran beneath his arm and past Latosha also.

Watching Kim disappear through the open door, Calbert staggered hard and before he could straighten was pressed against one of the many photographs hanging along the walls down the hallway. He recovered fast and gained a focus on Latosha.

"What the hell was he yelling about?"

His inquiry was giving no regards as Latosha went directly back to her pressing needs.

"Calbert see if you can get Slay to open this door so Clara and I can leave? They're in there giggling and acting silly like this is some type of game or something."

The eyes of Calbert were glossy as he attempted to hold a focus on the small girl standing before him practically consumed by an oversized football jacket that hid her hands completely and hung down to the back of her knees. He looked past Latosha to Gary Simms who after all the movement had positioned into plain sight on the arm of a chair in the living next to the door.

"Maybe she ain't ready to leave Latosha, you ever think about that?" Calbert slurred while smashing into the bathroom door directly next to the room Solomon and Clara could be heard whispering from. "Just leave her. Big Simms can drop her off when they go home."

"But she's spending the night at my house and my mom will not allow anyone to just drop her off there after my curfew."

"Latosha go on and leave . . . I'm staying with Slay."

The breathless burrowed voice came from behind the locked door.

After waiting for close to ten minutes for some form of response, the one Latosha was provided heightened her concern.

"I guess you've forgotten about our curfew, and about our test; school and pretty much everything. That's what your plans are Clara? Are you just into laying in there and getting pregnant by the preacher's boy? Is that what you want? I just wish you hadn't told my mom that you'd be home by curfew."

Calbert was struggling to navigate the hallway, with anger on full display; Latosha twisted by him and pointed a finger in the direction of her boyfriend.

"Do you think you can manage to get off of your drunk behind and walk me to my car, I need you to hear one last thing before I go?"

A MOVEMENT MADE BY Lawrence to gain a little more distance from my position pulled my thoughts away from the sad events that had exploded at Sunken Lake years ago and re-centered my attention back into the present.

Night had fallen hard and to my dismay there were no slow flying lightning bugs in flight.

Even in the darkness with my poor vision I could see the hurt Lawrence roughly backhanded away with swipes at his eyes. He accomplished this with one hand while holding onto his glasses with the other and all the while mumbling to himself like he had done from the beginning of my monologue.

Until moments ago, my full concentration had been years away and therefore enabling to clearly hear what he had been consistently uttering. My encounter into the present again rewarded me with what he had been muttering. I heard him in true clarity even though Lawrence had put aside the stool and moved several more feet from me.

"Child save those words . . . God already knows you're sorry. You don't have to keep reminding him . . . he's done given you forgiving."

I knew for a fact that Lawrence had heard my soothing words but in no way did he acknowledge them with his own. I sat quiet for a few moments and then pushed down on the arms of my chair and used them as a brace to stand before taking several careful steps. I reached across the empty stool he had abandoned and into my home to push on small lamps that sat on a stand next to the door. When I made it back to my rocker, some of the light had reached out to provide a little brightness over one of my frail shoulders.

Not to my surprise, young Lawrence Blackmon had moved again. He moved out of the distance of the light to the very edge of the porch where it cornered into the home, but he was still close enough that if I wanted to reach out and touch him I could. His legs were uncrossed and they swung beneath the open space separating the porch from the ground as if he was on a swing. Lawrence heaved and bounced as his sorrow fell from his eyes.

I almost hated myself for having to continue telling all that I knew of him again, but I had too. It was information that Lawrence desperately needed to hear and could possible save his life if they could keep him out of those woods between Sunken Lake and Gulleytown searching for Solomon Builder.

This awful tale had been tightly tied in a handkerchief knot against my bosom for so long and finally being able to release it was providing me a form of healing relief. I blinked away tears of my own and as they streamed away a cleansing scrubbed at my vision. I could feel the gray tint cracking and slowly chipping away.

I picked up again on what Calbert had told me like I had never stopped.

THE TRAUMA FROM the night had captured both Calbert and Lawrence as they sat shoulder to shoulder in emotional shock on the small dock that stretched a few feet out over Sunken Lake below the cabin Solomon Builder was left laying in his own blood in. The night had spun completely out of control and the events that shaped it had sobered them so that neither could remember drinking themselves silly.

Henly Blackmon had instructed the teenagers to remove Solomon's body from within the lake front home before his return but the order had been disobeyed and both boys had returned to the dock. They peered out into the darkness over the lake, looking but not really concentrating on what direction Henly had paddled away with their unconscious friends. Calbert and Lawrence were disturbed and had not exchanged a word since their hasty departure towards the cabin and immediate return to the dock.

Calbert was soaked in stress and it weighted him into a slouch. It was his words that finally divided their silence and what he said in a protected voice nearly clogged his friend's healthy heart vessel.

"He might not be dead Lawrence."

Everything inside of Lawrence Blackmon shifted.

"What . . . who are you talking about?"

"Slay. He moved, I think."

The legs of both teenagers were plunged midway to their shins into the lake for the second time that night. Lawrence pulled his up beneath him with such force that he almost toppled into the water while getting to his feet.

"When . . . I mean . . . what'd you see?"

"His f-f-foot."

Calbert was up on his feet also.

"What about it?"

"The last time we were in the room, it moved. I think it did anyway."

"Are you sure about that Calbert? You sure, because we looked at him and I didn't see nothing different about him when me and daddy went back in there to get Clara?"

Clutching at the elbows of Calbert, Lawrence begged, "Why didn't you say something?"

"Cause I could be dead wrong and just thought I saw him move."

"C'mon Calbert, you let my dad take Big Simms and Clara out onto the lake and you won't sure!?"

"No. He did that on his own." Calbert yelled. "Your-your dad is a-acting crazy. No matter what we try to tell him, he still wants to kill everybody over just an accident." His voice went from one of assuredness to childish. "I t-t-told you not to call him . . . you know he hates black people."

Tears brimmed in the eyes of Lawrence. His concentration went from Calbert to back out over the lake and it appeared as if he was about to scream out for his father but Lawrence didn't. He looked back to Calbert instead.

"Come on!"

They attacked the steep incline of the lake's bank and soon were spilling into the cabin one behind the other in wet shoes. They ended their erratic run at the empty spot that Solomon Builder had lain motionless in.

The skin color of Lawrence turned suddenly powdery white. He kneeled to pick up the fire tool that had forced a cavity in his friend's skull but allowed it to fall away from his grasp to thump hard against the floor as he stood again.

"What have we done Calbert, what the hell have we done?"

Watching Lawrence handle the instrument he had used to Strike Solomon made Calbert nauseous and he trembled all over after hearing him speak.

"I just hit him Lawrence . . . my eyes were closed. I di-d-didn't mean it."

The tear wells of Calbert Davis had burst again. He turned from Lawrence like he had been pulled away and without making another sound wandered from the room and down the narrow hallway. Distraught, Calbert never realized that he was following a trail of golf ball size blood spatters that led into the kitchen. Calbert proceeded past the kitchen counter cluttered with beer cans and a wood burning stove. The kitchen door was open and he continued through it and out to the rear of the home.

It only took a few moments for Calbert to readjust his vision to the night again. He remembered the landscape of the home and how the woods practically came right up to where he stood. The only structure within the small space that separated the backyard from the trees was a storage shelter made of logs where the paddle boats had leaned against.

Step for step Lawrence had followed Calbert outside into the ankle high grass without making a sound.

"We better hurry down and tell my dad."

The statement chilled Calbert but he stood tall in spite of it and did not offer a reply. He kept Lawrence at his rear while calling out in a guarded voice.

"Slay. Can you hear me?"

"Lawrence!"

The shout came from somewhere in the front of the cabin.

"Oh man Biggun . . . my dads back."

Lawrence spun in his heels to race back towards the call.

Calbert moved quicker and grabbed Lawrence at the upper portion of the thin gray running jacket where the logo stretched across the back and flung his surprised friend so that Lawrence faced him. Calbert then seized large fistfuls of Lawrence's chest, enough to make his friend grimace.

The skin of Lawrence had filled with color again as the warm breath and spittle of Calbert landed against it.

"Slay's out here somewhere and he's got to be scared and hurting. He's not dead, and you better make it your business he stays that way or so help me I'll find a way to kill you and your crazy ass daddy!"

Lawrence Blackmon was speechless and for the first time in his life frighten of Calbert. While looking into the lost watered eyes of his old friend, he was convinced that every word Calbert had spoke was meant and meant with malice from his heart.

"Lawrence, get out here and give me a hand."

The threatening voice wrung out with heavy angst.

"I heard you Biggun, but you got to let me go. I've got to go see what he wants."

The balls of his feet contacted the ground first and it was not until he felt the weight of his body come beneath him did Lawrence become aware that he had been lifted from his feet. Calbert's eyes flashed hatred and Lawrence got tangled in them while backing away timidly. Slowly, he swiveled before bouncing into a run that took him racing around the cabin as he was being yelled for again.

The departure of Lawrence meant that Calbert was alone for the first time since the early hours of the previous morning when he left home to catch the school bus; however, he still guarded his search for Solomon Builder. In a rush he searched in every place imaginable in back of the home but ended his hunt with suddenness after only several minutes had passed. By the time Calbert had fronted the cabin,

Henly Blackmon was dragging Lawrence on a straight line for his direction and moments later, they were all inside the cabin.

WITH THE USE OF a Sleeve, Lawrence wiped the last of his tears away. If there were anymore remaining inside of him, I truly believe they would have come forth also for revisiting the night that he had believed that they had killed Solomon Builder had him in a world of hurt. His athletically fit body continued to appear as if it was withering seated there on the edge of my porch and his back was to me when he offered his words to part through my disastrous journey.

"When my father got back, Calbert was trying his hardest to find someway to stop him. I should have been trying to help him. I knew my dad hated everyone out there including Calbert. Mrs. Sadie I wasn't helping him. I was just standing around doing nothing."

On the floor there was a glass filled almost to the top with water next to me that I had placed there before the daylight hours were over and before the arrival of Lawrence Blackmon to my home. My throat had parched, so I watered it until the glass was empty and then placed it back near the wet circle it had been picked up from and then afterwards spoke my conviction to Lawrence.

"For the life of me, I don't know why hate didn't stick to your Uncle Ray, but your grand folks raised your poppa up mean to be a man filled with hate for everybody not like him. It fits him good too. You won't a man like you are now, you were just boys when all this happened and that's all you were. Neither you nor my grandchild couldna did much more excepting what you did to stop your poppa once he'd gotten himself out to that lake. Without hardly thinking twice about it that man woulda killed you child if you'd went against him in front of Calbert. Those just won't a waste of words he slung against you when you didn't run and jump into his hate circle, and what you saw down at that lake don't tell half the story as to how terrible that man really is. He's a heap worse than all them folks put together whose been keeping up all that ruckus down in Gulleytown. Your sister tried sassing up to him and got herself almost killed. Your momma got her behind outta here in the middle of that night to save her and she ain't been back. When you up against Henly Blackmon, you not up against just him. You're fighting all the old power that's always been ruling this town by hate and division. You don't go up against people that don't got no cares about nothing and expect to live."

For the first time since changing his seating location, Lawrence turned and looked over his shoulder towards me with an inquiring expression over the statement I had made as it related to his sister Sarah and her departure from the lives of his family. It took several moments for the expression to pass as it appeared he was confronted and took a moment to accept the truth I had given him about why and how Sarah was no longer in Rix or his life. And it was good for me to witness him release the doubt in his face for what I had given him was pure truth.

What I took in next from Lawrence was a tiny fraction of his shoulders squaring as his head tilted towards the night sky.

He inquired of me. "Has Slay ever told you of how I found him . . . way back there next to them little red hills?"

Prior to offering Lawrence a reply, I held one hand up as if about to give an answered under oath and then gave. "As God as my witness, that child ain't ever huffed a word to me 'bout nothing that went on down there on your poppa's property. When all this mess took place, it was Calbert that told me all I know. It was no more than a week or so after the army folks sent me all of his belongings from over in that desert where he was, was when Solomon showed up in the woods in back of here." I paused to shake away a shudder of just remembering the sight. "My days done allowed me to see some awful things that's made me sick to the stomach but seeing that child who was suppose to be dead standing up in back of here looking all fallen to pieces like some thrown away dog almost chased life right out of me like it did to my grandchild who went away to his maker believing that the child was dead and hanting him."

The interval of time that lead right up to Calbert taking his life are moments I reflect upon continuously. I've even come up with my own belief of how he did it and I was reviewing it at this time as I chatted with Lawrence Blackmon. It was not an easy task but I shook away the reoccurring sight and continued.

"Right up front, Calbert believed Solomon to be alive, but the more his mind troubled him the more he came around to believe he was dead. He held onto that until he couldn't hold it no more and he took himself away. You and me both know that folks around here were believing what they wanted about what happened to Solomon. A heap followed right behind what the sheriff told 'em but not you . . . bless your heart. You didn't know if he was alive but you sure 'nough knew that child didn't drown." Needing to wash my throat again, I swallowed hard. "That child had been showing up here for 'bout half a year just to stand up in the woods back there. In all that time I still didn't know where he'd been for so long 'cause he wouldn't come no closer or say nary a word until this one day when he just walked up a little farther and then he'd stop. He kept that up on visit after visit after visit and every once in awhile the child would take a little of the food I lay out to feed him. He'd take it and most of the time disappear for some days and then show back up and even sleep out back. The child is real particular 'bout every move he makes and a never take nothing when it's coming straight out your hands, and he's never set foot in this house. My mind was made up that what ya'll had done to him had chased all of his words away for good 'cause he never said nothing until this one day late in the Summer. He walked up from in back of me while I was stretching out clothes on the line. Solomon came right up to my ear and said."

He said, "Mrs. Sadie."

"And I said yes child what is it?"

He said, "They've killed my mom and my dad. Burnt them up inside of the house because they believed my parents were hiding me. I miss them Mrs. Sadie, miss them real bad. I was raised me to stand up and be my own man and that's what I've been trying to do. I've been trying my best to do my best but it's real hard. I miss my momma Mrs. Sadie . . . can't nobody replace all that she means to me and I just wish that sometimes we could talk again. It's the one thing I keep needing the most and can't get past. I don't mean you or no one else any harm, but I do want to be able to talk to you sometimes."

"He placed a hand on top of mind along the clothes line before saying another word."

"Could you, would you be my momma?"

"I was crying up something awful holding to that child and he just stood there and let me and I balled out my tears. Since that day forward we've been talking up a storm 'bout everything you can imagine but never nothing 'bout what happened on your folks property. With his whole heart I can tell that the child loves me but he don't trust with it. He never has allowed me to see which way he gets back down to town. He leaves here when he's for sure I'm asleep and won't take nothing from here with him except food and some old clothes of my grandchild's he saw me rummaging through. One day he went out back and put on a pair of Calbert's army clothes and ain't come up out of 'em yet."

I intentionally paused and reached way over to place a hand on one of the shoulders of Lawrence because I wanted his eyes on me to make sure I had earned his full attention.

He gave it to me.

"A few years ago the child asked if I could get a hold of you. I didn't know much how but I figured that uncle of yours did if anybody knew. His wife was still with us then. She brought me over an address to some clinic you were schooling at, and that's when you got the letter I mailed you. And listen child . . . Solomon was originally set out on harming you. He told as much right before the first time ya'll set to meet up in Gulleytown. Something that must have had everything to do with the Lawd had to of got into that child between the time he left here and whatever time it took for you to get there to meet up with him near where his folk's old house use to be because thank goodness he changed his mind on putting death to you."

Even though he was looking up at me, I was no longer able to see Lawrence clearly anymore for nightfall had invaded but I knew he blinked really hard into those words and surely thought long and quietly about them.

Moments of uncomfortable dead time elapsed before Lawrence cleared his throat, skipped right over what I had informed him on the original intentions of Solomon Builder and went back to filling me in on how he had come across him after chasing after Solomon from the lake cabin.

"When I ran out after Slay, I couldn't tell you what my dad and Calbert were doing behind me but I did know that they were a long ways back. It was really dark out but I could see him a little ways up ahead falling down while holding on to the sleeve of Big Simms' football jacket that Latosha was wearing. Every time he'd fall, she would help him back up. Slay was solid and thick but he could run like a deer. It was obvious that all the blood he had lost was slowing them down. I kept yelling that I was coming to help but they wouldn't stop, they just kept running and running. When I made it to the end of the field, my mind didn't even flashback to all the times I'd been told never to go beyond there into the woods. I did look back though and what I saw was my dad and Calbert. They were both chasing behind me but were a ways off. Up ahead of me, Slay and Latosha were probably no more than thirty yards. I heard my dad's voice while standing there but couldn't make out anything he was saying, I just knew he was coming. I knew I had to catch Slay before he got anywhere close, so I started after them again and for some reason when I got in those woods, it seemed like they pulled farther ahead of me, but I came back up on them fast anyway. As I came around this big tree I couldn't see Slay anymore, the only thing I could see was that big jacket hanging off of Latosha. She was just a few feet ahead of me and wasn't running anymore. I reached for her but fell down before I could get to her. I thought I'd tripped over a root or something but I hadn't, it was Slay. He had fallen again and had reached out and tripped me. It kind of stunned me for a moment but I crawled over to him. Mrs. Sadie, He was trying to push further away from me while at the same time begging of me to not hurt Latosha. One of his hands was clutched to my wrist and the other one was pointing away from us towards her. I had to snatch away from him to cover my face because as soon as he started pointing I tried to go toward her. And all of a sudden, a burst of light came from out of nowhere and blinded me. The light was unreal, so unreal that I thought I was about to die. Something paralyzed me and even though I knew I could move, I didn't. I had this inner feeling telling me that I shouldn't. I can't even explained to you how scared I was because I don't know how and I couldn't adjust to the light even though I laid out there trying. I wasn't able to see but I could tell that once that light came down, everything out there had gotten this human-like nature to it. It was like the woods had become this big open heart that was hurting. The trees the bushes, everything had become frightening but it all had a spiritual essence to it and you could feel that more than anything. This is the first time I've ever spoken on what I experienced and felt out there. I never understood it and never thought anyone could ever help me too. I don't know what I was in the presence of out there, but it could drive you crazy if you lingered on it and I try my best not to.

My eyesight adjusted just a little bit and I was able to see only a glimpse of Latosha. She had run away out over those little red hills I told you about earlier. She lay down behind one of them and never came back up again. It was then when I heard my dad's voice again and all that seemed alive out there went back to being normal except for all that bright light shining over the hills. I knew I had to move fast to hide Slay before he got to us. I reached down under his arms and dragged him backwards a few feet from where he had fallen. He didn't look that scared anymore but he did look like he could die at any second. I didn't have time to do much more, so I propped him up on the side of a tree so I could go and get Latosha. Now this part might sound a little strange Mrs. Sadie, but I was walking towards those hills and could see my death. It was inside of them, but I was headed to get Latosha anyway. I don't know if I fell on my own or if I was tripped again but I fell forward on my face right before I got to the light. Those smooth hills were right there in front of me and I'll never forget the sight because they looked alive if that was possible. I stood up again and tried one more time to go after her but it felt like some invisible shield was blocking my way. Something kept me from going out there where she was Mrs. Sadie, and it wasn't me."

Lawrence Blackmon was truly a blessed individual in my sight, for with his own eyes he had observed and lived to tell about the well kept secret of what makes little Rix County so uniquely different from all other counties around our land. With all the death, hurt and separation his selfish actions had caused, his surviving everything that came after looking upon Sacred Hills is the one thing in particular that has given me a ray of hope about the young man. He had fought to overcome his father's hatred nature and willed his way through the powerful draw of the spiritual unknown which indicates to me that one of the angels from heaven is at his side constantly.

Lawrence had recessed, so I took the opportunity to pick up on my side of the story again.

"There was a reason the sky lit up down there. It was because of you chasing behind Solomon and that other child. I saw that light clear from up here. Scared me something awful, I thought the Lawd was coming right down here to start out on his walk over the earth."

After clearing my throat, I got as comfortable as I could in my old chair before giving of my knowledge again.

"Now you listen up good to what I'm about to tell you child. Way back to the time of my grand folks and probably way past them, his kind, and by that I mean the kind of folks that hate been hanging other folks in them woods ya'll was in on your poppa's property.

They never cared much for no law or being in any trouble for it cause they was much of the law or had their way of influencing it. Before the passing of my momma, she sat me down on this very porch and pointed down towards where the lake lies, and before she did, she made double sure that I knew about the black blood running through my veins beneath this white skin. She said even though I didn't look it on the outside, underneath I was as dark as her. She told me if I ever had trouble of any sort that I couldn't sort through with any of the kind of townsfolk that took away her parents then I should hide 'til the first chance I got to hightail it to the back of your poppa's property to what she called them Sacred Hills. That's show 'nuff what she said word for word. That's where I got the name for that place back there from. And let me tell you child, don't nobody know how them hills got back there or where they go when it ain't nobody being chased towards 'em. Momma told me that three townsfolk disappeared in 'em about sixty years ago chasing a black woman who'd got away after they'd had their way with her and killed off her children and husband. Since then whites won't go near 'em. They're scared to and I don't care what else they may tell you. None has been anywhere close until you followed that child out there them years back."

The grayness that distorted my vision washed away more and more the longer I sat there talking to Lawrence Blackmon. My vision was getting clearer and I concentrated hard on him for I expected him to crumble with guilt from my next inquiry. I swallowed hard on my saliva again and then tilted a little towards him to ask.

"Did you rape that young child after your poppa and the Sheriff pulled her from her momma's home?"

I was able to witness the tightening in Lawrence like the fist of a boxer. He was stiff and deafly quiet initially but when his response did emerge, he had scramble to his knees and was at the arm of my chair. And Lawrence Blackmon didn't crumble.

"No Mrs. Sadie I didn't. I have never in my life raped anyone."

His words were spoken softly and delicately delivered.

"The car that Latosha had driven back out to the cabin was the one my father took back to Gulleytown after we returned from those hills. The Sheriff drove behind him in his car. I had no idea that Latosha had went back home. I thought that she was still hiding in those hills and for good reason; it was obvious my father wasn't going in there after her. I didn't know she had left until they brought her back to the cabin in the sheriff's car."

The eyes of Lawrence were locked on my face but I really don't believe that he saw me at all at that moment. He was looking inside of his own being as he went forward explaining.

"Calbert and I were inside waiting for them to get back. We only came outside the cabin because we realized that they weren't coming in. My dad was really laughing it up like it was just some normal night until he looked up and saw us. He shouted that I was next in line and I didn't know what he was talking about until I got closer to the parking area and saw the sheriff on the trunk of the car with Latosha. I started running towards them screaming for him to stop when my dad put a gun in my face and pulled back the handle. Calbert jumped from the porch and took off running. I guess he ran all the way back home. I was in shock or something because I just stood there. I don't know for how long but I wasn't staring at what the sheriff was doing to Latosha, I was watching the evil look in my dad's eyes. It was right then and there when I knew he could hate me. I knew he would kill me too if he thought he had too. The gunshot is what drew me out of that stupor. I thought I'd been shot because the only gun I saw was in my face. But then I saw Latosha fall forward and hit against the car before sliding down to the ground.

My father screamed."

"Pete . . . what the fuck are you doing you stupid son of a bitch, now how do you think we gonna find out where she hid that boy!?"

"There was a lot more being said between them but nothing I remember. As soon as the gun was dropped from my face I ran towards Latosha and saw what had become of her. After that I took off running away also, but not in the direction Calbert went. I ran back across the field and didn't stop until I got to where I had left Slay. I knew I was in the right spot because I could feel some of his blood there on the tree I had leaned him against. I looked around back there up until daylight but never found him. There was no blood trail or nothing to indicate his whereabouts. From the way I had last seen him and even though there was never a body found, I thought for sure he was dead until you sent me that letter." Rubbing at his temples, Lawrence continued.

"They had to take the boat back out and put Latosha into the lake because she wasn't killed there. Her body was found further down from where Big Simms and Clara were found. The sheriff found her before dark but wouldn't bring her body out of the water until close to midnight, six hours after she had been found. He wanted to make sure the area had been mostly cleared of anyone on the banks but a few of his men. They had to continue the cover up. They got Mr. Jacobs to mask the bullet hole in her head. I know about this part because I was told of it about a month before we were to graduate. It was suppose to be my night of initiation into their brethren. My dad said that they drove into Gulleytown and parked Latosha's car in their drive. Like he had told her too when we were out near those hills, she was at her home when they drove up but she wouldn't come out to them. In the end she was forced into the car while the Sheriff circled the home pouring gasoline. He said that she was pretty hysterical and he beat her until she nearly passed out. The fire they set was already jumping all over the place before they started to drive away. It was told to the brethren that I killed Latosha. That lessened the complications of allowing me in. The rest of my personal hell broke when I refused to join. They would have gotten rid of me if it hadn't been for Uncle Ray. He had stopped by to drop off some fishing reels he had borrowed. Helping me out got him beaten pretty badly too but he still managed to get to his truck and held them off with a shotgun and get me up to his place. That was really the last time my dad and I exchanged any words and I don't know what my uncle told him to keep him backed off of me but they did let me graduate high school. The message was clear after that, show my face in Rix again and I'd end up buried beneath the lake."

Lawrence displayed a few tears that he had apparently kept on reserve. He mixed them in with his words and by the time he had finished covering the events of his past, his sweaty hands were wrapped into mine and his eyes went from mine down to the greenish tint on face of his wrist watch before he attempted to speak again.

"It's almost eleven-thirty Mrs. Sadie. Whitney is down at the cabin probably wondering what's happened to me. I've been turning it over in my head since leaving Uncle Ray's whether to give in to her and sleep overnight but this talk with you has pretty much settled that little issue for me. I don't feel like being here any longer, but I'm not running away this time, I'm just leaving. And don't worry Mrs. Sadie, you've convinced me, I'm not going looking for Slay. I know now that he's safe out there in his special place. He should be showing up around here sometime soon anyway. Tell him I'll be around his old house next Thursday to make up for the Thursday we missed."

Satisfied that my warning had been convincingly affective in preventing Lawrence from searching for Solomon Builder, I smiled and happily told him.

"I sure will child."

With his hands still in mine, Lawrence maneuvered up a little closer and whispered.

"Mrs. Sadie."

"Yes child."

"You're my momma too you know."

"Bless your heart child, yes."

He allowed a few more of his tears to escape as a large chunk of gray cleared from my own eyes.

Lawrence then smiled so handsomely through his tears up to me that I felt a blush, he then allowed.

"Momma Sadie, we've shared so much tonight, it just wouldn't be right if I didn't tell you this one last thing."

"Yes, what is it child?"

"Well, I've never tried to tell anyone this before and I guess it's because I really never knew how too but here it goes."

The smile that Lawrence had put forth was gone like it had been snatched away and he pressured hard down into my hands.

"Often when I'm all alone and just thinking about my life, I find myself feeling identical to the way Calbert use to say he was feeling . . . you know when he use to question why he was still living when all he did was stand around and did nothing while everybody else died."

His hands were pulling away from me. I tried to hold on to them but Lawrence got them away from me anyway and he got away from my porch even faster.

Listening to words like that coming from him, I knew in which direction his life was headed and where it would find an end. They were words I had heard from my grandson on a daily basis before he went off to a war and never came back to me.

I pleaded, "Don't talk like that child. You've got plenty of friends still living that's here for you and love you. You've got that young girl you fixing on marrying . . . you've got Ray and Slay . . . you know he calls you his brother and child you've got your momma Mrs. Sadie right here. And I love you. I surely do."

It was as if Lawrence never heard a word I said, he said not another word to me. He didn't stop his retreat and never even turned to look back at his Momma Sadie. After entering his vehicle, he drove away from my property in a manner like he never should have come in the first place.

More gray fell from my eyes as I cried for my Lawrence. Somehow, I should have stopped him. I surely should have.

CHAPTER 6

FRIDAY JUNE 14, 1999

DANDLER

FOR THE PAST TWELVE years Fanny Jacobs had been the chairwoman of a private club, the Ladies of Rix was its name. She chaired over forty women all of whom primary responsibilities as members amongst other duties were to arrange transportation for services for the less fortune and to provide meals for the elderly and sick throughout the communities.

The club met twice monthly in a second story room above a boutique owned by one of the members on the town square. Fanny had been a proud member for over twenty years. She had married young at twenty-two and had been faithfully committed to her marriage in spite of her husband's troubling fancy for young boys that arrived to him very much dead. She lived alone with Dennis in a four bedroom brick home. It was located on expansive property off of highway 44 and it stretched the boundary of Rix to its neighboring county. Other than her valued position within her club, Fanny held no other desirable titles besides wife of the county coroner. Fanny's parents had been well off and willed her the home and everything they owned which was the central reason she had never worked a day in her life, and with her husband's weakness, she had never wanted children and wasn't blessed with any.

During most of the day Friday, Fanny Jacobs was out visiting with old friends she had not seen in years who were still in town following the funeral of Sheriff Pete Crance. She had not been feeling very well as of late and after arriving home she ran a long bath to dispel the hugging sweat of a hot day and followed it up with a warm cup of tea and was in bed before nine that night.

Arriving home a half hour after his wife had fallen asleep, Dennis Jacobs got comfortable and went fast to sleep also.

Five years had passed since the first haunting encounter he could remember having with Solomon Builder. He had been driving when the headlights of his car sprayed over the presumed dead man's rugged face in front of the gulley that rounded Dead Man's curve. Following the encounter, Solomon Builder began appearing infrequently in and around his home. The appearances spiked over the past year where he began arriving sometimes as much as twice a week and always in the later hours of the night.

Dreadful dreams had become commonplace for Dennis, forcing breakage in his sleep and on this occasion it occurred around eleven. No more than two minutes later, Dennis Jacobs has rung the cell phone of Henly Blackmon three different times. They were frantic calls to the former mayor whom Dennis had not spoken with since much earlier in the morning when he watched as Henly set Solomon Builder to flames in the woods behind Sunken Lake.

Life had gotten far worse for Dennis since that particular event; fear ruled him completely as an individual long dead whom he knew no longer existed overwhelmed him with a presence within his home.

Two tall glasses of dry whiskey sent him running to the cold waters of a shower that lasted five terrifying minutes. Exiting the bathroom Dennis trembled in fright while tipping through his home and desperately attempting not to look directly at the horrible image coming toward him. He blinded one eye by closing it and squinted down the other while crawling back into bed and curling into a large ball. Dennis squirmed until his massive body was back against Fanny and at that point his green eyes jerked open. He felt skin that was sticky cold against his.

"Fanny!"

In an aggressive twisting maneuver Dennis shifted and was able to fill a hand with strands of his wife's short hair seeking her attention. His reward was the severed head of dear Fanny rolling into him.

In two shifting bounces that sent him upright, Dennis clawed his way free of the bed.

Poor Fanny Jacobs had been massacred, her flesh butchered at almost every inch, it was the purest form of beastliness the coroner had ever stood before and it had been practiced on the only individual that mattered to him. Blood pooled in their bed and it had expanded and soaked down through to the mattress where puncture holes were made by a large knife.

In desperation, Dennis got to a phone and using only one hand he punched in numbers that would contact Henly Blackmon again. His other hand clutched at the hair of Fanny's head and Dennis was never aware that it was there for he had been driven mad by images and his world overtaken. There was an individual that Dennis Jacobs looked upon, the sole human being that had committed such carnage. This person was never a part of his imagination and was very much alive and remained in the bedroom walking calmly past him covered in Fanny's blood.

More from a mental standpoint than a physical one, Coroner Jacobs was tired and it was absolute and complete exhaustion. He was desperate, afraid and now all alone with the loss of his wife and had not a soul to offer him comfort. Without Fanny to share life with, giving up on living would be easy for it had long ago given up on him.

SUNKEN LAKE,

LATE SATURDAY NIGHT, JUNE 15, 1999

THOUGH LAWRENCE HAD indicated that he had been under the weather earlier in the week, Whitney knew that he had not been straightforward and had not been ambushed by any physical ailment. Following her access back into his home, she noticed a darker side to him and it worried Whitney more than she let on. What exactly troubled Lawrence was a matter she was not of certain but she pinpointed the country store owned by his Uncle Ray Blackmon where it was apparent that whatever it was bothering him a decision was made to seek settlement of it before they took a departure from Rix.

Lawrence had not driven a half mile before making a decision to return to the old store and retrieve the keys to the cabin home on Sunken Lake. It was a decision Whitney mused over but didn't subject him to any questioning to a sudden change of heart. She did however inquire of his new plans and was given very little in reply other than he needed to make this visit alone.

At an hour before sunset at a cabin sitting in isolation above an enormous lake, Whitney Connors enjoyed the comfort of only herself. In the waning minutes of sunlight she walked along the lake enjoying the postcard views it offered from different angles. When the sun finally disappeared Whitney returned to the cabin for another of the sandwiches Ray Blackmon had white-bagged and before she knew it she had fallen easily to sleep minutes before nine from the weariness of not much sleep the previous night.

She slept comfortably on a sofa with many pillows in a room overrun with stuffed wildlife trophies and awakened on her own at just past eleven. With both hands pressed together beneath one side of her face, Whitney blinked in an attempt to gather a clearer focus on the unfamiliar face staring into hers.

Sitting in a chair across the room from Whitney with her hands resting on the inside of opposite knees was a woman with very dark eyes and pronounced cheeks that rounded down into her chin. Her face appeared young without a wrinkle and no telling age spots and she possessed skin that was brown like a pecan in color. Her hair was as dark as black ink and touched midway down her back in a loosely braided plat. She was an attractive woman in a country type way and more tiny than petite, attired in a faded denim shirt that tucked neatly into faded jeans that matched.

With her focus back in tact, Whitney continued her assessment of the visitor and before she could speak, she was spoken to in a voice that soothed like a mother brooding over a small child.

"Hi Sweetie, I'm so glad you woke yourself up, you looked so pretty and peaceful that I didn't want to wake you unless I had too."

Alarm bells were definitely ringing loud in Whitney as she adjusted upwards but got no further than her elbows before she was stroked by the soothing voice again.

"No, no Sweetie, don't be afraid . . . you're alright. I'm not here to bring you any harm at all."

Whitney had fallen asleep with her legs crossed. She uncrossed them to sit all the way up and to explore the room for the presence of anyone else.

"Lawrence, where's Lawrence!?"

"He ain't here Sweetie, but I'd bet he's up in Taylorsville visiting Mrs. Sadie."

"How would you know that, and how did you get in here?"

"Well, Sweetie I walked right in and sat down after you fell off to sleep. You left the door open. I'm around this cabin a lot, and that's especially when the Mayor is out here. I started making my way over this way after I saw you earlier in Gulleytown. I figured Lawrence to show up over this way eventually and I knew for sure he'd be going up to visit Mrs. Sadie."

"You saw me earlier; does that mean you're following us? And what does where Lawrence goes have to do with you? Walking into another person's home without being invited whether or not the door was open or not doesn't mean you're invited to take liberty."

"If there's one place I don't need an invitation too its here. I've been coming and will keep coming and you would too if the man that owned this house had burned up your babies."

At some point during their talk on Friday night, Lawrence had disclosed that entire families had lost their lives in an early morning fire after the tragedy on the lake. Whitney narrowed in on the presence of the small woman and wondered if what she had just been exposed to relate in anyway to what she had been told on the previous night. But could not be possible for no one had survived the fires, no one that Lawrence had mentioned to her anyway.

Whitney shifted her focus to where she remembered a telephone sat before a decision was made to say another word.

"If you don't offer a legitimate reason for being here, you'll force me to use that phone over there to call the police."

"The police, the phone, those things aren't important to me, what is important is the reason I'm here, and that's to keep a watch over you so you don't get yourself hurt out here too."

"I don't wish to call anyone because I don't feel threaten but at the same time you're not suppose to be here, and furthermore, you're not making sense for why you are. This matter of Lawrence's father hurting your kids is something I don't understand and you're not doing a good job of helping me."

"Not hurt my babies Sweetie, killed. The mayor killed all three of them."

After awakening to the audience of a total stranger, Whitney for the most part had remained reasonably calm, but this final statement cut into her with the precision of a surgeon's blade. Her unsettling was visible.

"Listen, other than his uncle, I've met none of Lawrence's family and of what I've heard of his father, I never want to meet him. I'm sorry about your family, really I am, but what does that have to do me and you doing out here?"

"Okay Sweetie, I'll clear things up so that you can understand. Has Lawrence ever mentioned the name Latosha Williams to you?"

She never waited for an answer.

"My name is Catherine Williams, Latosha was my oldest. My baby was raped . . . and she was killed, and it happened right here. You asked why I am in this house, and my answer is only to watch over you. You're on property owned by old Mayor Blackmon and he'll kill you dead and get away with it too for being on his land whether you was invited on it or not."

The decided comfort in the voice was no longer there and this sudden change frightened Whitney.

"If there was anybody the devil had its hands on it's that old bastard. Satan has to be his guide with all the crimes his hands are a part of in this town. I made it my personal business to stop by here and keep and eye on you. I'm here to make sure that what he done to my babies won't happen to nobody else's. He and his wife are the only two who've been in this cabin since they killed my family and I'm telling you information that can't be denied because I've been watching, and I don't mean looking, watching." With eyes narrowed, she added, "Real evil owns this property, the kind that gives birth to more of it."

There was certainty within Whitney; she was engaged in conversation with a woman she had been informed was dead. Nervousness invaded, but she did her absolute best to conceal it.

"Raped and murdered," Whitney quizzed. "By Lawrence's father, she didn't drown with their friends? That's what I was led to believe. And Lawrence has never spoken glowingly of his father, but he certainly never mentioned anything about him killing children. That's the work of someone horrible and if it's his father like you say, then something as equally as horrible will befall him. But Lawrence is nothing like that, I've known him for years and he's nothing like your description of his father."

"Huh, if that's the truth, then we can only thank Jesus for it. But that old mayor, he's the son of the devil like I told you."

Whitney had never heard Lawrence speak the name of Catherine Williams but at one point in the past she could recall him mentioning that Latosha's twin sisters and their mother all died in a fire the morning of her drowning, other than that, he had spoken nothing more about the tiny woman.

Whitney looked her over again and this time with complete compassion. Catherine Williams was somehow alive and Whitney was on the entrance of firsthand knowledge that was never forthcoming from Lawrence. The engaging woman's great loss warmed Whitney and influenced her guards to lower and the empathy was obvious in the manner she continued forward with Catherine Williams.

"I was told that you died in your home in a fire and that practically all of the community attended you and your children's funeral. Which is obviously a lie and it has me wandering if everything else that Lawrence has told me about what happened here was a lie also, or does he really not know you're alive."

Whitney's eyes were begging as she sat awaiting a reply.

"If it's not asking too much Mrs. Williams, would you tell me the truth about what took place the night or morning when your family was lost?"

It was nearly the beginning of summer but Catherine Williams was wrapped inside of a huge jacket that almost hid her entire body. The coat was burgundy and had a tweed pattern all over except for the sleeves which were tan leather. They were pushed back past her forearms. She pulled both hands from opposite knees and pushed them into the pockets of the jacket while pulling it around her more snuggly as though she were cold and then cleared her throat. Catherine Williams looked Whitney directly into her eyes but before speaking again she lost contact for the very first time.

"That's something I don't do very much . . . talking about that. But you laying up in this place and obviously not knowing where you really are might just mean you need to hear about the past and who you're involved with." She cleared her voice again, regained eye contact and continued.

"Even with all the hate the mayor had stuffed up in him, Lawrence was in Gulleytown, pretty much as much as he wanted and that was all the time. I watched him grow up just as I did the kids that stayed there. I don't believe it was ever his intent to be a bad seed like the mayor. Now that's just how I saw it from my eyes, you ask somebody else and you might hear something that's not the same as that." She stopped suddenly, lost eye contact but immediately regained it and then asked, "Sweetie what's your name?"

"It's Whitney, Mrs. Williams. My name is Whitney Connors."

She smiled. "Whitney . . . now that's a pretty name and you're a pretty girl. Is Lawrence somebody special to you Whitney?"

"We have a wedding planned this summer. He's very special to me."

"Marriage, you and Lawrence . . . well if that ain't something then ain't nothing is. A Blackmon getting married to a black woman . . . mmh, mmh, mmh."

A half smile that really wasn't a smile at all was on her face. Catherine Williams even pushed through a chuckle while adding, "Lawrence always has been kind of hard to figure, I guess this goes right along with it. As I was saying, he used to be in Gulleytown with Slay everyday like he lived there. Those two were crazy about one another, best friends despite of the old Mayor." She offered another of those smiles that really wasn't real and said, "Sweetie, your Lawrence for the most part was a good kid with a heart sort of like his Uncle that lives up in Taylorsville. I find fault in him because he knew plenty about how my babies were killed but chose to hold his tongue about it."

She went silent and stared at Whitney who waited for her to speak again while staring right back and after several moments words were put back into play.

"Lawrence doesn't know that I'm still alive. I know you wanted the answer to that question. There's been lots of talk about me especially around Gulleytown but I ain't showed myself on purpose to nobody except Glenda and Arnold Freeman. You know who they are?"

"I don't, but it's easy to guess. I assume that they're the parents of Clara Freeman, Slay's girlfriend. The other girl found in the lake."

"That's right Whitney. Remember when I said I saw you earlier, when you were in Gulleytown? Lawrence stopped in front of their home. He saw me inside looking out at ya'll but probably didn't believe what he was seeing. I use to be a seamstress, that's how I was raising my girls working for a fabric company here. We lost their daddy when the twins were two, so I was raising all of my children alone. For a little extra money which we always could use, I sewed a lot on the side. Latosha was a smart girl kind of like you with her heart set on being the first to make it out of college in the family. She liked sewing too. One of my teachers from high school got me into sewing. She taught me everything I know about it and I was teaching Latosha. My teacher died a few years after I finished up all my schooling but before she did she gave me this skeleton she used to hang her sewing on at home. I used it to hang finished jobs on too and that's what they pulled out of the ashes and said was me. They would have known right off that it wasn't if they all would've done their jobs right instead of rushing but nobody did. They were all to busy covering up a mess of lies they had scattered, just hurrying through everything trying to get it behind them."

The large coat wriggled further up her small shoulders and through the pockets she again pulled the opening together closer.

"I drove over to this cabin because it was the proper thing to do. I guess because Latosha had not long left everybody figured it was her that came back but it wasn't. It was me. A month or so before they commenced to playing any football that year, Latosha told me about Mayor Blackmon taking a rifle shot at the boys for being out here with Lawrence on his property. Nobody from Gulleytown should have been up on this land in the first place. My child sure wouldn't have been if I had any knowledge of a plan to meet up out here and no matter what, Latosha for no reason should have left Clara here."

The eye focus remained on Whitney but it became obvious that Catherine Williams was looking through all that was before her and back into the past as she carried forward.

"I thought the girls were together when Latosha got home. I was in my room sewing on something while waiting up for them when she yelled down the hallway that she'd made it in. I took for granted that they both were in her room until I went in later to check on them and found Latosha there alone. It was two or could have been three in the morning then. I don't hold to much to that exact memory but I know I waited just a little time, maybe a minute or two to see if the boys were gonna drop her off like Latosha said. I left all of my babies behind and that included my oldest and drove over here to get

Clara like I know her folks would of done for my baby under the same circumstances."

There was another momentary pause. A second loss of eye contact came with it as Catherine looked down over her small brown hiking boots.

"I didn't turn off the lights or the car when I drove up because I didn't expect to be here for more than a minute but I didn't get much of a chance to do anything. As soon as I got out, Slay slammed into me from behind and almost knocked the breath out of me. I figured out later that he came from hiding beneath an old pick-up truck but at the time I didn't know where he'd come from. I screamed but it went into his hands because he had covered my mouth. I was scared for my own life when he knocked me to the ground because I didn't know who'd hit me. When I found out who he was, I was more scared for him than I was for me because that boy didn't look like he should be living with how his head looked. Blood was just a flowing from it. I ain't never been that scare for nobody in all my life. The first thing he said was if I cared anything about living I'd better shut up and lay still. I did while he got up to one knee and looked in my car like he was about to get in it but he didn't. As he was snatching me up to my feet like some little toy, he told me to get ready to run. And that's exactly what we did; we set out running across that field out there. He was pretty much carrying me at first because it seemed like my feet hardly touched the ground, but before long I was dragging him. Blood was just everywhere, I didn't think we would make it out of the field but we did and on towards Gulleytown we headed. He was giving it his all but Slay was just hurt too bad to go any further. Right when Lawrence caught up to us was when he finally collapsed but he pushed me on ahead.

Lawrence looked like death too . . . his face was all bruised up and swollen . . . but he didn't look nothing like Slay. I didn't know why they both looked the way they did or why Lawrence was chasing us or what to think, because the only words Slay had spoken to me was what he said when he knocked me over. I remember Lawrence crying but I don't remember him saying much because something happened out there and it had him scared half to death I only looked back for a moment and I saw him dragging Slay away. I had hidden when I started hearing the old mayor's voice. I heard Calbert's too. They'd caught up. They couldn't see me but I could have seen them if I wanted and I heard everything they were saying. They thought they were running after Latosha. They had no idea it was me. When they walked away from where I was hiding I knew they were on their way to get my babies and believe me young lady, I tried to get there to protect them but the place that offered me safety wouldn't allow me to take one step towards Gulleytown or no place else no matter how hard I tried. I couldn't even cry a tear or show any of the emotions I was suppose to be feeling. I felt a spirit settling in over me and it was my babies' father. He was letting me know to not worry about our babies. He was letting me know that he was gonna take care of them from now on. I released them to his spirit and I felt good about doing it even though I would never have them again. I knew where they were going and they would be fine there.

Lawrence didn't tell where he had hid Slay but it wasn't far from where they all were standing. After they left, I went out and found him. He was plain suffering, shaking like he was freezing. He skin was cold, his lips were white and he was about to die in front of me and I knew it. I tried but I couldn't move him, he was too heavy. All I could think about was to just pray for him. I closed his eyes and then closed mine, hugged him real tight and went to praying. When I finished and open my eyes, I was still holding him but we'd been moved to the place I'd hid. Slay was healing up and I mean right there in my arms. It was all a miracle. Everything that happened once we ran into those woods was a miracle."

In quiet amazement Whitney had sat there, she opened her mouth to speak but was curtail.

"You want to ask me about the place where I hid, don't you?"

"Yes Mrs. Williams. What type of place is this?"

"Sweetie, I can't give you an answer because there's no way you would understand. There ain't no way you could and that's just how it is. I'll say this though, me and Slay been dead to the rest of the world and we would have been that for real if Mayor Blackmon found out we were still alive. We didn't have nobody but ourselves. They killed his mom and dad the same way they thought they'd killed me and that left us nobody to trust. For a bunch of years we hid where we could until this one day Glenda came home early from delivering the mail and caught me inside their home. It turned out to be a blessing. The Freemans began giving me almost everything we needed to survive. There's been a few people who've seen us and there's been lots of talk but nobody that meant us harm would even fly a crop plane over the area where we most of the time hide. We were surviving, we had our little area. Never told the Freemans that Slay was still alive and he said nothing to Mrs. Sadie about me being out in the woods with him. That way we thought we were protecting each other."

Whitney pushed forward like a child who had been lost from her mother and hurried over to wrap herself into Catherine Williams.

She had just received information that made the man she loved out to be a liar and possibly a participant in the murder of his friends. Lawrence Blackmon had been re-described and the description was hardly the individual Whitney had intended to share the rest of her life with. At this moment, this part of her torn emotions did not surface.

"Mrs. Williams, I'm so sorry the way that you've lost your family."

Whitney withdrew her head from one of Catherine's shoulders and it was at that moment her concentration fell to the stenciled name of Gary Simms produced in cursive lettering across the breast of the jacket. Her attention lasted there for such a period of time that it drew words.

"Before leaving my home, Latosha followed me outside and gave me this coat to wear. She was the last of my babies I laid eyes on and this jacket is the only thing I've got that connects me to any of them." A large letter R was on the opposite breast that she patted. "No matter what it feels like outside, I've wore it every single day since she pushed it into my arms."

"I just wish that there was something else I could do, something else I could say besides how sorry I am for this happening to you, and Lawrence; I had no idea that his involvement in this was so terrible."

"Sweetie, I thank you for your caring, but don't worry about me, as I told you my family is fine where they've gone onto with their dad, and I find a way to make it no matter how tough it gets."

"I admire that. That's a testament of strength. You and Slay lost everything but you still have each other and I guess that's a lot when you've lost everything else." After a pause, Whitney offered, "I can't believe that Lawrence hid all of this from everyone, that's just not the person I fell in love with. In no way does he deserve it for what he's put you through, but he's going to be very excited to learn that Slay is still alive after all of these years."

"Whitney I can tell that you're such a sweet young woman from the outside all the way into your heart. One that doesn't deserve to be lied to and treated the way you have." She held Whitney a little tighter by both of her arms before adding, "For some reason, Lawrence has chosen to feed you a bunch of lies. Slay ain't alive anymore but he was up until a day or two ago before somebody killed him, but Lawrence already knew he was alive. For at the least three years he's known about Slay and he's been coming over here from Athens late up in the night three or four times a year to see him. They meet up somewhere close to where Slay's old home use to be."

With a bit of force, Whitney pulled clear of Catherine's grip and stood to loop behind the chair the older woman relaxed on to release some of her hurt.

"I just can't believe how deliberately he's lied to me."

While wringing her hands, Whitney had spoken with anger.

Catherine Williams could hear her clearly but was not able to see the small lines of hurt streaming down the younger ladies' face.

Using both hands, Whitney forced away her tears while recalling a statement to the center of her thoughts.

"You mentioned that Slay was alive until sometime earlier this week?"

The inquiry produced a trace of sadness on the face of Catherine Williams as she responded.

"I could always tell when it was time for him to meet up with Lawrence. The whole day he wouldn't eat nothing or say hardly much, he'd just spend the day pacing back and forth until it got late in the night and then he'd leave. Tuesday night of this week was the last time I saw him alive. Up until I found him back in the woods I'd thought he'd went off on one of his angry spells and this time killed Lawrence. He threatens to do that sometimes. He gets over those spells though and afterwards goes up to stay a stretch with Mrs. Sadie."

Whitney looked incredulous while rounding the chair and appearing back in front of Catherine Williams.

"Kill Lawrence . . . why?"

"They may have been still friends and I mean the best of friends, and Slay loved him as much as he always did, but at times he'd get all caught up in what he saw Lawrence doing to Clara and it gets the best of him. But I knew I was wrong about Slay killing him when I saw you two over in Gulleytown."

"What do you mean? What did Slay see Lawrence doing to his girlfriend?"

"I'm sorry Whitney; I keep forgetting you don't know about everything that happened out here. It all started because of rape. My babies and all those other folks were killed because of that. Slay walked in on Lawrence and Calbert with Clara."

Whitney nearly fainted while Catherine Williams swiped at her own brow as she continued releasing her tragedy.

"The way Slay was acting the last time I saw him alive had me worried. I couldn't find him anywhere so I figured he had to be up in Taylorsville with Calbert's grandmother until I found him this evening coming through the woods to get here."

There was an attempt to catch the hurt but a single stream of it escaped and crested over one cheek to fall upon the old letterman jacket of Gary Simms.

"He's out there in the woods with those old clothes of Calbert he liked to wear piled up next to him. Somebody has burned him up to almost nothing and left him real close to that same spot Lawrence hid him at." She looked convincingly at Whitney before adding, "Only two people that's still alive that could have done that to him. One is old Mayor Blackmon because he's the only person I know foolish enough to go back there, and if it wasn't him, it was his seed, Lawrence."

Frustration had reached a peak within Whitney. It spurn from a cruel mixture of the deceit peddled by Lawrence coupled with the hurt of not having any legs to stand on to defend him anymore. There was no denying that she knew very little about who he really was. The part of Lawrence that he had so skillfully hidden from her for so long could almost be described as monstrous. Her voice was breaking when she spoke again.

"Do you really believe that Lawrence is capable of killing Slay or for that matter, anyone?"

"Sweetie, I believe that you're the best person to answer your own question, you're the one that's marrying him."

Whitney didn't respond. She couldn't. Her eyes were low and searching near her feet until the voice of Catherine Williams pulled them upwards to her again.

"For your sake Whitney, I pray that he's not. But if that's not the case, he should have never left you here alone in this house. He should never have even brought you near here knowing the type of creature the old mayor is."

"A reliable source has guaranteed that his father is away for the weekend, I'm pretty sure that's the only reason he left me here."

"Mayor Blackmon may have left town but I don't think he's gone anymore. Last night I was by a friend of his home and I heard that man begging the mayor to get back here now and I believe Mayor Blackmon listened. Remember Sweetie what I told you when you asked why I was here. I told you I was here to protect you."

"Well thank you Mrs. Williams but I don't need your protection anymore, I've been fine to this point and I think I'll be fine from moving forward and again, I'd like to thank you for your concern."

The anger Whitney displayed was not against Catherine Williams even though she was forced to bare it. It was at Lawrence and the deception he had spun that was flushing all of her dreams away.

"Lawrence is not a murderer," she shouted. "And in my heart I know that he has never raped anyone either. Please Mrs. Williams; you would be allowing me the greatest favor if you would just leave right now before he returns."

Walking briskly, Whitney positioned between the front door of the home and Catherine Williams.

Quietly and without further protest, the older woman displaced from the chair and followed the instructional finger of the younger woman at the doorway who appeared much shaken. Catherine Williams stopped however before exiting.

"Sweetie, what's before you I know is hard, and I don't blame you for asking me to leave. I guess if I was in your shoes I'd probably stand by the man I love too because that's what love does. You stay here and wait for Lawrence if that's what you believe you need to do but I want you to do me a favor too." She waited until their eye contact was solid and consistent before she gave, "While you're waiting don't for one second forget about what I told you about where you are. This is a house of death, and I'm serious about that. The only reason I'm leaving you in it is because my presence here troubles you, but while you are here, if you feel threatened by anybody, I want you to run out of here and keep running across the field out there. And don't you stop running even after you cross it until you don't have to run no more, and I promise that you'll know exactly when that time is. Do that for me Sweetie."

Without another word spoken, she stepped through the doorway and away from the home. Catherine Williams tugged at her large jacket so that it circled her more completely and almost instantly became a shadowy figure as she disappeared into the night without even a glance backwards.

Whitney closed the door of the cabin and there she struggled with her emotions and the disheartening reality of the possibility of murder and rape existing in the only individual she loved as much as she loved herself.

A chair with a winged back and wooden arm rest was beneath a rounded mirror right next to the door. Whitney positioned there but was up and down from its location every thirty seconds searching for any sign that indicated Lawrence had returned.

Nearly fifteen minutes following the departure of Catherine Williams, Lawrence made his return to the cabin owned by his father.

A dry dizziness swept through Whitney as she stood and watched his vehicle pull slowly into the parking area of the home.

The ride back from Taylorsville had been a cruel one for Lawrence. His thoughts were everywhere. They were of Mrs. Sadie and the topics they had discussed only minutes earlier. Weighing heavily on Lawrence also were his memories of Calbert Davis and his many demons. The two of them appeared to have almost as much in common through his death as they did when he was still alive for many of the pressures Calbert experienced exploding through his thoughts had been experiences of Lawrence as well. But what captured up his thoughts more than anything else as Lawrence traveled back to Rix from Taylorsville and the home of Mrs. Sadie was Solomon Builder. The friend he needed desperately to speak with in order to continue to save his own mentality.

In a physical form, Lawrence Blackmon had indeed arrived back around Sunken Lake, but in the ways that mattered most which were all mental, he had not really arrived back at all.

The ignition to the vehicle was ended and the lights had been switched to off but he never emerged.

The door to the cabin opened and Whitney stood there somberly with arms crossed within its frame awaiting. She didn't know what to exactly believe in anymore as it regarded them as a unit of one but she imagined the worst and for the first time since they had become permanent fixtures in one another's' lives, a twinge of the unknown with the feel of fear crept into her. An eventful day had born a depressing night and the latter had welled up inside of her and latched to her core. Dispirited by the individual she had fallen deeply in love with who was hidden by nightfall behind the dark windows of a vehicle; as she recalled the events of the week, Lawrence was not even the same individual to himself anymore, no less her.

Her impatience grew as she quickly became aware that Lawrence had made no attempt to exit the vehicle. Whitney called out for him but Lawrence offered no response and remained as he was. In her bare feet, Whitney walked in the direction of the parking area in small carefully placed steps and never stopped until she arrived as close as she could to the vehicle without touching it and waited patiently for the window to inch all the way down and no glass separated them. Whitney then initiated an action she had not anticipated taking, after unfolding her arms, she eased a hand over to Lawrence to lift his chin from its resting place on his chest. And from the guidance of her touch, Lawrence allowed his focus to rise to capture her eyes.

"Damn," Lawrence almost said to himself. There in her beautiful black eyes was an ugly image of exactly how he felt. He could feel his soul being carved out and the exact feeling matched what he looked upon in Whitney's eyes.

He pondered there momentarily at the possibility of her somehow knowing that he had circled Dead Man's curve twice prior to his arrival back in search of his own death. More than once he attempted to offer his thoughts but the quiver of his lips and sunken emotions held them at bay and when they finally did break forward, hollowness owned them.

"Whitney I am so sorry," he said with an enormously heavy sigh and looked away from her before continuing.

"We've got to talk. There's so much I need to tell you and I don't even know where to start. Let me just try to start with today . . . I mean earlier when we were in Gulleytown. I saw someone today and I wasn't mistaken. The person I saw has been dead since I left this place and I know she has because my father was one of the individuals that killed her. He and the sheriff that was murdered this week burned down a house with her and her kids inside."

Lawrence stopped and reflected for a few moments and then tonelessly added. "Before killing himself, Calbert use to always tell me that he felt like people were watching him. He even used to say haunting him." He paused again before adding, "You know I been to visit his grandmother, and the conversation with her helped me to realize how right he was. Somebody was watching him and riding back here I just kept thinking how I feel the same damn way Calbert did. It's a feeling that could drive you crazy Whitney and I want it to end but I just don't know how to stop it."

Lawrence swallowed hard with his pause this time.

"I've got to let you know this Whitney; I've got to let you know what really happened out here to all of my friends, all of it, everything."

His eyes were still hovering low when he included, "Whitney you're going to hate me for this . . . I know you are and you should."

As Lawrence looked back, Whitney had inquiries of her own that would probably carry through the remainder of the night. But she was no fool, she realized the suffering before her and Lawrence's inclusion would probably include all the things she wanted to know. Whitney set her questions aside in order to gain whatever it was Lawrence was attempting to give.

With one of her hands remaining inside of the window, Whitney traced his face with it and decided to assist Lawrence a bit and tabled an issue he had already made mention of.

"Lawrence, you're not seeing dead people coming back to life again and you're not being haunted. That person you think is haunting you was not in the fire that killed her two smallest children. You're talking about Catherine Williams, and she's still alive and doing as well as she can with the challenges she has. It wasn't Latosha that you were chasing; it was her mother running with your friend away from you."

"How . . . ."

Lawrence sat frozen, his mouth open and his thoughts on the reality that Whitney Connors had knowledge of his secret.

After the talk with Mrs. Sadie and the failed attempts at killing himself, Lawrence was nearly an empty shell and from what remained another portion of his emptiness died from existence as he turned his memory to the final moments of his pursuit of his friend Slay Builder years earlier.

Licking his dry lips, Lawrence swallowed hard on the bitter realization of what Whitney's statement would have on his life and theirs together and as if he was speaking back through the past, he offered, "That had to be Latosha."

"Sorry Lawrence but no it wasn't. It was her mother. Mrs. Williams was here not long before your arrival."

And while exposing Lawrence to those facts, Whitney began to cry. "Why Lawrence, why did you think you had to lie to all of the people here, all of the families that were hurt? People were murdered, and you and Calbert were right in the middle of it all."

"We didn't gather everyone up out here with the intention on hurting anyone. These were our friends, everybody that came out. Things got very much carried away but we never wanted anyone killed, but we messed up. No . . . I messed up . . . and when my dad got here," he whimpered, "uuugh, I should have died out here too."

"But why," Whitney screamed. Her gentleness surviving no longer, "Why did you let this happen?"

"I don't know why and I've never known. We just weren't thinking clearly. After what we did to Slay I went numb and then I got terrified of what my dad might do to us if I didn't let him know because he was going find out, but I didn't expect his reaction to be what it was. Everything, the entire incident started as just a misunderstanding and an accident during a fight but once he got here he made it something totally different than what it really was. He started this thing about mistrust and hate and told us he wouldn't protect us if we didn't do what he said. It seemed like everyday of the week they were burning crosses around Mrs. Sadie's home sending messages to Calbert, and a lot of nights they'd come after me by waking me up and they'd be standing around my bed in hats and robes. Sometimes Calbert and I did discuss telling someone else but we never followed up." Lawrence thought of Calbert's grandmother and her full knowledge of their acts and then added, "At least I didn't ever tell anyone."

"But why didn't you Lawrence? Why didn't you tell someone? This wasn't some teenage game, people's lives were taken."

"I don't know Whitney," he cried.

Whitney pressed onward past the elevated emotions on display before here and pushed for more answers.

"Then what about raping Latosha Williams, Lawrence, are you a rapist?"

Lawrence Blackmon flattened as his breathing passages collapsed and air needed for survival just pressed right out of him and silence took its place. He used it as a buffer for self pity but Whitney Connors would not allow him to linger for long there.

180

"I won't waste a thought over believing your capability of murdering anyone, but you tell me right now Lawrence if you've ever raped anyone?"

"I haven't Whitney. I promise you I haven't."

Lawrence paused and looked as stiff as a corpse before easing back into a breathing pattern. He then spilled out, "I didn't rape Latosha, but I believe I would have done it to Clara." His fist pounded into the ceiling of the jeep. I'm sorry Whitney but that's what I was fighting with Slay about before Calbert hit him!"

There was a wide open gap that led directly to a past that had been heavily suppressed and it increased the sorrows of Lawrence by mountains.

"I was drunk. We all had been really drinking except for Slay. I'm not making that an excuse. Clara was out of it, I mean so out of it that she didn't even feel when I was trying to force myself on her. I had gone inside of the room with her after I saw Slay leave out. He came back in and that's when all hell broke loose. We were fighting and it wasn't even a match, and after awhile, Calbert hit him with a fire tool. Slay was just laying there, never responding. We thought we'd killed him. Panic took over from the moment he was he hit and that's how the rest of the night went. Nothing was logical; I did everything in a panic."

"Pretty much everything you ever told me about Sunken Lake has been a lie?"

"It's been a lie. Most of it has been that, but I swear to you that we never killed anyone. And Calbert and I never raped Clara or Latosha."

Lawrence had tilted his head down again and his fists were white-knuckled gripping the steering wheel.

"But I don't feel like I didn't kill anyone. It feels like I killed all of my friends Whitney. I was completely wrong for what I allowed to happen and for my actions that started this whole mess. I was wrong, I know I was wrong. And I'm sorry . . . God I'm sorry!"

Lawrence Blackmon sat there heaving while crying and spitting out apologizes whenever he managed breath for them.

Whitney stood there quietly and allowed him to loiter in his sorrows but again she didn't permit it for very long before plowing a wide pathway right through the center of it.

"You've got to be heir to someone very powerful to keep something this ugly bottled up in silence for so long. Is there anymore of it, are there anymore lies you've not come forward with?"

Positioning his head to normal, Lawrence's eyes showed a sliver of what looked to be happiness hidden in the deepest midst of his existence, and with pride he proclaimed, "Slay is still alive."

The statement was dropped from his lips like he never wanted it held as a secret there in the first place.

"He never died. Everyone was wrong about that. I don't know where he came from but he showed up at Mrs. Sadie's house after Calbert died."

Seeking it all, Whitney pressed, "So the best friend you thought you'd killed was alive all along?"

"Yes. Slay was alive, and that saved my life when I found out."

Whitney had backed a few feet away. This acknowledgement drew her closer again.

"What do you mean it saved your life, how did it do that?"

"It's a kind of strange thing, but the moment Calbert killed himself I felt it. On the inside of me I felt it. Please don't ask me how because I don't know, it's just something that happened kind of spiritually. What's strange also is that I knew why he did it and I had planned something similar. But it obvious, I'm more of a coward than Calbert. I didn't kill myself for killing everybody. Years after he died I did get up the courage. I had gotten drugs, stole them from the clinic, and I was ready. That very same day, I got this letter, it was from Mrs. Sadie. She wrote of this person that wanted to see me. Someone whose life I had saved by hiding him from my father."

As Lawrence ended his revelation, Whitney realized that she was still very much in love with him in spite of the lies he had offered and the many failures that contributed to his existence. After disposing of her own tears, she lovingly reached out to push away the tears Lawrence still easily produced and then gathered his face in her hands to speak softly to him.

"Is Slay aware of everything that happened out here and did he forgive you for what you did to him and all of your friends?"

"Slay knows everything . . . and yes . . . somehow, he's forgiven me. I mean, I can tell he still hurts over losing his parents. Really he hurts over losing everyone and what I tried to do to Clara. I was the only person pushing to be with his girlfriend. Calbert and Big Simms didn't want to have anything to do with it. That's got to hurt him because we looked at each other like brothers and I crossed the line and destroyed everyone's future. He won't allow any discussion about what my father really did to Clara, Big Simms or any of them. He likes to act like they're alive and living their lives some place else and that's just one of the things that's special about seeing him. We laugh and carry on and talk about just about anything. Just like we did when we use to hang out in his backyard, and he makes it feel like that night never happened.

Whitney searched. "You really love this guy don't you, and you could never do anything else to hurt him could you Lawrence?"

For the first time since making a hasty departure from Taylorsville, Lawrence felt hope. He looked up and saw something in Whitney's eyes that wasn't emptiness and then quickly offered a reply.

"Even when Calbert was alive, believing that we had killed Slay was killing me. I miss Calbert like crazy and even sometimes open up and just start talking to him like he was with me, but Slay, no one has ever been as close to me as him. I wish Calbert had known that we didn't kill Slay. It probably would have saved his life. What I want now is for Slay to get back into a normal life. I want to take him to someplace far off where he'll feel comfortable. A place where there's no one that knows anything about us like where you've been offered a job in San Diego. The only thing is . . . he'll never go."

A smile appeared through the tears of Whitney, her search had ended.

"I believe you Lawrence, and I believe in you. I don't know why I continue to after all the lies you've told me, but I do. And if your friend has forgiven you with all he's lost, then I'm sure I can do the same. But Lawrence, only after you've taken this to the authorities so that it can be settled properly."

Lawrence cracked open the door to the vehicle and Whitney gave ground to allow him out and then wrapped tightly into his chest.

"You didn't give up on me. Thank you."

"Never babe, we're about to be married and you better never give up on that."

"You don't know how much I needed to hear you say those words. And I can face the world with this with you by my side. I definitely need you."

Whitney nodded while responding, "Lawrence I'm angry with you but proud of you also for being ready to stand up to this matter. And yes we'll do it together and it doesn't' matter how long it takes to get it behind us or who threatens us in the process."

A tiny smile eased into Lawrence as he recalled a recent event.

"I was on the verge of loosing it right in front of you earlier in Gulleytown out in front of the Freeman's home."

"Are you referring to when you saw Latosha's mom?"

"That rattled me. I mean I was spooked out. Where is she and where has she been? I need to talk to . . . ."

"Don't Lawrence. Don't attempt to do anything. She's the type that will contact you if it's necessary but please don't try bothering her."

"But I've got to tell her . . . ."

"No." Whitney interrupted him again. "Trust me on this babe. She desires to be left alone."

Lawrence bit down on his lip at the request for it was a challenging one for him, and after several moments headed the discussion in another direction.

"On three month intervals, Slay and I meet up in Gulleytown. We had a scheduled meeting set up for the past Thursday but somehow missed each other which have never happened before. If you've noticed any strangeness to my behavior, that's mostly the reason. I don't know where the heck he was but hopefully before long he'll get out to Mrs. Sadies' and we'll see if we can schedule another hook up as fast as possible. And I will tell him that Mrs. Williams is alive and about you knowing what happened and our plans to move forward. You've got to give me the opportunity to inform him before we go to the authorities."

Lawrence hugged his love strongly into the woman he thought he had lost forever only moments ago. And with every ounce of strength she owned, Whitney clutched back to him. She never wanted to let him go again and hated with all of her heart what she had to deliver to her Lawrence. While gritting her teeth she turned once against his chest and then twice before allowing her statement to release from her deepest depths.

"He's dead Lawrence."

Lawrence Blackmon had stiffened all over before pushing backwards. He held Whitney at arms length and murmured, "What? What did you say?"

Whitney tried forcing her way back but was disallowed as Lawrence moved further back to stand within his vehicles' door.

"Someone has taken his life babe. Latosha's mom explained it to me while she was here."

Originally Whitney couldn't decipher the facial expression offered by Lawrence and then it suddenly became crystal clear as his anger made an exit by way of his hands and into the shoulders of his fiancée. There was a forceful shout.

"You're lying! You didn't even know he was alive and you're making that up to hurt me because you think I raped Latosha and Clara."

"Lawrence, you're hurting me." Whitney attempted to wrestle free. "I'm telling you the truth Lawrence. He's in the woods somewhere near wherever you chased them."

The shouting continued as Lawrence held to Whitney with more firmness.

"You're lying and I want you to say you are! No one can even get close to him out in the woods because he knows them too well and you're going to stand here and lie and say that someone killed him in them. No. You're lying and I want you to tell me you are."

"Lawrence, I told you that you were hurting me and I'm not lying to you. Mrs. Williams said that someone had found him. Babe, I'm sorry."

"You liar!" Lawrence flung her from his grasp and went around the vehicle in a hard run as Whitney twisted down to the ground.

"Come back here! Lawrence . . . Lawrence . . . where are you going?"

Whitney yelled after him but Lawrence never answered back. He was gone. He ran mindlessly. The emptiness that had captured him earlier in the night in Taylorsville was back and Lawrence heard not a single word begging for his focus from his beloved Whitney.

In search of the direction he was tearing off in, Whitney made it back to her feet. Grabbing her attention were lights that flashed over her from a vehicle that was pulling into the dark drive and rolling slowly over to her.

Whitney brushed small bits of dirt and gravel from her hands while running back towards the cabin.

Her shoes were in front of the sofa where she had lain and Whitney went directly for them and was back out of the home instantly and running like a woman on fire.

Henly Blackmon had ended the ignition to his long white car and managed his way out and was more stunned than alarmed at the sight of the tiny woman sprinting away from his lake cabin.

"Hey . . . hey you . . . stop! Damn it girl I know you hear me. I said stop," he yelled.

Whitney Connors never slowed her pace, nor did she ever look in his direction.

Infuriated, Henly made a reactionary attempt in the direction of the young woman but ended it at the front bumper of the only other vehicle parked on his property. His lunge was only the length of a car but it gave rise to a nasty cough and hack.

The cabin had been left unsecured, the front door open. Henly made his way for it and after only a few moments inside he returned in a rush for the jeep. The door was never closed and stenciled on it in large letters was the name of Lawrence Blackmon. At recognition Henly's flesh stung, and beneath his banana hat the wide pulsating vein that traveled up the center of his forehead looked as though it would burst with red hatred.

One liver-spotted hand of Henly looped around his waist to displace a handgun from his belt and he clicked off the safety while he slammed the other hand against his chest to check the thundering rhythm of his heart. Henly then embarked on a lumbering trot in the direction of Gulleytown.

FULLY EXPOSED, THE MOON glowed low over Rix late Saturday night and the light it provided was desperately needed by each of the individuals running in carbon darkness into the woods dividing Sunken Lake from Gulleytown. Lawrence Blackmon led the chase and was in a state of mind that was so cloudy he could see very little anyway. Minimum attention was granted to all things he came across until Lawrence came within one hundred feet of the remains of Slay Builder. His torrid pace slowed as the very first haunting image exploded through his conscious and it damaged him less than fifteen minutes after Whitney had assured him he was not being haunted but Lawrence truly was. Above him in the trees and behind every bush Lawrence encountered disturbing sounds to match troubling sights of suffering not belonging to this world and further unbalancing him. The images twisted down into his emptiness in ways he never imagined possible. Lawrence could hear voices that were strangled as they tirelessly grasped for breath and he got a clear visual of the churning legs of small children as they ran seeking the protection of their mothers. But there was no escaping from the evil that sought them. There was a crackle and hiss of human flesh burning, the smell of it forced Lawrence to a stop and stricken him down to a knee.

Lawrence looked from one direction to the next and was invaded with more and more sickening sounds and images that overloaded him. There appeared no escaping from what haunted him. He looked towards the heavens and for all he was worth, Lawrence Blackmon wished he could have taken the decision back for it was far too late, he had already committed.

Death came down to smother him from almost every large tree. He encountered repulsive death of the very young and old at its ugly beginning to the very end.

Desperate frightened men spun through air in circles like large fiery tops while hanging from strong ropes. Below them on the ground stood men that looked in many ways like Lawrence's father, they held torches and wore plastered smiles. Swinging from limbs next to their mothers were the smallest of little ones, kids who were barely old enough to be called little boys. They were entangled in rope in odd broken positions with cattle wire twisting cruelly about their tiny arms.

As he remained down on one knee Lawrence was haunted by these god-awful sights but he was especially brought to mercy by the sight of tiny little girls not yet even of age to enter school but saddled with confused abysmal looks as their tiny legs churned in airy space while attempting to remain alive as they hung next to their ax-broken fathers like disturbing ornaments.

Lawrence Blackmon was somehow able to get to his feet again and managed to force his way forward ascertain that every tree he passed uprooted from the soil to follow his every step.

Calbert Davis had long ago described these haunting sights and sounds to Lawrence for he had lived with them everyday since venturing within feet of the place referred to as Sacred Hills. Lawrence also had been near this particular area and had become transfixed with all he saw but his experience had been nothing like what Calbert had lived with. All had now changed and the uniquely special place was granting him full exposure. The vexing images boring down into him had snatched the true focus and direction away from Lawrence and he had fallen so deeply into this new world that he had not noticed that his travel had delivered him upon the burned remains of his friend until a lone leaf displaced from a tree came falling slowly before him. Its descent delivered his reality back. Lawrence followed its twisting movements down to where a muddy pair of boots and military fatigues had been discarded against a fallen tree. All were items he was very familiar with. Slay Builder had always worn them.

And then Lawrence saw what was left of his old friend and the night opened up.

"Ooooooowww!"

The cry Lawrence emitted was a defeated, wounded one and it blended with perfection with every inhuman sound that had captured his arrival as he traveled deeper into the woods. Lawrence had used several things to help prop up his own existence but in this death of Slay Builder all of his foundation crumbled. Lawrence Blackmon again looked up for the heavens and this would be the mistake he would never recover from.

For years, death had sought Lawrence to settle the injustices of his past. His body as hollowed as it had become had finally been found and its entry came fast, much to fast.

TAYLORSVILLE

LAWRENCE BLACKMON HAD RACED from my presence and my property a little more than an hour ago but I remained pretty much as he had left me. I made entry to my home to retrieve a housecoat but came immediately back to the very spot that my grandchild Calbert and I enjoyed more than any other. I am a recipient of a blessing tonight that I am very thankful. My eyes are allowing me to take in the world again with only a semblance of gray remaining. Lawrence Blackmon saw to that blessing, bless his heart.

My presence out this late is a repetitive activity that I have not exposed myself too since first acquiring the grayish shade and although I was not aware of it at the time, Lawrence had saw to that also.

I have not taken leave of my position for several reasons and the first of them are the deep concerns I felt transmitting from Lawrence before he pulled away from this old home of mine. The coldness in his touch and the deadness in his words reminded me to much of what I had felt and heard my Calbert repeat over and over all the way up to the point when he ran away from this county to hide behind another one far away.

Wrongfully, my troubled grandchild believed that if he could just leave this little town far enough behind and distance himself from those red hills that lay between Gulleytown and Sunken Lake that all that troubled him would somehow shed away from him like dead skin.

As I relayed earlier on in this tale, lying is something that has no place in my life, so what I convey to you now comes under the sincerest belief. Soon after my Calbert took his own life, I felt him enter me through the marrow of my bones. His spirit traveled out of that hot desert in that faraway place and crossed back over that wide body of water to show up back here in Taylorsville to live on with me. And that is the second and the purest reason I remain outside sitting in my position at this ungodly hour for me. Calbert wanted to be here. He wanted us here together. Only moments ago he took leave of my body for the very first time since his arrival and I felt his presence down next to me on his small stool, the very one that Lawrence Blackmon had sat beneath me on. From there my beautiful grandchild has kept my attention focused in the direction of those black woods that back Gulleytown, and his spirit had asked me to keep a careful watch over that hallowed place down there that holds so many ghosts.

The unnatural process of offspring succumbing to death before elders is a path laid by my family. My daughter and grandson expired prior to me and Calbert left no legacy. But he did leave his spirit and I remain sitting here tonight for his spirit and for Calbert. I'm watching for him and his spirit waited with me.

IT APPEARED TO WHITNEY that the further she pushed into the woods, the deeper they shaded into blackness. When her charge after Lawrence had begun, she could see several yards ahead but after entering the dense woods that advantage was lost and she was restricted to seeing only what was directly in front of her. She stopped once momentarily to catch her breath and to try to gain some point of reference as to what direction to continue on in. She found none but pushed on irregardless in a calling search for her Lawrence.

Trees of a variety were everywhere and some as tall as she had ever seen. Onward she advanced, splitting pines and squeezing by small bushes. Whitney ducked beneath a low branch as she palmed the hairy bark of a large tree to adjust around it while at the same time lowering her focus to balance over a fallen tree that lay across the path she had chosen. Whitney wasn't able to make another step after colliding into to someone she had not seen.

Her scream was deafening, loud enough to wake up the dark and shrink every tree in the woods to the height of her shoulders.

FOR A MALE of his age and size with so many ailments, Henly Blackmon advanced fluidly across his property until a screaming cry slowed his advance. Sweating profusely, he stopped to cough and wheeze for several moments before resuming the deliberate pace that had him shuffling directly towards the location he had ended the life of Slay Builder a few nights ago which was in the direction of the scream.

As he had aged, Henly's large pinkish presence had gotten disturbingly worse to look upon and was one of the central factors why it was a rarity to see him at any social gathering or public events. In fact, he would have been relaxing and enjoying another day of fishing two counties over from Rix if not for the consistent and painstaking phone calls from a hysterical Dennis Jacobs. The distressing calls had pulled Henly home a full day earlier than he had originally planned. After arriving back into the county, Henly had gone immediately to the Jacob's home and had discovered his life long friend lying face up in the pond in back of his home with a large hole where his lower jaw once was. The horror was magnified even more at the scene of Dennis Jacobs' death; large catfish nibbled away at his blotted flesh and the sight that Henly would never forget was the severed head of Fanny Jacobs clutched in one of his hands. Shaken, Henly disappeared purposely from the property without ever stepping inside the quiet home to view the remainder of the destroyed body of Fanny Jacobs.

Being a shrewd man was something that Henly always fancied himself as and his instincts were a big part of the man that he had become. Some of the final beliefs that Dennis Jacobs shared with him were that his home continued to be haunted and that so was the cabin that Henly himself owned. The information alone had pushed Henly over to his lake property after his hasty exit from the Jacobs' home.

THE YOUNG LADY that was seen racing away from the cabin had been located, but Henly was denied full observance of her by heavy foliage compounded by intense darkness. Her sobs were breathless and Henly circled the point of origin to gain a better view.

WHITNEY HAD NOT TAKEN the same route into the woods that Lawrence had. Instead of chasing on a straight path after him, she had zigzagged her way through and had come across him by pure accident.

As she had ran away from the cabin, Whitney had given a glimpse of notice to a large man shouting towards her but had no idea who he was or that he had followed her and at that very moment she had absolutely no knowledge of his presence in back of her.

The gun Henly held in his hand remained there and it was the same one he had held against Latosha Williams, the exact revolver he had threaten the life of Lawrence with and the very weapon he had taken the life of Slay Builder with.

Henly had positioned at about ten yards behind her, where he could observe Whitney clearly and steadied his gun at the back of her head. Even though he had made somewhat of a circle to get a clearer view of her, Henly had taken almost the exact route into the woods that his son had to come immediately upon them.

Utilizing her entire body, Whitney strained and her face was in a fixed grimace as sweat sprinkled the middle section of her back. From a squatted stance she pushed down into her heels with all her might, fighting her hardest to steady Lawrence's legs against her body as she struggled with strength she never knew she owned to balance his feet back up on to the fallen tree he had stepped away from. Lawrence Blackmon had hung himself from the noose left hanging over Slay Builder.

From the frigid blue eyes of Lawrence came a dishearten stare, the loop of his spectacles had fallen from one of his ears and had tilted the glasses across his reddened nose. They were enlarged eyes that illustrated strain as they protruded outwards. His tongue had darkened and circled backwards in a curl, Whitney could see it from the slight opening to Lawrence's mouth. To her it looked as if something deep inside of him had attached an anchor to it and was pulling it from his mouth down into him. Just observing Lawrence and the manner he swayed quiet and all alone in the darkness was crippling to Whitney for it was the most crippling sight she had ever captured. The look on his face was horrific and just immobilizing. Whitney hated having to keep looking up into his stare but did so with regularity while willing a belief that if she could just get his back securely on the tree that Lawrence had stepped away from, then the man she loved would some how breathe to life again. In a voice filled with hurt and shock she cried out.

"Lawrence you've got to help me! Please step back . . . you can't do this to us . . . not now!"

Over the course of his lifetime, Henly Blackmon had seen his share of individuals hanging from trees to realize that his only son was dead and that nothing anyone could do would bring him back. Lawrence hung heavy in his death before him and although at a time earlier Henly had wanted his son dead by any manner, this sight saddened him and it softened Henly enough that he had lowered his weapon. The hardened hostility within him dispersed and Henly was overcome by memories he had once treasured of some of the childhood of his son. There was truly a side of gentleness to Henly Blackmon, one that few had ever seen, but this placid showing didn't last for more than a few moments before his raging anger returned with abruptness. Snarling, Henly stepped in a few feet closer to the charred remains of Slay Builder which were only a few feet from where Whitney was.

"What business you got on this property and what you doing with my Youngun?"

Since stumbling upon Lawrence, Whitney's entire focus had been lost, however, through her haze; she realized that someone had spoken. Whitney hadn't made out a word of what was said but she did swivel enough to gather a glimpse of the khaki pants the man looming behind her was wearing before retuning her efforts to Lawrence, and even if she had fully observed Henly, Whitney would still have only seen Lawrence for he was truly her only focus. The young woman had no idea that her life was on the verge of being taken. She begged.

"Can you please help me? I'm trying but I can't lift him on my own. Lawrence," Whitney yelled up into a death stare again. "Hold on babe . . . someone's here to help us."

With one hand flattened over his chest, Henly coughed until his eyes watered and then disposed of a mouthful of yellow bile. Beneath clammy skin, his fury could be seen rising like scalding

192

steam. While stepping over the remains of Slay Builder to come right up to Whitney, he aimed his revolver again and then spoke through clenched teeth.

"Help yourself to this nigger."

While one of Henly's fingers circled the trigger to his weapon, his view of what was taking place on his property suddenly changed. He looked up from Whitney and past his son and there was much activity taking place above them and it was extreme in every aspect. The haunting images that Calbert Davis lived with were there. The burning bodies of the children Pete Crance had bared witness too and carried around like his cross were present. Henly could also see the horrific sightings that Dennis Jacobs could never escape as they pushed down out of the trees and mandated that he give up his life as he had.

The black woods had exploded with death that had come screaming back to life again. Henly twisted and twisted more seeking an escape but it was to no avail because from each direction he was greeted with a similar death of the innocent coming back to life. On the soil of the woods below him the decaying body of Slay Builder began a reform and drew large heaving breaths. The young man crackled up laughter while wrapping his arms around the sock-less ankles of Henly. Disoriented, Henly yelled out and pushed backwards to widen his stance but the effort did not break him free of Slay nor anything else he was imagining that had gained a hold of him.

Henly aimed and fired several death-carrying slugs into the corpse of Slay Builder which only heightened the laughter brimming up from below.

The gunshots served to force a bit of reality back into Whitney Connors. She shuddered and screamed as she released Lawrence and rolled away to sit with both feet flat and her hands up cupping her ears.

In the midst of all that had begun to confuse Henly, he did realize that it was his rope hanging above him that held his son. In bitter frustration, he emptied several more bullets into old trees making bark scatter. Henly did this in fear of the trees, he felt that they were closing in on him and afterwards he coughed up more of his insides.

An array of activity continued up above Henly. Bodies hung oddly from tree branches in every direction and they begun to become untwisted from the ropes of death and jumped from the trees. Some drew his gunfire.

"Stop it. Would you please just stop shouting," Whitney screamed. "What are you firing at, there's nothing there? Nothing, look around."

Whitney pushed out her hands indicating to Henly their surrounding.

Attempting to reload his revolver, Henly lost as many bullets to the woods as he got to fit into the weapon. He was befuddled in his fear of what he was convinced he was observing take place, but the voice of Whitney dictated his attention and then his focus and the short barrel of his gun back to her.

"You fuckin' crawlin' nigger . . . you're the one that's behind all of this."

"Don't you dare blame your nasty evil on this beautiful girl."

Appearing from Whitney's left, Catherine Williams stepped closer and it was like she had surfaced from a hole in the darkness. The exact gentle nature canvassed her face that Whitney had observed earlier and the tiny woman had taken on and even younger appearance in those forever dark woods.

Her hands were hidden inside of her varsity football jacket and even in this instance of peril; Catherine Williams shared an easy smile that was out of place for that particular moment. It spread her lips thin and served as a tool to whiten the red skin around the twitching eyes of Henly Blackmon.

The caring, petite mother of three murdered children had keen knowledge of the tendencies of Henly for over the years of her disappearance from society she had studied him immensely and before leaving it all behind had already survived and experience with the hatred that was now staring her down.

"And don't you for one moment believe that you killed Slay. He killed himself. You just lit the match because you ain't man enough to defeat him on your own. I can't say I ever saw it coming to end this way 'cause I didn't and I'm not putting much effort towards understanding why he let it happen because there are some things in this world that just ain't meant to be figured out. And Slay ain't the one that cut open that old dirty sheriff in Gulleytown. You standing here looking at the ghost that killed that baby rapist. And I'm the same little ghost that saw the Jacobs fellow fall dead in his pond carrying around a head in his hand."

The revelations settled in on Henly as Catherine Williams paused her thoughts to allow him to really concentrate on her presence. She wanted Henly to completely take in her existence.

"What's wrong with you Mayor, having some kind a problem remembering me? How could you forget the night that you and your old Sheriff drove off with Latosha and left my other two babies burning in Gulleytown?"

That unbecoming smile that Catherine Williams gave off had disappeared.

"You remember now don't you Mayor Blackmon? Thought you had killed me off didn't you? Well you were wrong and that's what you are and that's all you've ever been. You may have burned down that home but I found a better one. Right here out on your property with all of my babies is where I live now and I know the good lord is letting you get a good look at 'em now. You hear 'em crying? They've been doing that since you left 'em."

From her seated position, Whitney looked around again and took in the environment. She could see nothing other than the forest and no one besides the three of them, the remains of Slay Builder on the ground and Lawrence swaying from a tree branch. And it was at that point that the reality of his death found its rightful place on her and the pain of it filled her body and welled all the way up to her throat. Whitney swallowed hard on it before shifting her focus towards the deranged man with the firearm but he couldn't hold it for long, for Catherine Williams was in demand of both their attention.

"The way the spirit of the lord works is so amazing," she exclaimed while smiling again. "There ain't no other way to explain why this land was chosen out of all others to be a home for wandering spirits to come to get whatever peace they want on probably the most hateful man that's ever lived property."

Henly Blackmon continued to be tangled up by Catherine Williams and he had not to that moment offered a word in reply.

Rotating a focus to them both was Whitney Connors who was very much surprised to notice a form of true hatred in the eyes of Catherine Williams.

"If its one thing I know about you Mayor Blackmon, it's that you ain't in no way human like the lord intended us all to be. But I want you to imagine something if you can. Imagine how it might feel to be hunted down and treated worse than an animal just because you don't look like somebody else. Can you just imagine how small children felt, not knowing why they had to run but running out in these woods and running for their lives, wondering if the breath they was breathing would be the last? That's exactly how I felt when I was running out into these woods with Slay away from you."

She stopped momentarily to force a hand from one of her pockets and pointed it toward Henly.

"You ain't nothing but the devil Mayor Blackmon and you rotten all the way down to the core."

"And you a little witch," Henly finally gave to open up his thoughts. But he had turned from Catherine Williams and was addressing them to Whitney instead.

"She ain't real because they pulled her stinking bones out of the fire."

Henly was nervous and it was evident. He fumbled his gun from one hand to the other as haunting images of the dark woods continued a relentless pursuit of him and with a belief that Catherine Williams was one of these images and did not exist at, he continued to address Whitney.

"Now I want you to get all these other things away from me!"

"You saw what you wanted in those ashes Mayor and that old dirty sheriff of yours had been of late trying to tell you, you should have listened."

"You better get all of these other smutty niggers to leave me alone you stinking witch." He pointed the gun down at the remains of Slay Builder. "You ain't had nothing to do with what happened to Pete, this boy down here killed him."

Whitney stood and while doing so brushed into Lawrence and forced his body into a larger sway, but her concentration was properly jetted towards the delirious man in front of her with the gun. She took a tiny peek at the burned remains of Slay Builder that lay in the position she had originally encountered them.

"Slay might of killed a lot of flies as a small boy but that's as far as his killing goes. I never saw him kill anything else in his life except for deer and rabbit and whatever else he could trap for us to survive on. He didn't have the kind of heart to kill a person."

The arms of Catherine Williams had been spread wide before she exclaimed, "You see Mayor Blackmon, you been having folks searching all over the place for the wrong ghost of Gulleytown. The one you really wanted is right here in front of you."

Henly reacted to the unnatural events occurring around him in a purely natural frightened manner although he believed all of it to be witchcraft that he could not explain and it most definitely included the existence of Catherine Williams. Burning in anger, he attempted a step forward but went stumbling backwards instead. After regaining balance, he kicked out wildly while squeezing down on the trigger of the revolver to send three more slugs into the remains of Slay Builder and he kept firing even when only empty clicks could be heard. He yelled.

"Let go of me you stinkin' nigger."

Soon after hearing the empty clicks from the handgun, Whitney decided to take a chance. She ducked beneath a swinging arm of Henly and ran over to Catherine Williams who waited to receive her.

More empty clicks sounded off behind her reinforcing the fact that there were no more bullets remaining on Henly's person.

With a specific aim on Whitney, Henly continued to squeeze on the handguns' trigger and only stopped to swing madly at some haunting image that had apparently gotten too close to him. The forcefulness of his attempt took him clumsily off balance to land in a giant spill atop Slay Builder, with whom he immediately unleashed his fight upon.

Without a single rugged cough, Henly rolled about the ground doing battling against foes and spirits that only his eyes could see.

With an exhausted grunt, he kicked out at something before rolling to one side to click the trigger one final time towards the face of a confounded Whitney Connors.

"It's empty Mayor," Catherine Williams flatly offered. "Just like the life you done lived. You've either run off or killed everybody who's ever tried to care something about you." She pointed. "Look up at what you've done to your boy. Lawrence may have jumped in that rope but you the one that killed him."

The focus of Henly was on Whitney but following this statement he allowed his eyes to close down and settle on only Lawrence. Thought buried deep in his heart; there still was a bit of compassion cavities for his son there. In a touching display of it, Henly held his hand up and reached out towards Lawrence.

The moment of empathy was immediately extinguish as he snatched away his hand to pull a long knife from a sheath strapped to his legs. An ugly cough ousted a steam of yellowish hate from his mouth as Henly pounced to his feet like a cornered animal.

Whitney screamed at the sight of the enraged man bent forward charging towards her.

Henly had cut the distance in half that separated them before either woman could properly react.

In one motion tight with aggression, Whitney was literally drug out of one of her shoes by a determined Catherine Williams.

"Run Sweetie!"

Stumbling, Henly fell towards them, spilling awkwardly on his upper body. He twisted in his fall and eventually rolled over near Whitney's heels and was up to his feet again fast as if he had planned the hard tumble. After missing on an attempt to seize her, he slung his empty handgun in her direction and was already chasing again before the gun met with force against the small of the young lady's back.

The pain was sharp and it forced Whitney forward.

Catherine Williams snatched at her arm again, dragging Whitney while encouraging her back up right.

"Keep your balance. We've got to keep moving."

With a hand out grasping forward, Henly grunted as he came up fast on them a second time.

Peeking over her shoulder and watching the large man come up so close behind them prompted Whitney to believe that it was a foregone conclusion that he was merely taunting them first before unleashing his venom.

Catherine Williams turned to admonish Whitney once more.

"Stop looking back and run."

Whitney obeyed. In union the two women easily jumped a sinkhole and ducked several tree branches.

Whitney was terrified and couldn't be faulted for looking over her shoulders again. Scanning back her horror was realized. The taunting had come to an end. She captured in full the sickening sight as the crazed man behind them reared back to plunge his knife down into her. The fear of it pulled a chilling scream from within Whitney that could have awakened the entire county.

TAYLORSVILLE

THE SPIRIT OF Calbert was right here with me when I pushed away from my rocker. I got to my feet and I mean I got to them fast. The night sky down there above my beloved Rix burst into brightness like God almighty had laid palms on it, and for all I know he had.

I no longer possess much strength, but the little that remained emptied out of me and I was rendered down to my knees like I had been tossed like a sack of feed. My eyes though were allowed to continue a strengthened hold to the near distance and for the first in years there was nothing there any longer to cloud my vision. I could see perfectly. Every remaining encumbrance of gray was immediately cleansed away. I was given strength back to rise but I remained on my knees and I prayed.

"Lord God almighty give 'em strength . . . please heavenly father . . . help somebody, please?"

A CHANGE HELD INFLUNCE over Whitney and the life she would endure and it didn't occur over any stretch of time. It happened instantly. The people that cared for her were no longer a thought. Her manner of living held no importance. Where she was given birth and by whom and all the precious gifts of life that mattered had been lost. While lunging forward to escape the knife driving down for her, Whitney had encountered a light form so magnificently pure that it erased away her sight and the inability was only the beginning of what transpired into being.

Complete calm had captured her and spread to wash away her every fear past and present and Whitney's marvel began as her vision cleared.

Her presence illuminated in a faultless light and that emanated a celestial glow. Whitney pondered whether she had reached the afterlife. She sat weightless and unblemished in deafening quiet and was without even a stain of sweat anymore. In wonder and not yet ready to remove her focus from the magnificent glow that held her in capture, Whitney's thoughts evolved from there. She endured a sudden fulfillment of aged wisdom that was totally pure as she positioned to sit straight up on red dirt that was without impression which Whitney could not feel beneath her.

Sitting motionless and quiet beside Whitney was Catherine Williams aglow in her presence also. As Whitney looked over to her, the older woman directed her focus over their shoulders to where Henly Blackmon was still clutching to his knife with one hand. With disbelief masking his face, Henly teetered on the line of where the woods abruptly ended and Sacred Hills began, he remained at the exact point where Whitney had last turned to capture the deadly action he presented against her in the darkest forest she had ever entered.

Only feet away from Henly Blackmon were small Georgia red clay mounds that numbered in the hundreds and all looked as though they were cloned from one another. They jumped up out of the earth in remarkable fashion as far as he could see beneath a majestic light that narrowed down to cover only the area that they were in.

This wonder and these hills were not unfamiliar to Henly for he had encountered them before in the presence of Lawrence and Calbert Davis. He was aware that the hills only were viewable when the dark night above them lit up with light. Henly also knew of the mystery that surrounded them but instead of turning and walking away like he had done before, he decided to refocus his concentration on Whitney. She had been the lone individual he had seen running away from his cabin and the very same person he believed to have at least something to do with Lawrence swinging from a rope behind him. Henly continued to relegate Catherine Williams as just another ghostly image created by witchcraft like all the others he had encountered over the night intent on altering his thoughts. As he looked down on Whitney, Henly didn't observe the existence of placid calm she was at rest in. His vision offered up a woman stricken in fear sitting right before him. He envisioned her in the same manner of fear he had seen in Latosha Williams before he had raped her in the back of the sheriff cruiser driven by Pete Crance after they had stolen her from her mother's home.

The unwelcome presence of the disabling light had ended his pursuit of Whitney momentarily but he had not given up on destroying her.

From the small hill directly in front of Henly, Whitney Connors touched the arm of the tiny woman that sit right next to her before speaking.

"Mrs. Williams?"

A respond came to Whitney but Catherine Williams never looked her way.

"Yes Sweetie."

"I can't feel anything. I'm touching you but I don't feel you. What's happened to me . . . why did we stop running? Please help me understand what's taken place?"

"Whitney we didn't stop running we were stopped and we were stopped because there's no need to run any further. We've made it where we need to be and he can't do nothing to harm us now and he won't be fool enough to make a mistake that can he never take back by coming any further."

"I don't understand. Why can't he?"

An answer was not provided. Catherine Williams however did look over to Whitney and then immediately returned her focus to the place where Henly Blackmon remained. Whitney did likewise and for the very first time really searched the face of the man who sought to end her life. What she took in reminded her much of the man she had fallen in love with. The high cheekbones, Henly's nose, the dimple that centered his chin and those sea blue eyes all described her Lawrence. Everything about the face she looked upon except the scowl of bitter hate reminded her of the man she had wished to marry. After several moments Whitney turned calmly from Henly to search the mystic place she had settled in and after several more moments had more questions to present.

"Where are we? This place, what is this?"

A smile that truly belonged on the face of Catherine Williams came easily and she provided Whitney a reply in her very motherly manner.

"You've been given a little piece of God. You can call it heaven, home or whatever you want because right now it belongs to you. And no harm can come to you here because we're in a place he can't ever visit. Circled around us are spirits and they'll never let him in. Where we are my Sweetie is wrapped up in the arms of heaven. That's what we called it, me and Slay. Only people in need can come in here with God's angels to be protected." Her smile continued even though it had faded some as she finished off. "The only other thing you need to know about where we are is that it's blessed, and you are too for being let in."

Henly Blackmon had moved several feet back and Catherine Williams watched as he did and afterwards spoke directly to him what was on her heart.

"Lawrence has passed on Mayor Blackmon and he passed over in a troubling way. His passing left a heap of unanswered questions plus it left you with a taste of loosing a baby you was blessed to birth. I didn't kill your baby like you did mine but I'm ready to move on from it. I count five people dead in the last week and that's too much killing. This all needs to come to an end. Keep out of Gulleytown and you won't have to worry about seeing this face no more and we'll let everybody in this town live in peace like they want."

The scowl Henly hid beneath disappeared and a hint of color showed in his face. He slumped away from his intensity as he looked directly at Whitney and then finally bowed his head and hid his eyes beneath the brim of his hat. Henly never responded by use of his words but a small nod acknowledged his agreement to what he had heard. The knife dropped from his hand and like someone was remotely controlling his abilities; Henly turned and began a slumbered walk in the direction of his cabin without ever looking up again.

The retreat signaled an instant disappearance of the light cascading down from the heavens and the small hills were gone likewise as all returned to normal in the small area between Sunken Lake and Gulleytown.

It occurred suddenly as if a switch had been flicked from off to on again. Pure brightness was back and it showed Whitney in an embrace with Catherine Williams sitting in peace in Sacred Hills. The re-emergence of light also highlighted the return of the terrifying presence of Henly Blackmon lurching beastly through mid air towards the two ladies.

With his long knife in hand again, one of his elbows was bent dangerously back near his head.

Neither woman broke their embrace nor did they move one inch. It was as though they never saw the attack coming or the reappearance of the light and what took place around them occurred in frames of motion that were slowed down like a slide show.

As Henly entered the light totally outstretched, he became frozen in levitation. His emotion of massive hatred went to the complete fear of the unknown. A flame sparked first from the hand Henly grasped to the knife with and from there it traveled up his arm to the shoulder and eventually throughout his entire body. The last to burn was Henly's face, and when it did it burned to the reddish color of red before completely blackening. In a large hovering ball Henly began melting away, but nothing that burned from him ever touched the hollowed grounds of Sacred Hills. Everything smoldered upwards instead of down and eventually so did Henly.

He had burned suspended no more than four feet above the ground before beginning to rise. Henly was pitched upwards slowly at first and then faster as he cleared the trees. He was being held up and pushed backwards by the strong winds of angels flapping their wings. Angels that always appeared with the arrival of Sacred Hills and they had surrounded Catherine Williams and Whitney Connors.

Henly had been lifted high and pushed back over the dark woods of his property. As he passed over his cabin, the lower half of him dropped away and exploded the lake home into a raging fire that went out of control immediately.

The illumination diving down from the heavens ended again for a final time as what remained of Henly Blackmon landed in a burning splash in the dead center of Sunken Lake. The dark water gulped him down but hurriedly spit Henly back up to the surface where he continued to burn through the night and was still aflame when the sun appeared the following morning. At that point his remains were flushed down into a hole that miraculously cracked open in the bottom of the lake. With Henly inside, it sealed in a similar remarkable fashion.

The instant that Henly Blackmon went beneath the surface of the water, it thundered once and the air over the county got heavy and moist. The bursting thunder was like none ever heard. The sound from it vibrated into a humming sound that lasted for six full days. A horrendous smell invaded the county and it came in with a muggy fog. Both fell over Sunken Lake like a blanket and it killed everything with life that lived within it.

CHAPTER 7

TAYLORSVILLE

MAY 2000

Early on in this tale you were enlightened on how the depiction of a homer befits me. That description is not as accurate anymore as it once was. I lifted away from my rocker and finally journeyed away from this clay road and found a way out to a place called California and the city of San Diego. From east Georgia that's about as far I could get before dropping off into the sea.

There is a beautiful child who has become pretty much the center of my life and my traveling to San Diego was due in every aspect to her. Ms. Whitney Connors has taken me to quite a few other places also and they all appeared to be kingdoms of other worlds when compared to Rix County.

My Whitney has a spirit about her that seems as if it's as old as mine and that's probably the reason why we get along so well. About four months after the Saturday Lawrence introduced her to Rix, Whitney showed up in Taylorsville. I felt the comforting presence of my Calbert immediately after her arrival and once Whitney and I sat down and began talking, we didn't stop for two entire days. It didn't take us very long to develop affection for one another.

Before her first visit with me, Whitney had accepted a position that would send her to live in San Diego and before I knew it she had educed a promise from me to visit her there. To ensure our very spiritual bond remains strong, twice this year I have already gone west for a visit and she has been back to Taylorsville twice.

It has been almost a year since a tunnel of light channeled through the Rix night for all to see and a good many did from every section of the county. They witnessed the miracle as I had and it's made a positive difference that is easily seen in all our lives, for we are certain now that they do occur.

Henly Blackmon had been broken in half. The lower portion of his body had fallen onto his cabin and it burned there until the moment his other half was swallowed down by the lake. The second afterwards, it rained for six straight days. Black storm clouds dumped a river of rain water into the cabin but it continued to simmer irregardless and stayed hot even past the rain. When the home finally did release its burn, there were no remains of Henly Blackmon.

County residents marvel over what we witnessed take place in our small town and because of it the jails and criminal courts have remained empty and not even a verbal assault has been recorded between anyone. That's a lot more of a miracle to me than anything else that's happen here.

The estate of Henly Blackmon was settled six months earlier. All that he had accumulated in life including his inheritance were left to his brethren in hatred but they all renounced it and it eventually ended up in the hands of his older brother Ray Blackmon.

With Whitney's assistance, it took Ray Blackmon less than a month to locate Lawrence's sister Sarah Planster. The only surviving child of Henly now lived in Provo, Utah. Once Sarah was found, Ray signed over all of the assets and properties to her and her husband Kenneth and their three children.

THE MORNING FOLLOWING the death of Henly Blackmon, the flat clearing on the edge of his property had filled in with thick grass and tiny pine trees were growing from the soil there. The open space was no longer there and with its disappearance, Rix had lost the amazing place that distinguished it from any other city, place or town anywhere. Sacred Hills was no longer.

There is not a single night that passes that I don't pray a few words for just one opportunity to sit down with the wandering Catherine Williams. I would welcome the chance to learn of some of her secrets and that goes especially for her knowledge of those small red hills and her special relationship with the angels that lived in the midst of them. But she disappeared from Rix right along with them. Even my lovely child Whitney doesn't know the exact moment of her departure, she just looked around the morning after Lawrence had hung himself and Catherine Williams, the small woman that had protected her, was no longer there.

The spirit of my beautiful grandchild Calbert Davis escaped from my inner beings for good when the heavens went dark and Henly Blackmon began burning away from this world. And aside from the initial day when Whitney showed up at my home, Calbert's spirit hasn't come around to keep me company anymore. With all my heart I believe that my grandchild hung around this old home with me for all of those years just for the purpose of witnessing pure evil being put to death. I miss Calbert and always will but just not as much as I use to now that I know he's at rest.

I am finally enjoying the latter years of my life like I guess I should have been doing all along. I don't do very much differently than I did years ago other than a time or two a week manage a way down to the old country store of Ray Blackmon. When I arrive I sit across the checker table from my good friend Ray and we talk about what has become of our town and go on and on about our young child Whitney Connors. But I'm always sure to be back at my home in time to watch those beautiful lightning bugs burn the tail off the evenings. They sure do make a pretty sight in a country night. I know because I own a set of aged blue eyes that can see them ever so clearly again.

THE END